Mudbound

Hillary Jordan grew up in Texas and Oklahoma and received her MFA in fiction from Columbia University. *Mudbound* is her first novel. She lives in Tivoli, New York.

Mudbound

HILLARY JORDAN

WINDMILL BOOKS

Published by Windmill Books 2008

2 4 6 8 10 9 7 5 3 1

Copyright © Hillary Jordan 2008

Hillary Jordan has asserted her right under the Copyright, Designs and
Patents Act, 1988, to be identified as the author of this work

First published in the United States under the title Mudbound by Hillary Jordan.
Published by arrangement with Algonquin Books of Chapel Hill, a division of
Workman Publishing Company, New York

First published in Great Britain in 2008 by
William Heinemann

Windmill Books
The Random House Group Limited
20 Vauxhall Bridge Road, London SW1V 2SA

Addresses for companies within The Random House Group Limited can be
found at: www.randomhouse.co.uk/offices.htm

The Random House Group Limited Reg. No. 954009

www.rbooks.co.uk

A CIP catalogue record for this book
is available from the British Library

ISBN 9780099524687

The Random House Group Limited supports The Forest Stewardship Council
(FSC), the leading international forest certification organisation.
All our titles that are printed on Greenpeace approved FSC certified paper carry
the FSC logo. Our paper procurement policy can be found at:
www.rbooks.co.uk/environment

Printed and bound in Great Britain by
CPI Cox & Wyman, Reading, RG1 8EX

To Mother, Gay and Nana,
for the stories

If I could do it, I'd do no writing at all here. It would be photographs; the rest would be fragments of cloth, bits of cotton, lumps of earth, records of speech, pieces of wood and iron, phials of odors, plates of food and of excrement. . . .

A piece of the body torn out by the roots might be more to the point.

—JAMES AGEE, *Let Us Now Praise Famous Men*

I.

JAMIE

HENRY AND I DUG the hole seven feet deep. Any shallower and the corpse was liable to come rising up during the next big flood: *Howdy boys! Remember me?* The thought of it kept us digging even after the blisters on our palms had burst, re-formed and burst again. Every shovelful was an agony— the old man, getting in his last licks. Still, I was glad of the pain. It shoved away thought and memory.

When the hole got too deep for our shovels to reach bottom, I climbed down into it and kept digging while Henry paced and watched the sky. The soil was so wet from all the rain it was like digging into raw meat. I scraped it off the blade by hand, cursing at the delay. This was the first break we'd had in the weather in three days and could be our last chance for some while to get the body in the ground.

"Better hurry it up," Henry said.

I looked at the sky. The clouds overhead were the color of ash, but there was a vast black mass of them to the north, and it was headed our way. Fast.

"We're not gonna make it," I said.

"We will," he said.

That was Henry for you: absolutely certain that whatever he wanted to happen *would* happen. The body would get buried before the storm hit. The weather would dry out in time to resow the cotton. Next year would be a better year. His little brother would never betray him.

I dug faster, wincing with every stroke. I knew I could stop at any time and Henry would take my place without a word of complaint—never mind he had nearly fifty years on his bones to my twenty-nine. Out of pride or stubbornness or both, I kept digging. By the time he said, "All right, my turn," my muscles were on fire and I was wheezing like an engine full of old gas. When he pulled me up out of the hole, I gritted my teeth so I wouldn't cry out. My body still ached in a dozen places from all the kicks and blows, but Henry didn't know about that.

Henry could never know about that.

I knelt by the side of the hole and watched him dig. His face and hands were so caked with mud a passerby might have taken him for a Negro. No doubt I was just as filthy, but in my case the red hair would have given me away. My father's hair, copper spun so fine women's fingers itch to run through it. I've always hated it. It might as well be a pyre blazing on top of my head, shouting to the world that he's in me. Shouting it to me every time I look in the mirror.

Around four feet, Henry's blade hit something hard.

"What is it?" I asked.

"Piece of rock, I think."

But it wasn't rock, it was bone—a human skull, missing a

big chunk in back. "Damn," Henry said, holding it up to the light.

"What do we do now?"

"I don't know."

We both looked to the north. The black was growing, eating up the sky.

"We can't start over," I said. "It could be days before the rain lets up again."

"I don't like it," Henry said. "It's not right."

He kept digging anyway, using his hands, passing the bones up to me as he unearthed them: ribs, arms, pelvis. When he got to the lower legs, there was a clink of metal. He held up a tibia and I saw the crude, rusted iron shackle encircling the bone. A broken chain dangled from it.

"Jesus Christ," Henry said. "This is a slave's grave."

"You don't know that."

He picked up the broken skull. "See here? He was shot in the head. Must've been a runaway." Henry shook his head. "That settles it."

"Settles what?"

"We can't bury our father in a nigger's grave," Henry said. "There's nothing he'd have hated more. Now help me out of here." He extended one grimy hand.

"It could have been an escaped convict," I said. "A white man." It could have been, but I was betting it wasn't. Henry hesitated, and I said, "The penitentiary's what, just six or seven miles from here?"

"More like ten," he said. But he let his hand fall to his side.

"Come on," I said, holding out my own hand. "Take a break. I'll dig awhile." When he reached up and clasped it, I had to stop myself from smiling. Henry was right: there was nothing our father would have hated more.

HENRY WAS BACK to digging again when I saw Laura coming toward us, picking her way across the drowned fields with a bucket in each hand. I fished in my pocket for my handkerchief and used it to wipe some of the mud off my face. Vanity—that's another thing I got from my father.

"Laura's coming," I said.

"Pull me up," Henry said.

I grabbed his hands and pulled, grunting with the effort, dragging him over the lip of the grave. He struggled to his knees, breathing harshly. He bent his head and his hat came off, revealing a wide swath of pink skin on top. The sight of it gave me a sharp, unexpected pang. *He's getting old,* I thought. *I won't always have him.*

He looked up, searching for Laura. When his eyes found her they lit with emotions so private I was embarrassed to see them: longing, hope, a tinge of worry. "I'd better keep at it," I said, turning away and picking up the shovel. I half jumped, half slid down into the hole. It was deep enough now that I couldn't see out. Just as well.

"How's it coming?" I heard Laura say. As always, her voice coursed through me like cold, clear water. It was a voice that belonged rightfully to some ethereal creature, a siren or an angel, not to a middle-aged Mississippi farmwife.

"We're almost finished," said Henry. "Another foot or so will see it done."

"I've brought food and water," she said.

"Water!" Henry let out a bitter laugh. "That's just what we need, is more water." I heard the scrape of the dipper against the pail and the sound of him swallowing, then Laura's head appeared over the side of the hole. She handed the dipper down to me.

"Here," she said, "have a drink."

I gulped it down, wishing it were whiskey instead. I'd run out three days ago, just before the bridge flooded, cutting us off from town. I reckoned the river had gone down enough by now that I could have gotten across—if I hadn't been stuck in that damned hole.

I thanked her and handed the dipper back up to her, but Laura wasn't looking at me. Her eyes were fixed on the other side of the grave, where we'd laid the bones.

"Good Lord, are those human?" she said.

"It couldn't be helped," Henry said. "We were already four feet down when we found them."

I saw her lips twitch as her eyes took in the shackles and chains. She covered her mouth with her hand, then turned to Henry. "Make sure you move them so the children don't see," she said.

WHEN THE TOP of the grave was more than a foot over my head, I stopped digging. "Come take a look," I called out. "I think this is plenty deep."

Henry's face appeared above me, upside down. He nodded. "Yep. That should do it." I handed him the shovel, but when he tried to pull me up, it was no use. I was too far down, and our hands and the walls of the hole were too slick.

"I'll fetch the ladder," he said.

"Hurry."

I waited in the hole. Around me was mud, stinking and oozing. Overhead a rectangle of darkening gray. I stood with my neck bent back, listening for the returning squelch of Henry's boots, wondering what was taking him so goddamn long. *If something happened to him and Laura,* I thought, *no one would know I was here.* I clutched the edge of the hole and tried to pull myself up, but my fingers just slid through the mud.

Then I felt the first drops of rain hit my face. "Henry!" I yelled.

The rain was falling lightly now, but before long it would be a downpour. The water would start filling up the hole. I'd feel it creeping up my legs to my thighs. To my chest. To my neck. "Henry! Laura!"

I threw myself at the walls of the grave like a maddened bear in a pit. Part of me was outside myself, shaking my head at my own foolishness, but the man was powerless to help the bear. It wasn't the confinement; I'd spent hundreds of hours in cockpits with no problem at all. It was the water. During the war I'd avoided flying over the open ocean whenever I could, even if it meant facing flak from the ground. It was how I won all those medals for bravery: from being so scared of that vast, hungry blue that I drove straight into the thick of German antiaircraft fire.

I was yelling so hard I didn't hear Henry until he was standing right over me. "I'm here, Jamie! I'm here!" he shouted.

He lowered the ladder into the hole and I scrambled up it. He tried to take hold of my arm, but I waved him off. I bent over, my hands on my knees, trying to slow the tripping of my heart.

"You all right?" he asked.

I didn't look at him, but I didn't have to. I knew his forehead would be puckered and his mouth pursed—his "my brother, the lunatic" look.

"I thought maybe you'd decided to leave me down there," I said, with a forced laugh.

"Why would I do that?"

"I'm just kidding, Henry." I went and took up the ladder, tucking it under one arm. "Come on, let's get this over with."

We hurried across the fields, stopping at the pump to wash the mud off our hands and faces, then headed to the barn to get the coffin. It was a sorry-looking thing, made of mismatched scrap wood, but it was the best we'd been able to do with the materials we had. Henry frowned as he picked up one end. "I wish to hell we'd been able to get to town," he said.

"Me too," I said, thinking of the whiskey.

We carried the coffin up onto the porch. When we went past the open window Laura called out, "You'll want hot coffee and a change of clothes before we bury him."

"No," said Henry. "There's no time. Storm's coming."

We took the coffin into the lean-to and set it on the rough plank floor. Henry lifted the sheet to look at our father's face one last time. Pappy's expression was tranquil. There was nothing to show that his death was anything other than the natural, timely passing of an old man.

I lifted the feet and Henry took the head. "Gently now," he said.

"Right," I said, "we wouldn't want to hurt him."

"That's not the point," Henry snapped.

"Sorry, brother. I'm just tired."

With ludicrous care, we lowered the corpse into the coffin. Henry reached for the lid. "I'll finish up here," he said. "You go make sure Laura and the girls are ready."

"All right."

As I walked into the house I heard the hammer strike the first nail, a sweet and final sound. It made the children jump.

"What's that banging, Mama?" asked Amanda Leigh.

"That's your daddy, nailing Pappy's coffin shut," Laura said.

"Will it make him mad?" Bella's voice was a scared whisper.

Laura shot me a quick, fierce glance. "No, darling," she said. "Pappy's dead. He can't get mad at anyone ever again. Now, let's get you into your coats and boots. It's time to lay your grandfather to rest."

I was glad Henry wasn't there to hear the satisfaction in her voice.

LAURA

WHEN I THINK of the farm, I think of mud. Limning my husband's fingernails and encrusting the children's knees and hair. Sucking at my feet like a greedy newborn on the breast. Marching in boot-shaped patches across the plank floors of the house. There was no defeating it. The mud coated everything. I dreamed in brown.

When it rained, as it often did, the yard turned into a thick gumbo, with the house floating in it like a soggy cracker. When the rains came hard, the river rose and swallowed the bridge that was the only way across. The world was on the other side of that bridge, the world of light bulbs and paved roads and shirts that stayed white. When the river rose, the world was lost to us and we to it.

One day slid into the next. My hands did what was necessary: pumping, churning, scouring, scraping. And cooking, always cooking. Snapping beans and the necks of chickens. Kneading dough, shucking corn and digging the eyes out of potatoes. No sooner was breakfast over and the mess cleaned up than it was time to start on dinner. After dinner came supper, then breakfast again the next morning.

Get up at first light. Go to the outhouse. Do your business, shivering in the winter, sweating in the summer, breathing through your mouth year-round. Steal the eggs from under the hens. Haul in wood from the pile and light the stove. Make the biscuits, slice the bacon and fry it up with the eggs and grits. Rouse your daughters from their bed, brush their teeth, guide arms into sleeves and feet into socks and boots. Take your youngest out to the porch and hold her up so she can clang the bell that will summon your husband from the fields and wake his hateful father in the lean-to next door. Feed them all and yourself. Scrub the iron skillet, the children's faces, the mud off the floors day after day while the old man sits and watches. He is always on you: "You better stir them greens, gal. You better sweep that floor now. Better teach them brats some manners. Wash them clothes. Feed them chickens. Fetch me my cane." His voice, clotted from smoking. His sly pale eyes with their hard black centers, on you.

He scared the children, especially my youngest, who was a little chubby.

"Come here, little piglet," he'd say to her.

She peered at him from behind my legs. At his long yellow teeth. At his bony yellow fingers with their thick curved nails like pieces of ancient horn.

"Come here and sit on my lap."

He had no interest in holding her or any other child, he just liked knowing she was afraid of him. When she wouldn't come, he told her she was too fat to sit on his lap anyway, she might break his bones. She started to cry, and I imagined that old man in his coffin. Pictured the lid closing on his face, the box being lowered into the hole. Heard the dirt striking the wood.

"Pappy," I said, smiling sweetly at him, "how about a nice cup of coffee?"

BUT I MUST START at the beginning, if I can find it. Beginnings are elusive things. Just when you think you have hold of one, you look back and see another, earlier beginning, and an earlier one before that. Even if you start with "Chapter One: I Am Born," you still have the problem of antecedents, of cause and effect. Why is young David fatherless? Because, Dickens tells us, his father died of a delicate constitution. Yes, but where did this mortal delicacy come from? Dickens doesn't say, so we're left to speculate. A congenital defect, perhaps, inherited from his mother, whose own mother had married beneath her to spite her cruel father, who'd been beaten as a child by a nursemaid who was forced into service when her faithless husband abandoned her for a woman he chanced to meet when his carriage wheel broke in front of the milliner's where she'd gone to have her hat trimmed. If we begin there, young David is fatherless because his great-great-grandfather's nursemaid's husband's future mistress's hat needed adornment.

By the same logic, my father-in-law was murdered because I was born plain rather than pretty. That's one possible beginning. There are others: Because Henry saved Jamie from drowning in the Great Mississippi Flood of 1927. Because Pappy sold the land that should have been Henry's. Because

Jamie flew too many bombing missions in the war. Because a Negro named Ronsel Jackson shone too brightly. Because a man neglected his wife, and a father betrayed his son, and a mother exacted vengeance. I suppose the beginning depends on who's telling the story. No doubt the others would start somewhere different, but they'd still wind up at the same place in the end.

It's tempting to believe that what happened on the farm was inevitable; that in fact all the events of our lives are as predetermined as the moves in a game of tic-tac-toe: Start in the middle square and no one wins. Start in one of the corners and the game is yours. And if you don't start, if you let the other person start? You lose, simple as that.

The truth isn't so simple. Death may be inevitable, but love is not. Love, you have to choose.

I'll begin with that. With love.

THERE'S A LOT of talk in the Bible about cleaving. Men and women cleaving unto God. Husbands cleaving to wives. Bones cleaving to skin. Cleaving, we are to understand, is a good thing. The righteous cleave; the wicked do not.

On my wedding day, my mother—in a vague attempt to prepare me for the indignities of the marriage bed—told me to cleave to Henry no matter what. "It will hurt at first," she said, as she fastened her pearls around my neck. "But it will get easier in time."

Mother was only half-right.

I was a thirty-one-year-old virgin when I met Henry McAllan in the spring of 1939, a spinster well on my way to petrifaction. My world was small, and everything in it was known. I lived with my parents in the house where I'd been born. I slept in the room that had once been mine and my sisters' and was now mine alone. I taught English at a private school for boys, sang in the Calvary Episcopal Church choir, babysat my nieces and nephews. Monday nights I played bridge with my married friends.

I was never beautiful like my sisters. Fanny and Etta have the delicate blonde good looks of the Fairbairns, my mother's people, but I'm all Chappell: small and dark, with strong Gallic features and a full figure that was ill-suited to the flapper dresses and slim silhouettes of my youth. When my mother's friends came to visit, they remarked on the loveliness of my hands, the curliness of my hair, the cheerfulness of my disposition; I was that sort of young woman. And then one day—quite suddenly, it seemed to me—I was no longer young. Mother wept the night of my thirtieth birthday, after the dishes from the family party had been cleaned and put away and my brothers and sisters and their spouses and children had kissed me and gone home to their beds. The sound of her crying, muffled by a pillow or my father's shoulder perhaps, drifted down the hallway to my room, where I lay awake listening to the whippoorwills, cicadas and peepers speak to one another. *I am! I am!* they seemed to say.

"I am," I whispered. The words sounded hollow to my ears, as pointless as the frantic rubbings of a cricket in a matchbox. It was hours before I slept.

But when I woke the next morning I felt a kind of relief. I was no longer just unmarried; I was officially unmarriageable. Everyone could stop hoping and shift the weight of their attention elsewhere, to some other, worthier project, leaving me to get on with my life. I was a respected teacher, a beloved daughter, sister, niece and aunt. I would be content with that.

Would I have been, I wonder? Would I have found happiness there in the narrow, blank margins of the page, habitat of maiden aunts and childless schoolteachers? I can't say, because a little over a year later, Henry came into my life and pulled me squarely into the ink-filled center.

My brother Teddy brought him to dinner at our house one Sunday. Teddy worked as a civilian land appraiser for the Army Corps of Engineers, and Henry was his new boss. He was that rare and marvelous creature, a forty-one-year-old bachelor. He looked his age, mostly because of his hair, which was stark white. He wasn't an especially large man, but he had density. He walked with a noticeable limp which I later learned he'd gotten in the war, but it didn't detract from his air of confidence. His movements were slow and deliberate, as if his limbs were weighted, and it was a matter of great consequence where he placed them. His hands were strong-looking and finely made, and the nails wanted cutting. I was struck by their stillness, by the way they remained folded calmly in his lap or planted on either side of his plate, even when he talked politics. He spoke with the lovely garble of the Delta—like he had a mouthful of some rich, luscious dessert. He addressed most of his remarks to Teddy and my parents, but I felt his gray eyes on my face all through dinner, lighting there briefly, moving away and then returning again. I remember my skin prickling with heat and damp beneath my clothes, my hand trembling slightly when I reached for my water glass.

My mother, whose nose was ever attuned to the scent of male admiration, began wedging my feminine virtues into the conversation with excruciating frequency: "Oh, so you're a college graduate, Mr. McAllan? Laura went to college, you know. She got her teaching certificate from West Tennessee State. Yes, Mr. McAllan, we all play the piano, but Laura is by far the best musician in the family. She sings beautifully too, doesn't she Teddy? And you should taste her peach chess pie." And so on. I spent most of dinner staring at my plate. Every time I tried to retreat to the kitchen on some errand or another, Mother insisted on going herself or sending Teddy's wife, Eliza, who shot me sympathetic glances as she obeyed. Teddy's eyes were dancing; by the end of the meal he was choking back laughter, and I was ready to strangle him and my mother both.

When Henry took his leave of us, Mother invited him back the following Sunday. He looked at me before he agreed, a measuring look I did my best to meet with a polite smile.

In the week that followed, my mother could talk of little else but that charming Mr. McAllan: how soft-spoken he was, how gentlemanly and—highest praise of all from her—how he did not take wine with dinner. Daddy liked him too, but that was hardly a surprise given that Henry was a College Man. For my father, a retired history professor, there was no greater proof of a person's worth than a college education. The Son of God

Himself, come again in glory but lacking a diploma, would not have found favor with Daddy.

My parents' hopefulness grated on me. It threatened to kindle my own, and that, I couldn't allow. I told myself that Henry McAllan and his gentlemanly, scholarly ways had nothing to do with me. He was newly arrived in Memphis and had no other society; that was why he'd accepted Mother's invitation.

How pathetic my defenses were, and how paper-thin! They shredded easily enough the following Sunday, when Henry showed up with lilies for me as well as for my mother. After dinner he suggested we go for a walk. I took him to Overton Park. The dogwoods were blooming, and as we strolled beneath them the wind blew flurries of white petals down on our heads. It was like a scene out of the movies, with me as the unlikely heroine. Henry plucked a petal from my hair, his fingers lightly grazing my cheek.

"Pretty, aren't they?" he said.

"Yes, but sad."

"Why sad?"

"Because they remind us of Christ's suffering."

Henry's brows drew together, forming a deep vertical furrow between them. I could tell how much it bothered him, not knowing something, and I liked him for admitting his ignorance rather than pretending to know as so many men would have done. I showed him the marks like bloody nail holes on each of the four petals.

"Ah," he said, and took my hand.

He held it all the way back to my house, and when we got

there he asked me to a performance of *The Chocolate Soldier* at the Memphis Open Air Theatre the following Saturday. The female members of my family mobilized to beautify me for the occasion. Mother took me to Lowenstein's department store and bought me a new dress with a frothy white collar and puffed sleeves. On Saturday morning my sisters came to the house with pots of color for my cheeks and eyes, and lipsticks in every shade of red and pink, testing them out on me with the swift, high-handed authority of master chefs choosing seasonings for the sauce. When I was plucked, painted and powdered to their satisfaction, they held a mirror to my face, presenting me with my own reflection like a gift. I looked strange to myself and told them so.

"Just wait till Henry sees you," laughed Fanny.

When he came to pick me up, Henry merely told me that I looked nice. But later that day he kissed me for the first time, taking my face in his hands as naturally and familiarly as if it were a favorite hat or a shaving bowl he'd owned for years. Never before had a man kissed me with that degree of possession, either of himself or of me, and it thrilled me.

Henry had all the self-confidence that I lacked. He was certain of an astonishing number of things: Packards are the best-made American cars. Meat ought not to be eaten rare. Irving Berlin's "God Bless America" should be the national anthem instead of "The Star-Spangled Banner," which is too difficult to sing. The Yankees will win the World Series. There will be another Great War in Europe, and the United States would do well to stay out of it. Blue is your color, Laura.

I wore blue. Gradually, over the course of the next several months, I unspooled my life for him. I told him about my favorite students, my summer jobs as a camp counselor in Myrtle Beach and my family, down to the second and third cousins. I spoke of my two years at college, how I'd loved Dickens and the Brontës and hated Melville and mathematics. Henry listened with grave attention to everything I chose to share with him, nodding from time to time to indicate his approval. I soon found myself looking for those nods, making mental notes on when they were bestowed and withheld, and inevitably, presenting him with the version of myself that seemed most likely to elicit them. This wasn't a deliberate exercise of feminine wiles on my part. I was unused to male admiration and knew only that I wanted more of it, and all that came with it.

And there was so much that came with it. Having a beau — my mother's word, which she used at every possible opportunity—gave me cachet among my friends and relations that I'd never before enjoyed. I became prettier and more interesting, worthier somehow of every good thing.

How lovely you look today, my dear, they would say. And, *I declare, you're positively glowing!* And, *Come and sit by me, Laura, and tell me all about this Mr. McAllan of yours.*

I wasn't at all sure that he was my Mr. McAllan, but as spring turned to summer and Henry's attentions showed no sign of slacking, I began to allow myself to hope that he might be. He took me to restaurants and the picture show, for walks along the Mississippi and day trips to the surrounding countryside, where he pointed out features of the land and the farms

we passed. He was very knowledgeable about crops, livestock
and such. When I remarked on it, he told me he'd grown up
on a farm.

"Do your parents still live there?" I asked.

"No. They sold the place after the '27 flood."

I heard the wistfulness in his voice but put it down to nostalgia. I didn't think to ask if he was interested in farming his
own land someday. Henry was a College Man, a successful
engineer with a job that allowed him to live in Memphis—the
center of civilization. Why in the world would he want to
scratch out a living as a farmer?

"MY BROTHER'S COMING UP from Oxford this weekend,"
Henry announced one day in July. "I'd like for him to meet
you."

For *him* to meet *me*. My heart fluttered. Jamie was Henry's
favorite sibling. Henry spoke of him often, with a mixture of
fondness and exasperation that made me smile. Jamie was at
Ole Miss studying fine arts ("a subject of no practical use whatever") and modeling men's clothing on the side ("an undignified
occupation for a man"). He wanted to be an actor ("that's no
way to support a family") and spent all his spare time doing
thespian productions ("he just likes the attention"). Yet despite
these criticisms, it was obvious that Henry adored his little
brother. Something quickened in his eyes whenever he talked
about Jamie, and his hands, normally so impassive, rose from
his sides to make large, swooping shapes in the air. That he

wanted Jamie to meet me surely meant that he was considering a more permanent attachment between us. Out of long habit, I tried to stifle the thought, but it stayed stubbornly alive in my mind. That night, as I peeled the potatoes for supper, I imagined Henry's proposal, pictured him kneeling before me in the parlor, his face earnest and slightly worried—what if I didn't accept him? As I made my narrow bed the next morning, I envisioned myself smoothing the covers of a double bed with a white, candlewick-patterned spread and two pillows bearing the imprints of two heads. In class the next day, as I quizzed my boys on prepositional phrases, I pictured a child with Henry's gray eyes staring up at me from a wicker bassinet. These visions bloomed in my mind like exotic flowers, opulent and jewel-toned, undoing years of strict pruning of my desires.

The Saturday I was to meet Jamie I dressed with extra care, wearing the navy linen suit I knew Henry liked and sitting patiently while my mother tortured my unruly hair into an upswept do worthy of a magazine advertisement. Henry picked me up and we drove to the station to meet his brother's train. As we stood in the flow of disembarking passengers, I scanned the crowd for a younger copy of Henry. But the young man who came bounding up to us looked nothing like him. I studied the two of them as they embraced: one weathered and solid, the other tall, fair and lanky, with hair the color of a newly minted penny. After a time they clapped each other on the back, as men will do to break the intimacy of such a moment, then pulled apart and searched each other's face.

"You look good, brother," said Jamie. "The Tennessee air seems to agree with you. Or is it something else?"

He turned to me then, grinning widely. He was beautiful; there was no other word for him. He had fine, sharp features and skin so translucent I could see the small veins in his temples. His eyes were the pale green of beryl stones and seemed lit from the inside. He was just twenty-two then, nine years younger than myself and nineteen years younger than Henry.

"This is Miss Chappell," said Henry. "My brother, Jamie."

"Pleased to meet you," I managed.

"The pleasure's mine," he said, taking my offered hand and kissing the back of it with exaggerated gallantry.

Henry rolled his eyes. "My brother thinks he's a character in one of his plays."

"Ah, but which one?" Jamie said, raising a forefinger in the air. "Hamlet? Faust? Prince Hal? What do you think, Miss Chappell?"

I blurted out the first thing that came into my head. "Actually, I think you're more of a Puck."

I was rewarded with a dazzling smile. "Dear lady, thou speakest aright, I *am* that merry wanderer of the night."

"Who's Puck?" asked Henry.

Jamie shook his head in mock despair. "Lord, what fools these mortals be," he said.

I saw Henry's lips tighten. I suddenly felt sorry for him, standing there in his brother's shadow. "Puck's a kind of mischievous sprite," I said. "A troublemaker."

"A hobgoblin," Jamie said contritely. "Forgive me, brother, I'm only trying to impress her."

Henry put his arm around me. "Laura's not the impressionable type."

"Good for her!" Jamie said. "Now why don't you two show me this fine city of yours?"

We took him to the Peabody Hotel, which had the best restaurant in Memphis and a swing band on weekends. At Jamie's insistence we ordered a bottle of champagne. I'd had it only once before, at my brother Pearce's wedding, and I was light-headed after one glass. When the band started up, Jamie asked Henry if he could have a dance with me (Henry didn't dance, that night or any other, because of his limp). We whirled round and round to Duke Ellington, Benny Goodman and Tommy Dorsey, music I'd heard on the radio and danced to in the parlor with my brothers and young nephews. How different this was, and how exhilarating! I was aware of Henry's eyes following us, and others' too—women's eyes, watching me enviously. It was a novel sensation for me, and I couldn't help but revel in it. After several numbers, Jamie escorted me back to our table and excused himself. I sat down, flushed and out of breath.

"You look especially pretty tonight," Henry said.

"Thank you."

"Jamie has that effect on girls. They sparkle for him." His expression was bland, his tone matter-of-fact. If he was jealous of his brother, I couldn't detect it. "He likes you, I can tell," he added.

"I'm sure he doesn't dislike anyone."

"Well, at least not anyone in a skirt," Henry said, with a wry smile. "Look." He gestured toward the dance floor, and I saw Jamie with a willowy brunette in his arms. She was wearing a satin dress with a low-cut back, and Jamie's hand rested on her bare skin. As she followed him effortlessly through a series of complicated turns and dips, I realized what a clumsy partner I must have been. I wanted to cover my face with my hands; I knew everything I felt was there for Henry to see. My envy and embarrassment. My foolish yearning.

I stood up. I don't know what I would have said to him, because at that moment he rose and took my hand. "It's late," he said, "and I know you have church in the morning. Come on, I'll take you home."

He was so gentle, so kind. I felt a rush of shame. But later, as I lay sleepless in my bed, it occurred to me that what I'd shown Henry so nakedly wasn't new to him. He must have seen it before, must have felt it himself a hundred times in Jamie's presence: a longing for a brightness that would never be his.

JAMIE RETURNED TO Oxford, and I put him out of my thoughts. I was no fool; I knew a man like him could never desire a woman like me. It was marvel enough that Henry desired me. I can't say whether I was truly in love with him then; I was so grateful to him that it dwarfed everything else. He was my rescuer from life in the margins, from the pity, scorn and crabbed kindness that are the portion of old maids. I should say, he was my potential rescuer. I was by no means sure of him, and for good reason.

One night at choir practice, I looked up from my hymnal and saw him watching me from one of the rear pews, his face solemn with intent. *This is it,* I thought. *He's going to propose.*

Somehow I got through the rest of the practice, though the director had to chide me twice for missing my entrance. In the choir room afterward, as I unbuttoned my robe with clumsy fingers, I had a sudden vision of Henry's hands undoing the buttons of my nightgown on our wedding night. I wondered what it would be like to lie with him, to have him touch my body as intimately as though it were his own flesh. My sister Etta, who was a registered nurse, had told me about the sexual act when I turned twenty-one. Her explanation was strictly factual; she never once referred to her own relations with her husband, Jack, but I gathered from her private smile that the marriage bed was not an altogether unpleasant place.

Henry was waiting for me outside the church, leaning against his car in his familiar white shirt, gray pants and gray fedora. That was all he ever wore. Clothes didn't matter to him, and his were often ill-fitting—pants drooping at the waist, hems dragging in the dirt, sleeves too long or too short. I laugh now when I think of the feelings his wardrobe aroused in me. I practically throbbed with the desire to sew for him.

"Hello, my dear," he said. And then, "I've come to say goodbye."

Goodbye. The word billowed in the space between us before settling around me in soft black folds.

"They're building a new airfield in Alabama, and they want me to oversee the project. I'll be gone for several months, possibly longer."

"I see," I said.

I waited for him to say something more: How he would miss me. How he would write to me. How he hoped I'd be here when he returned. But he said nothing, and as the silence stretched on I felt myself fill with self-loathing. I was not meant for marriage and children and the rest of it. These things were not for me, had never been for me. I'd been a fool to think otherwise.

I felt myself receding from him, and from myself too, our images shrinking in my mind's eye. I heard him offer to give me a lift home. Heard myself decline politely, telling him I needed the fresh air, then wish him the best of luck in Alabama. Saw him lean toward me. Saw myself turn my head so his kiss found my cheek instead of my lips. Watched as I walked away from him, my back as straight as pride could make it.

Mother pounced on me as soon as I came in the door. "Henry stopped by earlier," she said. "Did he find you at church?"

I nodded.

"He seemed eager to speak with you."

It was hard to look at her face, to see the hope trembling just beneath the surface of her bright smile. "Henry's going away," I said. "He doesn't know for how long."

"Is that . . . all he said?"

"Yes, that's all." I started up the stairs to my room.

"He'll be back," she called out after me. "I know he will."

I turned and looked down at her, so lovely in her distress. One pale, slender hand lay on the banister. The other clenched the fabric of her skirt, crumpling it.

"Oh, Laura," she said, with a telltale quaver.

"Don't you dare cry, Mother."

She didn't. It must have been a Herculean effort. My mother

weeps over anything at all: dead butterflies, curdled sauce. "I'm so sorry, darling," she said.

My legs went suddenly boneless. I sank down onto the top step and put my head on my knees. I heard the creak of her footsteps and felt her sit beside me. Her arm went around me, and her lips touched my hair. "We won't speak of him," she said. "We won't mention his name ever again."

She kept her promise, and she must have passed the word to the rest of the family, because no one said a thing about Henry, not even my sisters. They were just overly kind, all of them, complimenting me more often than I deserved and concocting ways to keep me busy. I was in great demand as a dinner guest, bridge partner and shopping companion. Outwardly I was cheerful, and after a time they began to treat me normally again, believing I was over it. I wasn't. I was furious—with myself, with Henry. With the cruel natural order that had made me simultaneously undesirable to men and unable to feel complete without one. I saw that my former contentment had been a lie. This was the truth at the core of my existence: this yawning emptiness, scantily clad in rage. It had been there all along. Henry had merely been the one who'd shown it to me.

I didn't hear from him for nearly two months. And then one day, I came home to find my mother waiting anxiously in the foyer. "Henry McAllan's come back," she said. "He's in the parlor. Here, your hair's mussed, let me fix it for you."

"I'll see him as I am," I said, lifting my chin.

I regretted that little bit of defiance as soon as I laid eyes on him. Henry looked tan and fit, more handsome than he ever had. Why hadn't I at least put on some lipstick? No—that was foolishness. This man had led me on, then abandoned me. I hadn't gotten so much as a postcard from him in all these weeks. What did I care whether I looked pretty for him?

"Laura, it's good to see you," he said. "How have you been?"

"Just fine. And you?"

"I've missed you," he said.

I was silent. Henry came and took my hands in his. My palms were damp, but his were cool and dry.

"I had to be sure of my feelings," he said. "But now I am. I love you, and I want you to be my wife. Will you marry me."

And there it was, just like that: the question I'd thought I would never hear. Granted, the scene didn't play out quite like I'd pictured it. Henry wasn't kneeling, and the question had actually come out as more of a statement. If he felt any worry over my answer, he hid it well. That stung a little. How dared he be so sure of himself, after such a long absence? Did he think he could simply walk back into my house and claim me like a forgotten coat? And yet, beside the enormity of his wanting me, my anger seemed a paltry thing. If Henry was certain of me, I told myself, it was because that was his way. *Meat should not be eaten rare. Blue is your color. Will you marry me.*

As I looked into his frank gray eyes, I had a sudden, unbidden image of Jamie grinning down at me as he'd spun me around the ballroom of the Peabody. Henry was neither dashing nor romantic; like me, he was made of sturdier, plainer stuff. But he loved me, and I knew that he would provide for me and be true to me and give me children who were strong and bright. And for all of that, I could certainly love him in return.

"Yes, Henry," I said. "I will marry you."

He nodded his head once, then he kissed me, opening my mouth with his thumb and putting his tongue inside. I clamped my mouth shut, more out of surprise than anything; it had been years since I'd been French-kissed, and his tongue felt foreign, thick and strange. Henry let out a little grunt, and I realized I'd bitten him.

"I'm sorry," I stammered. "I didn't know you were going to do that."

He didn't speak. He merely reopened my mouth and kissed me again exactly the same as before. This time I accepted his invasion without protest, and that seemed to satisfy him, because after a few minutes he left me to go and speak to Daddy.

WE WERE MARRIED six weeks later in a simple Episcopal ceremony. Jamie was the best man. When Henry brought him to the house he greeted me with a bear hug and a dozen pink roses.

"Sweet Laura," he said. "I'm so glad Henry finally came to his senses. I told him he was an idiot if he didn't marry you."

Jamie had spoiled me for the rest of the McAllans, whom I met for the first time two days before the wedding. From the moment they arrived it was clear they felt superior to us Chappells, who (it must be said) had French blood on my father's side and a Union general on my mother's. I didn't see much of Henry's father that weekend—Pappy and the other men were off doing whatever men do when there's a wedding on—but I spent enough time with the McAllan women to know we'd never be close, as I'd naïvely hoped. Henry's mother was cold, haughty and full of opinions, most of them negative, about everyone and everything. His two sisters, Eboline and Thalia, were former Cotton Queens of Greenville who'd married into money and made sure everybody knew it. The day before the wedding my mother gave a luncheon for the ladies of both families, and Fanny asked them whether they'd gone to college.

Thalia arched her perfectly plucked brows and said, "What good is college to a woman? I confess I can't see the need for it."

"Unless of course you're poor, or plain," said Eboline.

She gave a little laugh, and Thalia giggled with her. My sisters and I looked at each other uncertainly. Had Henry not told them we were all college girls? Surely they didn't know, Fanny said to me later; surely the slight had been unintentional. But I knew better.

Still, not even Henry's disagreeable relations could dampen the happiness I felt on my wedding day. We honeymooned in Charleston, then returned to a little house Henry had rented for us on Evergreen Street, not far from where my parents lived. And so my time of cleaving began. I loved the smallness of domestic life, the sense of belonging it gave me. I was Henry's now. Yielding to him—cooking the foods he liked, washing and ironing his shirts, waiting for him to come home to me each day—was what I'd been put on the earth to do. And then Amanda Leigh was born in November of 1940, followed two years later by Isabelle, and I became theirs more utterly even than I was their father's.

It would be six years into my marriage before I remembered that cleave has a second meaning, which is "to divide with a blow, as with an axe."

JAMIE

IN THE DREAM I'm alone on the roof of Eboline's old house in Greenville, watching the water rise. Usually I'm ten, but sometimes I'm grown and once I was an old man. I straddle the peak of the roof, my legs hanging down on either side. Snatched objects race toward and then around me, churning in the current. A chinaberry tree. A crystal chandelier. A dead cow. I try to guess which side of the house each item will be steered to by the water. The four-poster bed with its tail of mosquito netting will go to the left. The outhouse will go to the right, along with Mr. Wilhoit's Stutz Bearcat. The stakes of the game are high: every time I guess wrong the water rises another foot. When it reaches my ankles I draw my knees up as much as I can without losing my balance. I jockey the house, riding it north into the oncoming flood while the water urges me on in its terrible voice. I don't speak its language but I know what it's saying: It wants me. Not because I have any significance, but because it wants everything. Who am I, a skinny kid in torn britches, to deny it?

When the river takes me I don't try to swim or stay afloat. I open my eyes and my mouth and let the water fill me up. I feel my lungs spasm but there's no pain, and I stop being afraid. The current carries me along. I'm flotsam, and I understand that flotsam is all I've ever been.

Something glows in the murk ahead of me, getting brighter as I get closer to it. The light hurts my eyes. *Has a star fallen in the river?* I wonder. *Has the river swallowed everything, even the sky?* Five rays emanate from the star's center. They're moving back and forth, like they're seeking something. As I pass by them I see that they're fingers, and that what I thought was a star is a big white hand. I don't want it to find me. I'm part of the river now.

And then I'm not. I feel a sharp pain in my head and am yanked up, back onto the roof, or into a boat—the dream varies. But the hand is always Henry's, and it's always holding a bloody hank of my hair.

More than a thousand people died in that flood. I survived it, because of Henry. I wasn't alone on Eboline's roof, she and my parents were there with me, along with her husband, Virgil, and their maid, Dessie. The water didn't come and take me, I fell into it. I fell into it because I stood up. I stood up because I saw Henry approaching in the boat, coming to rescue us.

Because of Henry. So much of who I am and what I've done is because of Henry. My earliest memory is of meeting him for the first time. My mother was holding me, rocking me, and then she handed me to a large, white-haired stranger. I was afraid, and then I wasn't—that's all I remember. The way Mama always told it, I started to pitch a fit, but when Henry

held me up in front of him and said, "Hello, little brother," I
stopped crying at once and stuck my fingers in his mouth. I,
who howled like a red Indian whenever my father or any other
male tried to pick me up, went meekly into my brother's hands.
I was one and a half. He was twenty-one and just returned
from the Great War.

Because of Henry, I grew up hating Huns. Huns had tried to
kill him in a forest somewhere in France. They'd given him his
limp and his white hair. They'd taken things from him too—I
didn't know what exactly but I could sense his lack of them.
He never talked about the war. Pappy was always prodding him
about it, wanting to know how many men Henry had killed
and how he'd killed them. "Was it more than ten? More than
fifty?" Pappy would ask. "Did you get any with your bayonet,
or did you shoot em all from a distance?"

But Henry would never say. The only time I ever heard him
refer to the war was on my eighth birthday. He came home
for the weekend and took me deer hunting. It was my first
time getting to carry an actual weapon (if you can call a Daisy
Model 25 BB gun an actual weapon) and I was bursting with
manly pride. I didn't manage to hit anything besides a few
trees, but Henry brought down an eight-point buck. It wasn't
a clean kill. When we got to where the buck had fallen we
found it still alive, struggling futilely to get up. Splintered
bone poked out of a wound in its thigh. Its eyes were wild and
uncomprehending.

Henry passed a hand over his face, then gripped my shoulder hard. "If you ever have to be a soldier," he said, "promise

me you'll try and get up to the sky. They say battle is a lot cleaner up there."

I promised. Then he knelt and cut its throat.

From that day on, whenever the crop dusters flew over our farm, I pretended I was the pilot. Only it wasn't boll weevils I was killing, it was Huns. I must have shot down hundreds of German aces in my imagination, sitting in the topmost branches of the sweet gum tree behind our house.

But if Henry sparked my desire to fly, Lindbergh ignited it with his solo flight across the Atlantic. It was less than a month after the flood. Greenville and our farm were still under ten feet of water, so we were staying with my aunt and uncle in Carthage. The house was full, and I was stuck sleeping in a three-quarter bed in the attic with my cousins Albin and Avery, strapping bullies with pimply faces and buckteeth. Crammed between the two of them, I dreamed of the flood: the guessing game, the voice of the water, the big white hand. My moaning woke them, and they punched and kicked me awake, calling me a pansy and a titty baby. But not even their threats—to smother me, to throw me out the window, to stake me out over an anthill and pour molasses in my eyes—could stop the flood from coming to get me in my sleep. It came almost every night, and I always gave in to it. That was the part I dreaded: the part where I just let the water have me. It seemed a shameful weakness, the kind my brother would never give in to, even in a dream. Henry would fight with everything he had, and when his last bit of strength was gone he'd fight some more—like I hadn't done. At least, I was pretty sure I hadn't. That was the hell of it, I had no memory of what had happened between the time I fell in the water and when Henry pulled me out. All I had was the dream, which seemed to confirm my worst fears about myself. As the days passed and it kept recurring, I became more and more convinced it was true. I'd given myself willingly to the water, and would do it again if I had the chance.

I started refusing to take baths. Albin and Avery added "pig boy" to the list of endearments they had for me, and Pappy whipped my butt bloody with a switch, yelling that he wouldn't have a son who went around stinking like a nigger. Finally my mother threatened to bathe me herself if I wouldn't. The thought of Mama seeing me naked was enough to send me straightaway into the tub, though I never filled it more than a few inches.

It was during this time that stories about Lindbergh started to crop up in the papers and on the radio. He was going after the twenty-five-thousand-dollar Orteig Prize, offered by a Frenchman named Raymond Orteig to the first aviator to fly nonstop from New York to Paris, or vice versa. The purse had been up for grabs since 1919. A bunch of pilots had tried to win it. All of them had failed, and six had died trying.

Lindbergh would be the one to make it, I was positive. So what if he was younger and greener than the other pilots who'd tried? He was a god—fearless, immortal. There was no way he would fail. My confidence wasn't shared by the local papers, which dubbed him "the Flying Fool" for attempting it without a copilot. I told myself they were the fools.

The day of the flight, our entire family gathered around

the radio and listened to the reports of Lindbergh's progress. His plane was sighted over New England, then Newfoundland. Then he vanished, for sixteen of the longest hours of my life.

"He's dead," Albin taunted. "He fell asleep, and his plane crashed into the ocean."

"He did not!" I said. "Lindy would never fall asleep while he was flying."

"Maybe he got lost," said Avery.

"Yeah," said Albin, "maybe he was just too stupid to find his way."

This was a reference to the fact that I'd gotten lost a few days before. The two of them were supposed to take me fishing, but they'd led me in circles and then disappeared snickering into the woods. I was unfamiliar with the country around Carthage and it took me three hours to find my way back to the house, by which time my mother was out of her mind with worry. Albin and Avery had gotten a whipping, but that didn't make me feel any better. They'd bested me again.

They wouldn't this time. Lindbergh would show them. He would win for both of us.

And of course, he did. "The Flying Fool" became "the Lone Eagle," and Lindy's triumph became mine. Even my cousins cheered when he landed safely at Le Bourget Field. It was impossible not to feel proud of what he'd done. Impossible not to want to be like him.

That night after supper, I went outside and lay on the wet grass and stared up at the sky. It was twilight—that impossible shade of purple-blue that only lasts a few minutes before dulling into ordinary dark. I wanted to dive up into that blue and lose myself in it. I remember thinking there was nothing bad up there. No muck or stink or killing brown water. No ugliness or hate. Just blue and gray and ten thousand shades in between, all of them beautiful.

I would be a pilot like Lindbergh. I would have great adventures and perform acts of daring and defend my country, and it would be glorious. And I would be a god.

Fifteen years later the Army granted my wish. And it was not. And I was not.

RONSEL

THEY CALLED US "Eleanor Roosevelt's niggers." They said we wouldn't fight, that we'd turn tail and run the minute we got into real combat. They said we didn't have the discipline to make good soldiers. That we didn't have brains enough to man tanks. That we were inclined by nature to all kind of wickedness—lying, stealing, raping white women. They said we could see better than white GIs in the dark because we were closer to the beasts. When we were in Wimbourne an English gal I never laid eyes on before came up and patted me right on the butt. I asked her what she was doing and she said, "Checking to see if you've got a tail."

"Why would you think that?" I said.

She said the white GIs had been telling all the English girls that Negroes were more monkey than human.

We slept in separate barracks, ate in separate mess halls, shit in separate latrines. We even had us a separate blood supply—God forbid any wounded white boys would end up with Negro blood in their veins.

They gave us the dregs of everything, including officers. Our lieutenants were mostly Southerners who'd washed out in some other post. Drunkards, yellow bellies, bigoted no-count crackers who couldn't have led their way out of a one-room shack in broad daylight. Putting them over black troops was the Army's way of punishing them. They had nothing but contempt for us and they made sure we knew it. At the Officers' Club they liked to sing "We're dreaming of a white battalion" to the tune of "White Christmas." We heard about it from the colored staff, who had to wait on their sorry white asses while they sang it.

If they'd all been like that I probably would've ended up fertilizing some farmer's field in France or Belgium, along with every other man in my unit. Lucky for us we had a few good white officers. The ones out of West Point were mostly fair and decent, and our CO always treated us respectful.

"They say you're not as clean as other people," he told us. "There's a simple answer to that. Make damn sure you're cleaner than anybody else you ever saw in your life, especially all those white bastards out there. Make your uniforms look neater than theirs. Make your boots shine brighter."

And that's exactly what we did. We aimed to make the 761st the best tank battalion in the whole Army.

We trained hard, first at Camp Claiborne, then at Camp Hood. There were five men to a tank, each with his own job to do, but we all had to learn each other's jobs too. I was the driver, had a feel for it from the very first day. Funny how many of us farm boys ended up in the driver's seat. Reckon if you can get a mule to go where you want it to, you can steer a Sherman tank.

We spent a lot of time at the range, shooting all kind of weapons—.45s, machine guns, cannons. We went on maneuvers in the Kisatchie National Forest and did combat simulations with live ammo. We knew they were testing our courage and we passed with flying colors. Hell, most of us were more scared of getting snakebit than getting hit by a bullet. Some of the water moccasins they had down there were ten feet long, and that's no lie.

In July of '42 we got our first black lieutenants. There were only three of them but we all walked with our heads a little bit higher after that, at least on the base. Off base, in the towns where we took our liberty, we walked real careful. In Killeen they put up a big sign for us at the end of Main Street: NIGGERS HAVE TO LEAVE THIS TOWN BY 9 PM. The paint was blood red in case we missed the point. Killeen didn't have a colored section, only about half of them little towns did. The one in Alexandria near Camp Claiborne was typical—nothing to it but a falling-down movie theater and two shabby juke joints. Wasn't no place to buy anything or set and eat a meal. The rest of the town was off limits to us. If the MPs or the local law caught you in the white part of town they'd beat the shit out of you.

Our uniforms didn't mean a damn to the local white citizens. Not that I expected them to, but my buddies from up north and out west were thunderstruck by the way we were treated. Reading about Jim Crow in the paper is a mighty different thing from having a civilian bus driver wave a pistol in your face and tell you to get your coon hide off the bus to make room for a fat white farmer. They just couldn't understand it, no matter how many times we tried to explain it to them. You got to go along to get along, we told them, got to humble down and play shut-mouthed when you around white folks, but a lot of them just couldn't do it. There was this Yankee private in Fort Knox, that's where most of the guys in the battalion did their basic training. He got into an argument with a white storekeeper who wouldn't sell him a pack of smokes and ended up tied with a rope to the fender of a car and dragged up and down the street. That was just one killing, out of dozens we heard about.

The longer I spent around guys from other parts of the country, the madder I got myself. Here we were, about to risk our lives for people who hated us as bad as they hated the Krauts or the Japs, and maybe even worse. The Army didn't do nothing to protect us from the locals. When local cops beat up colored GIs, the Army looked the other way. When the bodies of dead black soldiers turned up outside of camp, the MPs didn't even try to find out who did it. It didn't take a genius to see why. The beatings, the lousy food and whatall, the piss-poor officers—they all added up to one thing. The Army wanted us to fail.

WE TRAINED FOR two long years. By the summer of '44, we'd about gave up hope that they were ever going to let us fight. According to the *Courier* there were over a hundred thousand of us serving overseas, but only one colored unit in combat. The rest were peeling potatoes, digging trenches and cleaning latrines.

But then, in August, word came down that General Patton had sent for us. He'd seen us on maneuvers at Kisatchie and wanted us to fight at the head of his Third Army. Damn, we were proud! Here was our chance to show the world something it'd never seen before. To hell with God and country, we'd fight for our people and our own self-respect.

We left Camp Hood in late August. I ain't never been so glad to see the back of a place. Only thing I'd miss about that hellhole was Mallie Simpson, she was a schoolteacher I kept company with in Killeen. Mallie was considerable older than me. She might've been thirty even, I never asked and didn't care. She was a tiny little gal with a big full-bellied laugh. She knew things the girls back home didn't have the first idea about, things to do with what my daddy calls "nature activity." Some weekends we didn't hardly leave her bed, except to go to the package store. Mallie liked her gin. She drank it straight up, one shot at a time, downing it in one gulp. She used to say a half-full glass of gin was a invitation to the devil. Seemed to me there was plenty of devilment going on with the glasses being empty, but I wasn't complaining. I said goodbye to her with real sadness. I reckoned it'd be a long while before I had another woman—from what I'd heard, Europe had nothing but white people in it.

But I reckoned wrong. There were plenty of white people over there all right, but they weren't like the ones back home. Wasn't no hate in them. In England, where we spent our first

month, some of the folks had never seen a black man before
and they were curious more than anything. Once they figured
out we were just like everybody else, that's how they treated
us. The gals too. The first time a white gal asked me to dance
I about fell out of the box.

"Go on," whispered my buddy Jimmy, he was from Los
Angeles.

"Jimmy," I said, "you must be plumb out of your mind."

"If you don't I will," he said, so I went on and danced with
her. I can't say I enjoyed it much, not that first time anyway. I
was sweating so bad I might as well to been chopping cotton. I
hardly even looked at her, I was too busy watching every white
guy in the place. Meantime my hand was on her waist and her
hand was wrapped around my sweaty neck. I kept my arms as
stiff as I could but the dance floor was crowded and her body
kept on bumping up against mine.

"What's the matter," she asked me after awhile, "don't you
like me?" Her eyes were full of puzzlement. That's when it hit
me: She didn't care that I was colored. To her I was just a man
who was acting like a damn fool. I pulled her close.

"Course I like you," I said. "I think you just about the prettiest gal I ever laid eyes on."

We didn't stay in their country long, but I'll always be grateful to those English folks for how they welcomed us. First time
in my life I ever felt like a man first and a black man second.

In October they finally sent us over to where the fighting
was, in France. We crossed the Channel and landed at Omaha
Beach. We couldn't believe the mess we seen there. Sunken

ships, blasted tanks, jeeps, gliders and trucks. No bodies, but we could see them in our heads just the same, sprawled all over the sand. Up till then we'd thought of our country, and ourselves, as unbeatable. On that beach we came face-to-face with the fact that we weren't, and it hit us all hard.

Normandy stayed with us during the four-hundred-mile trip east to the front. It took us six days to get there, to this little town called Saint-Nicholas-de-Port. We could hear the battle going on a few miles away but they didn't send us in. We waited there for three more days, edgy as cats. Then one afternoon we got the order to man all guns. A bunch of MPs in jeeps mounted with machine guns rolled up and parked themselves around our tanks. Then a single jeep came screeching up. A three-star general hopped out of it and got up onto the hood of a half-track. When I seen his ivory-handled pistols I knew I was looking at Ole Blood and Guts himself.

"Men," he said, "you're the first Negro tankers to ever fight in the American Army. I'd have never asked for you if you weren't the best. I have nothing but the best in my Army. I don't give a damn what color you are as long as you go up there and kill those Kraut sonsabitches."

Gave me a shock when I heard his voice, it was as high-pitched as a woman's. I reckon that's why he cussed so much—he didn't want nobody to take him for a sissy.

"Everybody's got their eyes on you and is expecting great things from you," he went on. "Most of all, your race is counting on you. Don't let them down, and damn you, don't let me down! They say it's patriotic to die for your country. Well, let's see how many patriots we can make out of those German bastards."

Course we'd all heard the scuttlebutt about Patton. How he'd hauled off and hit a sick GI at a hospital in Italy. How he was crazy as a coot and hated colored people besides. I don't care what anybody says, that man was a real soldier, and he took us when nobody else thought we were worth a damn. I'd have gone to hell and back for him, and I think every one of us Panthers felt the same. That's what we called ourselves: the 761st Black Panther Battalion. Our motto was "Come Out Fighting." That day at Saint-Nicolas-de-Port they were just words on a flag, but we were about to find out what they meant.

A TANK CREW'S like a small family. With five of you in there day after day, ain't no choice but to get close. After awhile you move like five fingers on a hand. A guy says, *Do this,* and before he can even get the words out it's already done.

We didn't take baths, wasn't no time for them and it was too damn cold besides, and I mean to tell you the smell in that tank could get ripe. One time we were in the middle of battle and our cannoneer, a big awkward guy from Oklahoma named Warren Weeks, got the runs. There he was, squatting over his upturned helmet, grunting and firing away at the German Panzers. The air was so foul I almost lost my breakfast.

Sergeant Cleve hollered out, "Goddamn, Weeks! We oughta load you in the gun and fire you at the Jerries, they'd surrender in no time."

We all about busted our guts laughing. The next day an armor-piercing shell blew most of Warren's head off. His blood and brains went all over me and the other guys, and all over the white walls. Why the Army decided to make the walls white I could never understand. That day they were red but we kept right on fighting, wearing pieces of Warren, till the sun went down and the firing stopped. I don't remember what battle that was, it was somewhere in Belgium—Bastogne maybe, or Tillet. I got to where I didn't know what time it was or what day of the week. There was just the fighting, on and on, the crack of rifles and the *ack ack ack* of machine guns, bazookas firing, shells and mines exploding, men screaming and groaning and dying. And every day knowing you could be next, it could be your blood spattered all over your buddies.

Sometimes the shelling was so ferocious guys from the infantry would beg to get in the tank with us. Sometimes we let them, depending. Once we were parked up on a rise and this white GI with no helmet on came running up to us. Ain't nothing worse for a foot soldier than losing your helmet in battle.

"Hey, you fellas got room for one more?" he yelled.

Sergeant Cleve yelled back, "Where you from, boy?"

"Baton Rouge, Louisiana!"

We all started hooting and laughing. We knew what that meant.

"Sorry, cracker," said Sarge, "we full up today."

"I got some hooch I took off a dead Jerry," said the soldier. He pulled a nice-sized silver flask out of his jacket and held it up. "This stuff'll peel the paint off a barn, sure enough. You can have it if you let me in."

Sarge cocked an eyebrow and looked around at all of us.

"I'm a Baptist, myself," I said.

"Me, too," said Sam.

Sarge hollered, "You want us to burn in hell, boy?"

"Course not, sir!"

"Cause you know drinking's a sin."

We all had plenty of reasons to hate crackers but Sarge hated them more than all of us put together. Word was he had a sister who was raped by a bunch of white boys in Tuscaloosa, that's where he was from.

"Please!" begged the soldier. "Just let me in!"

"Get lost, cracker!"

Reckon that soldier died that day. Reckon I should've felt bad about it but I didn't. I was so worn out it was hard to feel much of anything.

I didn't talk about none of that when I wrote home. Even if the censors would've let it through, I didn't want to fret Mama and Daddy. Instead I told them what snow felt like and how nice the locals were treating us (leaving out a few details about the French girls). I told them about the funny food they had over there and the glittery dress Lena Horne wore when she came and sang to us at the USO. Daddy wrote back with news from home: The skeeters were bad this year. Ruel and Marlon had grown two whole inches. Lilly May sang a solo in church. The mule got into the cockleburs again.

Mississippi felt far, far away.

LAURA

DECEMBER 7, 1941, changed everything for all of us. Within a few days of the attack on Pearl Harbor, Jamie and both of my brothers had enlisted. Teddy stayed with the Engineers, Pearce joined the Marines and Jamie signed up for pilot training with the Air Corps. He wanted to be an ace, but the Army had other plans for him. They made him a bomber pilot, teaching him to fly the giant B-24s called Liberators. He trained for two years before leaving for England. My brothers were already overseas by then, Teddy in France and Pearce in the Pacific.

I stayed in Memphis, worrying about them all, while Henry traveled around the South building bases and airfields for the Army. He remained a civilian; as a wounded veteran of the Great War he was exempt from the draft, for which I was grateful. I didn't mind his absences once I got used to them. I soon realized they made me more interesting to him when he was home. Besides, I had Amanda Leigh for company, and then Isabelle in February of '43. The two of them were as different as they could be. Amanda was Henry's child: quiet, serious-minded, self-contained. Isabelle was something else altogether. From the day she was born she wanted to be held all of the time and would start wailing as soon as I laid her in her crib. Her demanding nature exasperated Henry, but for me her sweetness more than made up for it.

I was bewitched by both of them, and by the beauty of ordinary life, which went on despite the war and seemed all the more precious because of it. When I wasn't changing diapers and weeding my victory garden, I was rolling bandages and sewing for the Red Cross. My sisters, cousins and I organized drives for scrap metal and for silk and nylon stockings, which the Army turned into powder bags. It was a frightening and sorrowful time, but it was also exhilarating. For the first time in our lives, we had a purpose greater than ourselves.

Our family was luckier than many. I lost two cousins and an uncle, but my brothers survived. Pearce was wounded in the thigh and sent home before the fighting turned savage in the Pacific, and Teddy returned safe and sound in the fall of '45. Jamie lost a finger to frostbite but was otherwise unharmed. He didn't come home after he was discharged, but stayed in Europe—to travel, he said, and see the place from the ground for a change. This baffled Henry, who was convinced there was something wrong with him, something he wasn't telling us about. Jamie's letters were breezy and carefree, full of witty descriptions of the places he'd seen and the people he'd met. Henry thought they had a forced quality, but I didn't see it. I thought it was natural Jamie would want to enjoy his freedom after four years of being told where to go and what to do.

Those months after the war were jubilant ones for us and for the whole country. We'd pulled together and been victorious. Our men were home, and we had sugar, coffee and gasoline again. Henry was spending more time in Memphis, and I was hoping to get pregnant. I was thirty-seven; I wanted to give him a son while I still could.

I never saw the axe blow coming. The downstroke came that Christmas. As we usually did, we spent Christmas Eve with my people in Memphis, then drove down to Greenville the next morning. Eboline and her husband, Virgil, hosted a grand family dinner every year in their fancy house on Washington Street. How I hated those trips! Eboline never failed to make me feel dull and unfashionable, or her children to make mine cry. This year would be even worse than usual, because Thalia and her family were driving down from Virginia. The two sisters together were Regan and Goneril to my hapless Cordelia.

When we pulled up at Eboline's, Henry's father came and met us at the car. Pappy had been living with Eboline since Mother McAllan died in the fall of '43. One look at his grim face and we knew something was wrong.

"Well," he said to Henry by way of greeting, "that stuck-up husband of your sister's has gone and killed himself."

"Good God," Henry said. "When?"

"Sometime last night, after we'd all gone to bed. Eboline found the body a little while ago."

"Where?"

"In the attic. He hanged himself," Pappy said. "Merry Christmas."

"Did he leave a note saying why?" I asked.

Pappy pulled a sheet of paper from his pocket and handed it to me. The ink had run where someone's tears had fallen on it. It was addressed to "My darling wife." In a quavering hand, Virgil confessed to Eboline that he'd lost the bulk of their money in a confidence scheme involving a Bolivian silver mine and the rest on a horse named Barclay's Bravado. He said he was ending his life because he couldn't bear the thought of telling her. (Later, when I was better acquainted with my father-in-law, I would wonder if what Virgil really couldn't bear was the thought of spending one more night under the same roof as Pappy.)

Eboline wouldn't leave her bed, even to soothe her children. That job fell to me, along with most of the cooking for a house full of people; Henry had kept the maid on for the time being, but he'd had to let the gardener and cook go. I did what I could. As much as I disliked Eboline, I couldn't help feeling terribly sorry for her.

After the funeral, the girls and I drove home to Memphis while Henry stayed on to help his sister sort out her affairs. He would just be a few days, he said. But a few days turned into a week, then two. The situation was complicated, he told me on the phone. He needed more time to settle things.

He took the train home in mid-January. He was cheerful, almost ebullient, and unusually passionate that night in our bed. Afterward he threaded his fingers through mine and cleared his throat.

"Honey, by the way," he said.

I braced myself. That particular phrase, coming out of Henry's mouth, could lead to anything at all, I never knew what: *Honey, by the way, we're out of mustard, could you pick some up at the store? Honey, by the way, I had a car accident this morning.*

Or in this case, "Honey, by the way, I bought a farm in Mississippi. We'll be moving there in two weeks."

The farm, he went on to tell me, was located forty miles from Greenville, near a little town I'd never heard of called Marietta. We'd live in town, in a house he'd rented for us there, and he'd drive to the farm every day to work.

"Is this because of Eboline?" I asked, when I could speak calmly.

"Partly," he said, giving my hand a squeeze. "Virgil's estate is a mess. It'll take months to untangle, and I need to be close by." I must have given him a dubious look. "Eboline and the children are all alone now," he said, his voice rising a little. "It's my duty to help them."

"What about your father?" I asked. Meaning, can't he help them?

"Eboline can't be expected to look after him now. Pappy will have to come and live with us." Henry paused, then added, "He'll be driving the truck up next week."

"What truck?"

"The pickup truck I bought to use on the farm. We'll need it to move the furniture. We won't be able to take everything at once, but I can make a second trip when we're settled."

Settled. In rural Mississippi. In two weeks' time.

"I bought a tractor too," he said. "A John Deere Model B. It's one hell of a machine—you won't believe how fast it can get a field plowed. I'll be able to farm a hundred and twenty acres by myself. Imagine that!"

When I said nothing, Henry propped himself up on one elbow and peered down at my face. "You're mighty quiet," he said.

"I'm mighty surprised."

He gave me a puzzled frown. "But you knew I always intended to have my own farm someday."

"No, Henry. I had no idea."

"I'm sure I must have mentioned it."

"No, you never did."

"Well," he said, "I'm telling you now."

Just like that, my life was overturned. Henry didn't ask me how I felt about leaving my home of thirty-seven years and moving with his cantankerous father in tow to a hick town in the middle of Mississippi, and I didn't tell him. This was his territory, as the children and the kitchen and the church were mine, and we were careful not to trespass in each other's territories. When it was absolutely necessary we did it discreetly, on the furthermost borders.

MOTHER CRIED WHEN I told her we were leaving, but it was hardly the squall I'd expected. It was more of a light summer shower, quickly over, followed by admonitions to buck up and make the best of it. Daddy merely sighed. "Well," he said,

"I guess we've had you with us longer than we had any right to expect." This was what happened to daughters, their expressions seemed to say. You raised them, and if you were lucky they found husbands who might then take them off anywhere at all, and it was not only to be expected, but borne cheerfully.

I tried to be cheerful, but it was hard. Every day I said goodbye to some beloved person or thing. The porch swing of my parents' house, where Billy Escue had given me my first real kiss the night of my seventeenth birthday. My own little house on Evergreen Street, with its lace curtains and flowered wallpaper. The roaring of the lions at the nearby zoo, which had made me uneasy when we first moved in but now provided a familiar punctuation to my days. The light at my church, which fell in shafts of brilliant color upon the upturned faces of the congregation.

My own family's faces I could hardly bear to look at. My mother and sisters, with their high Fairbairn foreheads and surprised blue eyes. My father, with his wide, kind smile and sloping nose that never could hold up his spectacles properly.

"It'll be an adventure," said Daddy.

"It's not that far away," said Etta.

"There are bound to be nice people there," said Mother.

"I'm sure you're right," I told them.

But I didn't believe a word of it. Marietta was a Delta town; its population—a grand total of four hundred and twelve souls, as I later learned—would consist mostly of farmers, wives of farmers and children of farmers, half of whom were probably Negroes and all of whom were undoubtedly Baptists. We would be miles from civilization among bumpkins who drank grape juice at church every Sunday and talked of nothing but the weather and the crops.

And as if that weren't bad enough, Pappy would be there with us. I'd never spent much time around my father-in-law, a blessing I didn't fully appreciate until that last week in Memphis, when I was forced to spend all day every day alone with him while Henry was at work. Pappy was sour, bossy and vain. His pants had to be creased, his handkerchiefs folded a certain way, his shirts starched. He changed them twice a day, not that they were ever soiled by anything but spilled food; he exerted himself only to roll cigarettes and instruct me on how to pack. I dug up some books I thought he'd like, hoping to distract him, but he waved them away contemptuously. Reading was a waste of time, he said, and education was for prigs and sissies. I wondered how he'd ever managed to produce two sons like Henry and Jamie. I hoped that once we got to Marietta, he'd be spending his days with Henry at the farm, leaving the house to me and the girls.

The house was the only bright spot in this otherwise bleak picture. Henry had rented it from a couple who'd lost their son in the war and were moving out west. He described it as a two-story antebellum with four bedrooms, a wraparound porch and, most enticing to me, a fig tree. I've always been crazy for figs. As I wrapped dishes in newspaper and boxed up lamps and books and linens, I spent many not entirely unpleasant moments picturing myself walking out my back door, plucking the ripe fruit from the branches and eating it unrinsed, like a greedy child. I imagined the pies and minces I would make, the preserves I would lay in for the winter. I said nothing of this to Henry; I wasn't about to give him the satisfaction. But every night at supper, he'd bring up some pleasing detail about the house that he'd neglected to mention before. Had he told me it had a modern electric stove? Did I know it was just three blocks from the elementary school where Amanda Leigh would start first grade the following year?

"That's nice, Henry," I would reply noncommittally.

The day of our departure, we rose before dawn. Teddy and Pearce came and helped Henry load the truck with our furniture, including my most prized possession—an 1859 Steiff upright piano with a rosewood case carved in the Eastlake style. It had belonged to my grandmother, who'd taught me to play. I'd just started giving lessons to Amanda Leigh.

Daddy arrived as I was making my last check of the house. I was surprised to see him; we'd said our goodbyes the night before. He brought biscuits from Mother and a crock of her apple butter. The eight of us ate the hot biscuits standing in the mostly empty living room, shivering in the chill, licking our sticky fingers between bites. When we were done my father and brothers walked us out to the car. Daddy shook Pappy's hand, then Henry's, then hugged the children. At last he turned to me.

Softly, in a voice meant for my ears alone, he said, "When you were a year old and you came down with rubella, the doctor told us you were likely to die of it. Said he didn't expect you'd live another forty-eight hours. Your mother was frantic, but I told her that doctor didn't know what he was talking about. Our Laura's a fighter, I said, and she's going to be just fine. I never doubted it, not for one minute, then or since. You keep that in your pocket and take it out when you need it, hear?"

Swallowing the lump in my throat, I nodded and embraced him. Then I hugged my brothers one last time.

"Well," Henry said, "the day's getting on."

"You take good care of my three girls," Daddy said.

"I will. They're my three girls too."

The children and I sang as we left Memphis. They sat beside me in the front seat of the DeSoto. Henry, Pappy, and all our belongings were in the truck in front of us. The Mississippi River was a vast, indifferent presence on our right.

"You've got to ac-cent-tchu-ate the positive," we sang, but the words felt as foolish and empty as I did.

IT WAS NEARING dusk when we turned onto Tupelo Lane. This, I knew, was the name of our street, and I felt a little ripple of excitement each time Henry slowed down. Finally he pulled the truck over and stopped, and I saw the house: a charming old place much as he'd described, but with many agreeable particulars he'd neglected to mention — probably because, being Henry, he hadn't noticed them in the first place. There was a large pecan tree in the front yard, and one side of the house was entirely covered in wisteria, like a nubby green cloak. In the spring, when it bloomed, its perfume would carry us down into sleep every night, and in the summer the lawn would be dotted with fallen purple blossoms. There were two bay windows on either side of the front door, and under them, clumps of mature azalea bushes.

"You didn't tell me we had azaleas, Henry," I chided him when I'd gotten the girls bundled up and out of the car.

"So we do," he said with a smile. I could tell he was feeling pleased with himself. I didn't begrudge him that. The house was truly lovely.

Amanda Leigh sneezed. She was leaning heavily against my leg, and her sister was half-asleep in my arms. Both of them had head colds. "The children are done in," I said. "Let's get them in the house."

"The key should be under the mat," he said.

As we started up the walk, the porch light went on and the front door opened. A man stepped out onto the porch. He was huge, with hunched shoulders like a bear's. A small woman came up behind him, peering from around his shoulder.

"Who are you?" he said. His tone wasn't friendly.

"We're the McAllans," Henry replied. "The new tenants of this house. Who are you?"

The man widened his stance, crossing his arms over his chest. "Orris Stokes. The new owner of this house."

"New owner? I rented this place from George Suddeth just three weeks ago."

"Well, Suddeth sold me the house last week, and he didn't say nothing to me about any renters."

"Is that a fact," Henry said. "Looks like I need to refresh his memory."

"You won't find him. He left town three days ago."

"I gave him a hundred-dollar deposit!"

"I don't know nothing about that," Orris Stokes said.

"You get anything in writing?" Pappy asked Henry.

"No. We shook on the deal."

The old man spat into the street. "How a son of mine could be such a fool, I'll never know."

I watched my husband's face fill with the knowledge that he'd been cheated, and worse, that he was powerless to make it right. He turned to me. "I paid him a hundred dollars cash," he said, "right there in the living room of that house. Afterward I sat down to dinner with him and his wife. I showed her pictures of you and the girls."

"You'd best be getting on," said Orris Stokes. "Ain't nothing for you here."

"Mama, I have to tinkle," Amanda Leigh said in a child's loud whisper.

"Hush now," I said.

The woman moved then, coming out from behind her husband. She was a tiny bird-boned thing with freckled skin and small, fluttering hands. No steel in her, I thought, until I saw her chin. That chin—sharply pointed and jutting forward like a trowel—told a different story. I imagined Orris had felt the sting of her defiance on more than one occasion.

"I'm Alice Stokes," she said. "Why don't y'all come in and have a little supper before you go?"

"Now, Alice," said her husband.

She ignored him, addressing herself to me as if the three men weren't there. "We've got stew and cornbread. It ain't fancy but we'd be pleased to share it with you."

"Thank you," I said, before Henry could refuse. "We'd be most grateful."

The house was cheaply furnished and deserved better. The ceilings were high and the rooms spacious, with lovely period details. I couldn't help but imagine my own things in place of the Stokeses': my piano beside the bay window in the living room, my Victorian love seat in front of the hand-carved mantel in the parlor. As I sat down to supper at Alice's crude pine table, I thought how much better my own dining set would have looked beneath the ornate ceiling medallion.

Over supper we learned that Orris owned the local feed store. That perked Henry up a bit. The two of them talked livestock for a while, discussing the merits of various breeds of pigs—a subject on which Henry was astonishingly well versed. Then the talk turned to farm labor.

"Damn niggers," Orris said. "Moving up north, leaving folks with no way to make a crop. Ought to be a law against it."

"In my day we didn't let em leave," Pappy said. "And the ones that tried sneaking off in the middle of the night ended up sorry they had."

Orris nodded approvingly. "My brother has a farm down to Yazoo City. Do you know, last October he had cotton rotting in the fields because he couldn't find enough niggers to pick it? And the ones he did find were wanting two dollars and fifty cents per hundred pounds."

"Two-fifty per hundred!" Henry exclaimed. "At that rate

they'll put every planter in the Delta out of business. And then what'll they do, when there's nobody to hire them and give them a roof over their heads?"

"If you're expecting sense from a nigger, you're gonna be waiting a good long while," said Pappy.

"You mark my words," said Orris, "they're gonna be asking for even more this year, now the government's done away with the price controls."

"Damn niggers," said Pappy.

It was eight o'clock by the time we finished supper, and the children were nodding into their bowls. When Alice offered to let us stay the night, I accepted quickly; it was a two-hour drive to Eboline's in Greenville, and I wasn't about to chance our flimsy wartime tires on those pothole-filled roads in the dark. Henry and Orris both looked like they wanted to object, but neither of them did. The three men went outside to cover the furniture in the truck against the dew, while Alice cleaned up and I put the girls to bed. After I got them tucked in, I helped her make up the bed Henry and I would share.

"This is a big house," I said. "Is it just you and Mr. Stokes?"

"Yes," she said in a low, sad voice. "Diphtheria took Orris Jr. in the fall of '42, and our daughter Mary died of pneumonia last year. Your girls are sleeping in their beds."

"I'm sorry." I busied myself with the pillowcases, not knowing what else to say.

"I'm expecting," she confided shyly after a moment. "I haven't told Orris yet. I wanted to be sure it took."

"I hope you have a fine strong baby, Alice."

"So do I. I pray for it every night."

She left me then, wishing me a good sleep. I went to the window, which looked out over the backyard. I could see the promised fig tree, its branches naked of leaves but still graceful in the moonlight. *If he had just signed a lease,* I thought. *If he were just a different sort of man.* Henry was never good at reading people. He always assumed everybody was just like him: that they said what they meant and would do what they said.

When the door opened I didn't turn around. He walked up behind me and laid his hand on my shoulder. I hesitated, then reached up and touched it with my own. The skin on top was soft and papery. I felt a rush of tenderness for him, for his aging hands and his wounded pride. He kissed the top of my head, and I sighed and leaned into him. How could I wish him to be other than he was? To be hard and suspicious, like his father? I couldn't, and I felt ashamed of myself for having had such thoughts.

"We'll find another house," I said.

I felt him shake his head. "This was the only place for rent in town. It's all the returning soldiers, they've taken all the housing. We'll have to live out on the farm."

"What about one of the other towns nearby?" I asked.

"I've got no time to look elsewhere," he said. "I have to get the fields broken. I'm already starting a month late."

He stepped away from me. I heard the snap of the suitcase opening. "The farmhouse isn't much, but I know you'll make it nice," he said. "I'm going to brush my teeth now. Why don't you get into bed?"

There was a brief pause, then the door opened and shut. As his footsteps receded down the hall, I looked at the fig tree and thought of the fruit that would begin ripening there come summer. I wondered if Alice Stokes liked figs; if she would gather up the fruit eagerly or let it fall to the ground and rot.

IN THE MORNING we said goodbye to the Stokeses and headed to the general store to buy food, kerosene, buckets, candles and the other provisions we would need on the farm. That's when I learned there was no electricity or running water in the house.

"There's a pump in the front yard," Henry said, "and some kind of stove in the kitchen."

"A pump? There's no indoor plumbing?"

"No."

"What about the bathroom?" I said.

"There is no bathroom," he said, with a hint of impatience. "Just an outhouse."

Honey, by the way.

A stout-bodied woman in a man's checked shirt and overalls spoke from behind the counter. "You the new owners of the Conley place?"

"That's right," said Henry.

"You'll be wanting wood for that stove. I'm Rose Tricklebank, and this is my store, mine and my husband Bill's."

She stuck her hand out, and we all shook it in turn. She

had a strong, callused grip; I saw Henry's eyes widen when her hand grasped his. Yet for all her mannish ways, from the neck up Rose Tricklebank resembled nothing so much as the flower whose name she bore. She had a Cupid's-bow mouth and a round face surrounded by a mop of curly auburn hair. A cigarette tucked behind one ear spoiled the picture, but only a little.

"You'll want to stock up good on supplies today," she said. "Big storm's coming in tonight, could rain all week."

"Why should that matter?" Pappy asked.

"When it rains and that river rises, the Conley place can be cut off for days."

"It's the McAllan place now," Henry said.

After we paid, Rose hefted one of our boxes herself and carried it out to the car, over Henry's protests. She pulled two licorice ropes out of her pocket and handed them to Amanda Leigh and Isabelle. "I've got two girls of my own, and my Ruth Ann is about your age," she said to Amanda, tousling her hair. "She and Caroline are in school right now, but I hope you'll come back and visit us soon."

I promised we would, thinking it would be nice to have a friend in town, and some playmates for the girls. As soon as she was out of earshot, Henry muttered, "That woman acts like she thinks she's a man."

"Maybe she is a man, and her husband hasn't cottoned to it yet," Pappy said.

The two of them laughed. It irritated me. "Well, I like her," I said, "and I plan on visiting her once we get settled in."

Henry's brows went up. I wondered if he would forbid me

to see her, and what I would say if he did. But all he said was, "You'll have a whole lot to do on the farm."

THE FARM WAS about a twenty-minute drive from town, but it seemed longer because the road was so rutted and the view so monotonous. The land was flat and mostly featureless, as farmers will inevitably make it. Negroes dotted the fields, tilling the earth with mule-drawn plows. Without the green of crops to bring it alive, the land looked bleak, an ocean of unrelieved brown in which we'd been set adrift.

We crossed over a creaky bridge spanning a small river lined with cypresses and willows. Henry stuck his head out the window of the truck and shouted back at me, "This is it, honey! We're on our land now!"

I mustered a smile and a wave. To me, it looked no different from the other land we'd passed. There were brown fields and unpainted sharecroppers' shacks with dirt yards. Women who might have been any age from thirty to sixty hung laundry from sagging clotheslines while gaggles of dirty barefoot children watched listlessly from the porch. After a time we came to a shack that was larger than the others, though no less decrepit. It had a deserted air. The truck stopped in front of it, and Henry and his father got out.

"Why are we stopping?" I called out.

"We're here," Henry said.

Here was a long, rickety house with a warped tin roof and shuttered windows that had neither glass nor screens. Here was a porch that ran the length of the house, connecting it to a small lean-to. Here was a dirt yard with a pump in the middle of it, shaded by a large oak tree that had somehow managed to escape razing by the original steaders. Here was a barn, a pasture, a cotton house, a corncrib, a pig wallow, a chicken coop and an outhouse.

Here was our new home.

Amanda Leigh and Isabelle scrambled out of the car and ran around the yard, delighted with everything they saw. I followed, stepping up to my ankles in muck. It would be weeks before I learned that on a farm, you always look before you step, because you never know what you might be stepping in or on: a mud puddle, a pile of excrement, a rattlesnake.

"Will we have chickens, Daddy? And pigs?" Amanda Leigh asked. "Will we have a cow?"

"We sure will," Henry said. "You know what else?" He pointed back to the line of trees that marked the river. "See that river we crossed over? I bet it's full of catfish and craw-dads."

There was some kind of structure on the river, about a mile away. Even from a distance I could tell it was much larger than the house. "What's that building?" I asked Henry.

"An old sawmill, dates back to before the Civil War. You and the girls stay out of there, it's liable to fall down any minute."

"It ain't the only thing," said Pappy, gesturing at the house. "That roof needs repairing, and them steps look rotten. And some of the shutters are missing, you better replace em quick or we're liable to freeze to death."

"We'll get the place fixed up," Henry said. "It'll be all right. You'll see."

He wasn't speaking to Pappy, but to me. *Make the best of it,* his eyes urged. *Don't shame me in front of my father and the girls.* I felt a stirring of anger. Of course I would make the best of it, for the children's sake if nothing else.

With the help of one of the tenants, a talkative light-skinned Negro named Hap Jackson, Henry unloaded the truck and moved the furniture in. I saw right away that we wouldn't be able to bring much more from Memphis. The house had just three rooms: a large main room that encompassed the kitchen and living area, and two bedrooms barely big enough to hold a bed and a chest of drawers each. There were no closets, just pegs hammered at intervals along the walls. Like the floors, the walls were rough plank, with gaps between the boards through which the wind and all manner of insects could enter freely. Every surface was filthy. I felt another surge of anger. How could Henry have brought us to such a place?

I wasn't the only one displeased with the accommodations. "Where am I gonna sleep?" demanded Pappy.

Henry looked at me. I shrugged. He had laid this egg all by himself; he could figure out how to hatch it.

"I guess we'll have to put you out in the lean-to," Henry said.

"I ain't sleeping out there. It don't even have a floor."

"I don't know where else to put you," Henry said. "There's no room in the house."

"There would be, if you got rid of that piano," Pappy said.

The piano just barely fit in one corner of the main room.

"If you got rid of that piano," Pappy said, "we could put a bed there."

"We could," Henry agreed.

"No," I said. "We need the piano. I'm teaching the girls to play, you know that. Besides, I don't want a bed in the middle of the living room."

"We could rig a curtain around it," Pappy said.

"True," Henry said.

They were both looking at me: Henry unhappily, his father wearing a smirk. Henry was going to agree. I could see it in his face, and so could Pappy.

"I need to speak to you in private," I said, looking at Henry. I went out onto the front porch. Henry followed, shutting the door behind him.

In a low voice, I said, "When you told me you were bringing me here, away from my people and everything I've ever known, I didn't say a word. When you informed me your father was coming to live with us, I went along. When Orris Stokes stood there and told you you'd been fleeced by that man you rented the house from, I kept my mouth shut. But I'm telling you now, Henry, we're not getting rid of that piano. It's the one civilized thing in this place, and I want it for the girls and myself, and we're keeping it. So you can just go back in there and tell your father he can sleep in the lean-to. Either that or he can sleep in the bed with you, because I am *not* staying here without my piano."

Henry was looking at me like I'd just sprouted antlers. I stared back, resisting the urge to drop my gaze.

"You're overtired," he said.

"No. I'm fine."

How my heart thumped as I waited him out! I'd never defied my husband so openly, or anyone else for that matter. It felt dangerous, heady. Inside the house I could hear the girls squabbling over something. Isabelle started crying, but I didn't take my eyes off Henry's.

"You'd better go to them," he said finally.

"And the piano?"

"I'll put a floor in the lean-to. Fix it up for him."

"Thank you, honey."

That night in our bed he took me hard, from behind, without any of the usual preliminaries. It hurt, but I didn't make a sound.

HENRY

WHEN I WAS SIX years old, my grandfather called me into the bedroom where he was dying. I didn't like to go in there—the room stank of sickness and old man, and the skeleton look of him scared me—but I was reared to be obedient so I went.

"Run outside and get a handful of dirt, then bring it back here," he said.

"What for?"

"Just do it." He waved one gnarled hand. "Go on now."

"Yes, sir."

I went and got the dirt. When I returned with it, he asked me what I was holding.

"Dirt," I said.

"That's right. Now give it to me."

He cupped his hands. They shook with palsy. I poured the dirt into them, trying not to spill any on the sheets.

"What am I holding?" he asked.

"Dirt."

"No."

"Earth?"

"No, boy. This is *land* I've got. Do you know why?" His eyebrows shot up. They were gray and bushy, tangled like wire.

I shook my head, not understanding.

"Because it's *mine*," he said. "One day this'll be your land, your farm. But in the meantime, to you and every other person who don't own it, it's just dirt. Here, take it on back outside before your mama catches you with it."

He poured it back into my hands. As I turned to leave, he grabbed ahold of my sleeve and fixed me with his rheumy eyes. "Remember this, boy. You can put your faith in a whole lot of things—in God, in money, in other people—but land's the only thing you can count on to be there tomorrow. It's the only thing that's really yours."

A week later he was dead, and his land passed to my mother. That land was where I grew to manhood, and though I left it at nineteen to see what lay outside its borders, I always knew I'd return to it someday. I knew it during the weeks I spent overseas with my face pressed in alien mud soaked in the blood of people not my own, and during the long months after, lying on my back in Army hospitals while my leg stank and throbbed and itched and finally healed. I knew it while I was a student up in Oxford, where the land doesn't lie flat, but heaves itself up and down like seawater. I knew it when I went to work for the Corps of Engineers, a job that took me many places that were strange to me, and some others that looked like home but weren't. Even when the flood came in '27, overrunning Greenville and destroying our house and that year's cotton crop, it never occurred to me that my father would do other than rebuild and replant. That land had been in my mother's family for nearly a hundred years. My great-great-grandfather and his slaves had cleared it, wresting it acre by acre from the seething mass of cane and brush that covered it. Rebuild and replant: that's what farmers do in the Delta.

My father did neither. He sold the farm in January of '28, nine months after the flood. I was living down to Vicksburg at the time and traveling a great deal for work. I didn't find out what he'd done till after it was too late.

"That damned river wiped me out," Pappy liked to tell people after he'd moved to town and started working for the railroad. "Never would've sold otherwise."

That was a lie, one of many that made up his story of himself. The truth was he walked away from that land gladly, because he feared and hated farming. Feared the weather and the floods, hated the work and the sweat and the long hours alone with his own thoughts. Even as a boy I saw how small he got when he looked at the sky, how he brushed the soil from his hands at the end of the day like it was dung. The flood was just an excuse to sell.

Took me nearly twenty years to save enough to buy my own land. There was the Depression to get through, and then the war. I had a wife and two children to provide for. I put by what I could and waited.

By V-J Day, I had the money. I figured I'd work one more year to give us a cushion and start looking for property the following summer. That would give me plenty of time to learn the land, purchase seed and equipment, find tenants and so on before the new planting season started in January. It would also give me time to work on my wife, who I knew would be reluctant to leave Memphis.

That's how it was supposed to be, nice and orderly, and it would have been if that good-for-nothing husband of Eboline's hadn't gone and hanged himself that Christmas. I never trusted my brother-in-law, or any man comfortable in a suit. Virgil was a great drinker and a great talker besides, and those are stains enough on anybody's character, but what sort of man ends his life with no thought for the shame and misfortune his actions will bring upon his family? He left my sister flat broke and my nephew and nieces fatherless. If he hadn't already been dead, I would have killed him myself.

Eboline and the children needed looking after, and there was no one to do it but me. As soon as we buried Virgil, I started searching for property nearby. There was nothing suitable for sale around Greenville, but I heard about a two-hundred-acre farm in Marietta, forty miles to the southeast. It belonged to a widow named Conley whose husband had died at Normandy. She had no sons to inherit the place and was eager to sell.

From the minute I set foot on the property, I had a good feeling about it. The land was completely cleared, with a small river running along the southern border. The soil was rich and black—Conley had had the sense to rotate his crops. The barn and cotton house looked sound, and there was a ramshackle house on the property that would serve me well as a camp, though it wouldn't do as a home for Laura and the girls.

The farm was everything I wanted. Mrs. Conley was asking ninety-five hundred for it—mostly, I reckoned, because I'd driven up in Eboline's Cadillac. I bargained her down to eighty-seven hundred, plus a hundred and fifty each for her cow and two mules.

I was a landowner at last. I could hardly wait to tell my wife.

But first, I had some things to take care of. Had to find us a rent house in town. Had to buy a tractor—I wasn't about to be a mule farmer like my father had been—and a truck. And I had to decide which tenants to keep on and which to put off. With the tractor I could farm more than half the acreage myself, so I'd only need three of the six tenants who were living there. I interviewed them all, checking their accounts of themselves against Conley's books, then asked the ones with the smallest yields per acre and the greatest talent for exaggeration to leave.

I kept on the Atwoods, the Cottrills, and the Jacksons. The Jacksons looked to be the best of the bunch, even though they were colored. They were share tenants, not sharecroppers, so they only paid me a quarter of their crop as opposed to half. You don't see many colored share tenants. Aren't many of them have the discipline to save for their own mule and equipment. But Hap Jackson wasn't your typical Negro. For one thing, he could read. The first time I met him, before he signed his contract, he asked to see his page in Conley's account book.

"Sure," I said, "I'll show it to you, but how will you know what it says?"

"I been reading going on seven years now," he said. "My

boy Ronsel learned me. I wasn't much good at it at first but he kept after me till I could get through Genesis and Exodus on my own. Teached me my numbers too. Yessuh, Ronsel's plenty smart. He's a sergeant in the Army. Fought under General Patton hisself, won him a whole bunch of medals over there. Reckon he'll be coming home any day now, yessuh."

I handed him the account book, as much to shut him up as anything. Underneath Hap's name, Conley had written, *A hardworking nigger who picks a clean bale.*

"Mr. Conley seemed to have a good opinion of you," I said.

Hap didn't answer. He was concentrating on the figures, running his finger down the columns. His lips moved as he read. He scowled and shook his head. "My wife was right," he said. "She was right all along."

"Right about what?"

"See here, where it says twenty bales next to my name? Mist Conley only paid me for eighteen. Told me that was all my cotton graded out to. Florence said he was cheating us, but I didn't want to believe her."

"You never saw this book before?"

"No suh. One time I asked Mist Conley to look in it, that was the first year we was here, and he got to hollering at me till it was a pity. Told me he'd put me off if I questioned his word again."

"Well I don't know, Hap. It says here he paid you for twenty."

"I ain't telling no part of a lie," he declared.

I believed him. A Negro is like a little child, when he tries to lie it's stamped on his face plain as day. Hap's face held nothing but honest frustration. Besides, I know it's common practice for planters to cheat their colored tenants. I don't hold with it myself. Whatever else the colored man may be, he's our brother. A younger brother, to be sure, undisciplined and driven by his appetites, but also kindly and tragic and humble before God. For good or ill, he's been given into our care. If we care for him badly or not at all, if we use our natural superiority to harm him, we're damned as surely as Cain.

"Tell you what, Hap," I said. "You stay on and I'll let you look in this account book any time you want. You can even come with me to the gin for the grading."

He gave me a measuring look and I saw that his eyes, which I'd thought were brown, were actually a muddy green. Between that and his light skin, I figured he must have had two white grandfathers. It explained a lot.

He was still looking at me. I raised my eyebrows, and he dropped his gaze. I was glad to see that. Smart is well and good, but I won't have a disrespectful nigger working for me.

"Thank you, Mist McAllan. That'd be just fine."

"Good, it's settled then," I said. "One more thing. I understand your wife and daughter don't do field work. Is that true?"

"Yessuh. Well, they help out at picking time but they don't do no plowing or chopping. Ain't no need for em to, me and my sons get along just fine without em. Florence is a granny midwife, she brings in a little extra thataway."

"But you could farm another five acres with them helping you in the fields," I said.

"I don't want no wife of mine chopping cotton, or Lilly May neither," he said. "Womenfolks ain't meant for that kind of labor."

I feel that way myself, but I'd never heard a Negro say so before. Most of them use their women harder than their mules. I've seen colored women out in the fields so big with child they could barely bend over to hoe the cotton. Of course, a colored woman is sturdier than a white woman to begin with.

Laura wouldn't have lasted a week in the fields, but I thought she'd make a fine farmwife once she got used to the idea. Shows you how smart I was.

SHE WAS AGAINST the move from the minute I told her about it. She didn't say so directly, but she didn't have to. I could tell from the way she started humming whenever I walked in the room. A woman will make her feelings known one way or another. Laura's way is with music: singing when she's content, humming when she isn't, whistling tunelessly when she's thinking a thing over and deciding whether to sing or hum about it.

The music got a lot less pleasant once we got to the farm. Slamming doors and banging pans, raising her voice to Pappy and me. Defying me. It was as if somebody had come in the night and stolen my sweet, biddable wife, leaving behind a shrew in her place. Everything I did or said was wrong. I knew she blamed me for losing that house in town, but was it my fault the girls got so sick? And the storm—I suppose that was my doing too?

It hit the middle of the night we arrived, making an ungodly racket on the tin roof. The girls' room was leaking, so we brought them into the bed with us. By morning they were both coughing and hot to the touch. They'd been sniffling for a few days but I hadn't thought much of it, kids are always catching something. The rain kept up all that day and the next, coming down in heavy sheets. Late that second afternoon I was out in the barn mending tack when Pappy came to fetch me.

"Your wife wants you," he said. "Your daughters are worse."

I hurried to the house. Amanda Leigh was coughing, high, cracking sounds like shots from a .22. Isabelle lay in the bed beside her, making a terrible wheezing noise with each indrawn breath. Their lips and fingernails were blue.

"It's whooping cough," Laura said. "Go and fetch the doctor at once. And tell your father to put a pot of water on to boil." I wanted to comfort her but her eyes stopped me. "Just go," she said.

I told Pappy to put the water on and ran out to the truck. The road was a muddy churn. Somehow I made it to the bridge without skidding off into a ditch. I heard the river before I saw it: a roar of pure power. The bridge was two feet underwater. I stood with the rain lashing my face and looked at the swollen brown water and cursed George Suddeth for a liar, and myself for a gullible fool. Never should have trusted him to begin with, that's what Pappy said, and I reckoned he was right. Still, it's a sorry world if you can't count on a man to keep his given word after you've sat at his table and broken bread with him.

It was on the way back to the house that I thought of Hap Jackson's wife, Florence. Hap had said she was a midwife, she might know something of children's ailments. Even if she didn't, she'd be able to help with the cooking and housework while Laura nursed the girls.

Florence herself answered my knock. I hadn't met her before, and her appearance took me aback. She was a tall, strapping Negress with sooty black skin and muscles ropy as a man's—an Amazon of her kind. I had to look up at her to talk to her. Woman must have been near to six feet tall.

"May I help you?" she said.

"I'm Henry McAllan."

She nodded. "How do. I'm Florence Jackson. If you looking for Hap, he's out in the shed, tending to the mule."

"Actually, I came to see you. My little girls, they're three and five, they've taken sick with whooping cough. I can't get to town because the bridge is washed out, and my wife . . ." *My wife is liable to kill me if I come home with no doctor and no help.*

"When they start the whooping?"

"This afternoon."

She shook her head. "They still catching then. I can give you some remedies to take to em but I can't go with you."

"I'll pay you," I said.

"I wouldn't be able to come home for three or four days at least. And then who gone look after my own family, and my mothers?"

"I'm asking you," I said.

As I locked eyes with her, I was struck by the sheer force of her. That force was banked now but I could sense it un-

derneath, ready to come alive at need. This wasn't your com-
monplace Negro vitality—the animal spirits they spend so
recklessly in music and fornication. This was a deep-running
fierceness that was almost warriorlike, if you can imagine a
colored farmwife in a flour-sack dress as a warrior.

Florence shifted, and I saw a girl of maybe nine or ten in the
room behind her, white to the elbows with flour from kneading
dough. Had to be the daughter, Lilly May. She was watching
us, waiting like I was for her mother's answer.

"I got to ask Hap," Florence said finally.

The girl ducked her head and went back to her kneading,
and I knew that Florence was lying. The decision was hers to
make, not Hap's, and she'd just made it.

"Please," I said. "My wife is afraid." I felt my face get hot as
she considered me. If she said no, I wouldn't ask her again. I
wouldn't stoop to beg a nigger for help. If she said no—

"All right then," she said. "Wait here while I get my
things."

"I'll wait in the truck."

A few minutes later she came out carrying a battered leather
case, a rolled-up bundle of clothes and an empty burlap bag.
She opened the passenger door and set the case and the clothes
inside.

"You got you any chickens yet?" she asked.

"No."

She closed the truck door and walked around to the chicken
coop on the side of the house, moving unhurriedly in spite of
the pouring rain. She stepped over the wire fence and tucked

the bag under one arm. Then she reached into the henhouse, pulled out a flapping bird and, with one sure twist of her big hands, wrung its neck. She put the chicken in the bag and walked back to the truck, still moving at that same steady, deliberate pace.

She opened the door. "Them girls gone need broth," she said, as she climbed inside. She didn't ask my permission, just got in like she had every right to sit in the cab with me. Under normal circumstances I wouldn't have stood for it, but I didn't dare ask her to ride in back.

FLORENCE

FIRST TIME I LAID eyes on Laura McAllan she was out of her head with mama worry. When that mama worry takes ahold of a woman you can't expect no sense from her. She'll do or say anything at all and you just better hope you ain't in her way. That's the Lord's doing right there. He made mothers to be like that on account of children need protecting and the men ain't around to do it most of the time. Something bad happen to a child, you can be sure his daddy gone be off somewhere else. Helping that child be up to the mama. But God never gives us a task without giving us the means to see it through. That mama worry come straight from Him, it make it so she can't help but look after that child. Every once in awhile you see a mother who ain't got it, who just don't care for her own baby that came out of her own body. And you try and get her to hold that baby and feed that baby but she won't have none of it. She just staring off, letting that baby lay there and cry, letting other people do for it. And you know that poor child gone grow up wrong-headed, if it grows up at all.

Laura McAllan was tending to them two sick little girls when I come in with her husband. One of em was bent over a pot of steaming water with a sheet over her head. The other one was just laying there in the bed making that awful whooping sound. When Miz McAllan looked up and seen us her eyes just about scorched us both to a crisp.

"Who's this, Henry? Where's the doctor?"

"The bridge is washed out," he said. "I couldn't get to town. This is Florence Jackson, she's a midwife. I thought she might be able to help."

"Do you see anybody giving birth here?" she said. "These children need a medical doctor, not some granny with a bag full of potions."

Just then the little one started gagging like they do when the whooping takes em real bad. I went right over to her. I turned that child onto her side and held her head over the bowl, but all that come out was some yellow bile. "I seen this with my own children," I told her. "We need to get some liquid down em. But first we got to clear some of that phlegm out."

She glared at me a minute, then said, "How?"

"We'll make em up some horehound tea, and we'll keep after em with the steam like you been doing. That was real good, making that steam for em."

Mist McAllan was just standing there dripping water all over the floor, looking like somebody stabbed him whenever one of them little girls coughed. Times like that, you got to give the men something to do. I asked him to go boil some more water.

"That tea'll draw the phlegm right on out of there," I told Miz McAllan. "Then once they get to breathing better we'll make em some chicken broth and put a little ground-up willow bark in it for the fever."

"I've got aspirin somewhere, if I can find it in all this mess."

"Don't fret yourself over it. Aspirin's made out of willow bark, they do the same work."

"I should have taken them to the doctor yesterday, as soon as they started coughing. If anything happens to them . . ."

"Listen to me," I said, "your girls gone be just fine. Jesus is watching over em and I'm here too, and ain't neither one of us going nowhere till they feeling better. Give em a week or so, they'll be right as rain, you'll see." I talked to her just like I talk to a laboring woman. Mothers need to hear them soothing words. They just as important as the medicines, sometimes even more.

"Thank you for coming," she said after awhile.

"You welcome."

After they had some tea and was quieted down some I went and started plucking the chicken I'd brought. I hadn't been in the house since the Conleys left and it was filthy from standing empty. Well, not altogether empty—plenty of creatures had been in and out of there. There was mouse droppings and snail tracks on the floor, cicada husks stuck to the walls and dirt all over everything. When Miz McAllan come in and seen me looking, I could tell she was ashamed.

"I haven't had time to clean," she said. "The children took sick as soon as we got here."

"We'll set it to rights, don't you worry."

Whole time I was plucking that chicken and cutting up the onions and carrots for the broth, that ole man was setting at the table watching me. Mist McAllan's father, that they called Pappy. He was a bald-headed fellow with hardly any meat on him, but he still had all his teeth—a whole mouthful of em, long and yellow as corn. His eyes was so pale they was hardly any color at all. There was something bout them eyes of his, gave me the willies whenever they was on me.

Mist McAllan had gone outside and Miz McAllan was back in the bedroom with the children, so it was just me and Pappy for a spell.

"Say, gal, I'm thirsty," he said. "Why don't you run on out to the pump and fetch me some water?"

"I got to finish this broth for the children," I said.

"That broth can do without you for a few minutes."

I had my back to him, didn't say nothing. Just lingered along, stirring that pot.

"Did you hear me, gal?" he said.

Now, my mama and daddy raised me up to be respectful to elderly folks and help em along, but I sure didn't want to fetch that water for that ole man. It was like my body got real heavy all of a sudden and didn't want to budge. Probably I would a made myself do it but then Miz McAllan come in and said, "Pappy, there's drinking water right there, in the pail by the sink. You ought to know, you pumped it yourself this morning."

He held his cup out to me without a word. Without a word

I took it and filled it from the pail. But before I turned around and gave it back to him I stuck my finger in it.

For supper I fried up some ham and taters they had and made biscuits and milk gravy. After I served em I started to make up a plate for myself to take out to the porch.

"Florence, you can go on home now," Miz McAllan said. "I'm sure you've got your own family to see to."

"Yes'm, I do," I said, "but I can't go home to em. It's like I told your husband when he come to fetch me. That whooping cough is catching, specially at the start like your girls is. They gone be contagious till the end of the week at least. If I went home now I could pass it to my own children, or to one of my mothers' babies."

"I ain't sleeping under the same roof as a nigger," Pappy said.

"Florence, why don't you go check on the girls?" Miz McAllan said.

I left the room but it was a small house and there wasn't nothing wrong with my ears.

"She ain't sleeping here," Pappy said.

"Well, we can't send her home to infect her own family," Miz McAllan said. "It wouldn't be right."

There was a good long pause, then Mist McAllan said, "No, it wouldn't be."

"Well then," Pappy said, "she can damn well sleep out in the barn with the rest of the animals."

"How could you suggest such a thing, in this cold?" Miz McAllan said.

"Niggers need to know their place," Pappy said.

"For the last few hours," she said, "her *place* has been by your granddaughters' bedside, doing everything she could to help them get better. Which is more than I can say for you."

"Now Laura," Mist McAllan said.

"We'll make up a pallet for her here, in the main room," Miz McAllan said. "Or you can sleep in here and we can put Florence out in the lean-to."

"And have her stinking up my room?"

"Fine then. We'll put her in here."

I heard a chair scrape.

"Where are you going?" Mist McAllan asked.

"To the privy," she said. "If that's all right with you."

The front door opened and then banged shut.

"I don't know what's gotten into your wife," Pappy said, "but you better get a handle on her right quick."

I listened hard, but if Mist McAllan said anything back I didn't hear it.

SLEPT FOUR NIGHTS in that house and by the end of em I'd a bet money there was gone be trouble in it. Soft citybred woman like Laura McAllan weren't meant for living in the Delta. Delta'll take a woman like that and suck all the sap out of her till there ain't nothing left but bone and grudge, against him that brung her here and the land that holds him and her with him. Henry McAllan was as landsick as any man I ever seen and I seen plenty of em, white and colored both. It's in their eyes, the way they look at the land like a woman they's itching for. White men already got her, they thinking, *You mine now, just you wait and see what I'm gone do to you.* Colored men ain't got her and ain't never gone get her but they dreaming bout her just the same, with every push of that plow and every chop of that hoe. White or colored, none of em got sense enough to see that she the one owns them. She takes their sweat and blood and the sweat and blood of their women and children and when she done took it all she takes their bodies too, churning and churning em up till they one and the same, them and her.

I knew she'd take me and Hap someday, and Ruel and Marlon and Lilly May. Only one she wasn't gone get was my eldest boy, Ronsel. He wasn't like his daddy and his brothers, he knowed farming was no way to raise hisself up in the world. Just had to look at me and Hap to see that. Spent our lives moving from farm to farm, hoping to find a better situation and a boss that wouldn't cheat us. Longest we ever stayed anywhere was the Conley place, we'd been there going on seven years. Mist Conley cheated us some too but he was better than most of em. He let us put in a little vegetable patch of our own, and from time to time his wife gave us some of their old clothes and shoes. So when Miz Conley told us she'd up and sold the farm we was real anxious. You never know what you getting into with a new landlord.

"I wonder if this McAllan fellow ever farmed before," Hap fretted. "He's from up to Memphis. Bet he don't know the eating end of a mule from the crapping end."

"It don't matter," I told him. "We'll get by like we always do."

"He could put us off."

"He won't, not this close to planting time."

But he could a done it if he'd had a mind to, that was the plain truth. Landlords can do just about anything they want. I seen em put families off after the cotton was laid by and that family worked all spring and summer to make that crop for em. And if they say you owe em for furnishings you don't get nothing for your labor. Ain't nobody to make em do right by you. You might as well not even go to the sheriff, he gone take the boss man's side every time.

"Even if he wants us to stay," Hap said, "we still might have to move on, depending on what type a man he is."

"I don't care if he's the Dark Man hisself, I ain't moving if we don't have to. Took me this long to get the house fit to live in and the garden putting out decent tomatoes and greens. Besides, I can't just go off and leave my mothers." I had four mothers due in the next two months and one of em, little Renie Atwood, was just a baby herself. Couldn't nary one of em afford a doctor and I was the only granny midwife for miles around.

"You'll move if I say so," Hap said. "For the husband is the head of the wife, even as Christ is the head of the church."

"Only so long as he alive," I said. "For if the husband be dead the wife is loosed from his law. Says so in Romans."

Hap gave me a sharp look and I gave him one right back. He's never once laid a hand to me and I always speak my mind to him. Some men need to beat a woman to get her to do what they want, but not Hap. All he has to do is talk at you. You can start off clear on the other side of something, and then he'll get to talking, and talking some more, and before long you'll find yourself nodding and agreeing with him. That was how I started loving him, was through his words. Before I ever knowed the feel of his hands on me or the smell of him in the dark, I used to lay my head on his shoulder and close my eyes and let his words lift me up like water.

Henry McAllan turned out not to be the Dark Man after all, but wasn't no use telling that to my husband. "Do you know what that man is doing?" Hap said. "He's bringing in one of them infernal tractors! Using a machine to work his land instead of the hands God gave him, and putting three families off on account of it too."

"Who?"

"The Fikeses, the Byrds and the Stinnets."

That surprised me about the Fikeses and the Stinnets, on account of them being white. Lot of times a landlord'll put the colored families off first.

"But he's keeping us on," I said.

"Yes."

"Well, we can thank the Almighty for that."

Hap just shook his head. "It's devilry, plain and simple."

That night after supper he read to us from the Revelations. When he got to the part about the beast with seven heads and ten horns, and upon his horns ten crowns and upon his heads the name of blasphemy, I knowed he was talking bout that tractor.

THE REAL DEVIL was that ole man. When Miz McAllan asked me to keep house for her like I done for Miz Conley,

I almost said no on account of Pappy. But Lilly May needed a special kind of boot for her clubfoot and Ruel and Marlon needed new clothes, they was growing so fast they was about to split the seams of their old ones, and Hap was wanting a second mule so he could work more acres so he could save enough to buy his own land, so I said I'd do it. I worked for Laura McAllan Monday to Friday unless I had a birthing or a mother who needed looking in on. My midwifing came first, I told her that when I took the job. She didn't like it much but she said all right.

That ole man never gave her a minute's peace, or me neither. Just set there all day long finding fault with everything and everybody. When he was in the house I thought up chores to do outside and when he was out on the porch I worked in the house. Still, sometimes I had to be in the same room with him and no help for it. Like one time I had ironing to do, mostly his ironing, he wore Sunday clothes every day of the week. He was setting at the kitchen table like always, smoking and cleaning the dirt from under his fingernails with a buck knife. Cept he couldn't a been getting em too clean cause he was too busy eyeballing me.

"You better be careful, gal, or you're gonna burn them sheets," he said.

"Ain't never burnt nothing yet, Mist McAllan."

"See that you don't."

"Yessuh."

He admired the dirt on the tip of the knife awhile, then he said, "How come that son of yours ain't home from the war yet?"

"He ain't been discharged yet," I said.

"Guess they still need some more ditches dug over there, huh?"

"Ronsel ain't digging ditches," I said. "He's a tank commander. He fought in a whole lot of battles."

"That what he told you?"

"That what he done."

The ole man laughed. "That boy's pulling your leg, gal. Ain't no way the Army would turn a tank worth thousands of dollars over to a nigger. No, ditch digger's more like it. Course that don't sound as good as 'tank commander' when you're writing the folks back home."

"My son's a sergeant in the 761st Tank Battalion," I said. "That's the truth, whether you want to believe it or not."

He gave a loud snort. I answered the only way I could, by starching his sheets till they was as stiff and scratchy as raw planks.

LAURA

FAIR FIELDS. That's what Henry wanted to call the farm. He announced this to me and the children one day after church, clearing his throat first with the self-consciousness of a small-town politician about to unveil a new statue for the town square.

"I think it has a nice ring to it, without being too fancy," he said. "What do you girls think?"

"Fair Fields?" I said. "Mudbound is more like it."

"Mudbound! Mudbound!" the girls cried.

They couldn't stop laughing and saying the name. Mudbound stuck; I made sure of it. It was a petty form of revenge, but the only kind available to me at the time. I was never so angry as those first months on the farm, watching Henry be happy. Becoming a landowner had transformed him, bringing out a childlike eagerness I'd rarely seen in him. He would come in bursting with the exciting doings of his day: his decision to plant thirty acres in soybeans, his purchase of a fine sow from a neighbor, the new weed killer he'd read about in the *Progressive Farmer*. I listened, responding with as much enthusiasm as I could muster. I tried to shape my happiness out of the fabric of his, like a good wife ought to, but his contentment tore at me. I would see him standing at the edge of the fields with his hands in his pockets, looking out over the land with fierce pride of possession, and think, *He's never looked at me like that, not once.*

For the children's sakes, and for the sake of my marriage, I hid my feelings, maintaining a desperate cheerfulness. Some days I didn't even have to pretend. Days when the weather was clear and mild, and the wind blew the smell of the outhouse away from us rather than toward us. Days when the old man went off with Henry, leaving the house to me, the girls and Florence. I depended on her a great deal, and for far more than housework, though I wouldn't have admitted it then. Each time I heard her brisk knock on the back door, I felt a loosening in myself, an unclenching. Some mornings I would hear Lilly May's more hesitant rapping instead, and I would know that Florence had been called away to another woman's house. Or I'd open the door to find an agitated husband standing on my porch, twisting his soiled straw hat in his hands, saying the pains had started, could she come right now? Florence would take her leather case and go, bustling with purpose and importance, leaving me alone with the girls and the old man. I accepted these absences because I had no choice.

"I got to look after the mothers and the babies," she told me. "I reckon that's why the Lawd put me on this earth."

She had four children of her own: Ronsel, her eldest, who was still overseas with the Army; the twins, Marlon and Ruel, shy, sturdy boys of twelve who worked in the fields with their father; and Lilly May, who was nine. There had been another boy, Landry, who'd died when he was only a few weeks old. Florence wore a leather pouch on a thong around her neck containing the dried remains of the caul in which he'd been born.

"A caul round a child mean he marked for Jesus," she told me. "Jesus seen the sign and taken Landry for His own self. But my son'll be watching over me from heaven, long as I wear his caul."

Like many Negroes, Florence was highly superstitious and full of well-meaning advice about supernatural matters. She urged me to burn my nail clippings and every strand of hair left in my brush to prevent my enemies from using them to hex me. When I assured her that wouldn't be necessary, as I had no enemies, she looked pointedly at Pappy across the room and replied that the Dark Man had many minions, and you had to be vigilant against them all the time. One day I smelled something rotten in the bedroom and found a broken egg in a saucer under the bed. It looked to have been there for at least a week. When I confronted Florence with it, she told me it was for warding off the evil eye.

"There are no evil eyes here," I said.

"Just cause you can't see em don't mean they ain't there."

"Florence, you're a Christian woman," I said. "How can you believe in all these curses and spirits?"

"They right there in the Bible. Cain was cursed for killing his brother. Womenfolks cursed on account of Eve listened to that ole snake. And we got the Holy Spirit in every one of us."

"That's not the same thing at all," I said.

She replied with a loud sniff. Later I saw her give the dish to Lilly May, who went and buried the egg at the base of the oak tree. Lord knows what that was supposed to accomplish.

There was no colored school during planting season, so Florence often brought Lilly May to work with her. She was a fey child, tall for her age, with purple-black skin like her mother's. The girls adored Lilly May, though she didn't talk much. She had a clubfoot, so she lacked Florence's slow heavy grace, but her voice more than made up for it. I've never heard anyone sing like that child. Her voice soared, and it took you along with it, and when it stopped and the last high, yearning note had shivered out, you ached for its passing and for your return to your own lonely, mortal sack of flesh. The first time I heard her, I was playing the piano and teaching the girls the words to "Amazing Grace" when Lilly May joined in from the front porch, where she was shelling peas. I've always prided myself on my singing voice, but when I heard hers, I was so humbled I was struck dumb. Her voice had no earthly clay in it, just a sure, sweet grace that was both a yielding and a promise. Anyone who believes that Negroes are not God's children never heard Lilly May Jackson sing to Him.

This is not to say that I thought of Florence and her family as equal to me and mine. I called her Florence and she called me Miz McAllan. She and Lilly May didn't use our outhouse, but did their business in the bushes out back. And when we sat down to the noon meal, the two of them ate outside on the porch.

• • •

EVEN WITH FLORENCE's help, I often felt overwhelmed: by the work and the heat, the mosquitoes and the mud, and most of all, the brutality of rural life. Like most city people, I'd had a ridiculous, goldenlit idea of the country. I'd pictured rain falling softly upon verdant fields, barefoot boys fishing with thistles dangling from their mouths, women quilting in cozy little log cabins while their men smoked corncob pipes on the porch. You have to get closer to the picture to see the wretched shacks scattered throughout those fields, where families clad in ragged flour-sack clothes sleep ten to a room on dirt floors; the hookworm rashes on the boys' feet and the hideous red pellagra scales on their hands and arms; the bruises on the faces of the women, and the rage and hopelessness in the eyes of the men.

Violence is part and parcel of country life. You're forever being assailed by dead things: dead mice, dead rabbits, dead possums, dead birds. You find them in the yard, crawling with maggots, and smell them rotting under the house. Then there are the creatures you kill for food: chickens, hogs, deer, quail, wild turkeys, catfish, rabbits, frogs and squirrels, which you pluck, skin, disembowel, debone and fry up in a pan.

I learned how to load and fire a shotgun, how to stitch up a bleeding wound, how to reach into the womb of a heaving sow to deliver a breached piglet. My hands did these things, but I was never easy in my mind. Life felt perilous, like anything at all might happen. At the end of March, several things did.

One night near to dawn, I woke to the sound of gunshots. I was alone with the children; Henry and Pappy had gone to

Greenville to help Eboline move into her new and considerably more humble abode—the big house on Washington Street had been sold to pay off Virgil's debts. I checked on the girls, but the shots hadn't wakened them. I went out to the porch and peered into the graydark. A half mile away, in the direction of the Atwood place, I saw a light moving. Then it stopped. Then, from that same direction, came two more gunshots. Thirty seconds later there was another. Then another. Then silence.

I must have stood on the porch for twenty minutes, hands clenched in a death grip around our shotgun. The sun rose. Finally I saw someone coming up the road. I tensed, but then I recognized Hap's slightly stooped gait. He was out of breath when he reached me. His clothes were covered with dirt, and he too was carrying a shotgun.

"Miz McAllan," he said. "Is your husband here?"

"No, he and Pappy went to Greenville. What's going on? Was that you firing your gun?"

"No, ma'am, it was Carl Atwood. He done shot his plow horse in the head."

"Good heavens! Why would he do that?"

"He been messing with that whiskey. Ain't no devilment a man won't get hisself into when he's full of drink."

"Please, Hap. Just tell me what happened."

"Well, Florence and I was asleep when we heard them first two gunshots. Both of us like to jump right out of our skins. I got up and looked out the window but I couldn't see nothing. Then we heard another two shots, sound like they coming from the Atwood place. I got my gun and went over there but I know them Atwoods is crazy so I snuck up on em. First thing I seen was that plow horse of Carl's, haring through the fields like the devil hisself was after it. I could hear Carl a-cussing that horse, hollering, 'You oughten not to done it, damn your hide!' Then here he come chasing after it with his shotgun. I could tell he'd been at the whiskey and I was afraid he was gone see me and shoot me too so I dropped down on the ground and laid there real still. He pointed the gun at that horse and bam! He missed again and fell over backwards. That horse let into whinnying, I could a swore it was laughing at him. Carl kept trying to get up and falling back down again, all the while just a-cussing that horse up and down. Finally he got up and aimed again and bam! This time that horse went down, wasn't twenty feet from where I was laying. Carl went over to it and said, 'Damn you to hell, horse, you oughten not to done it.' And then he pissed—begging your pardon Miz McAllan, I mean to say he done his business on that horse, right on its shot-up head, cussing and crying like a baby the whole time."

I hugged myself. "Is he still out there?" I asked.

"No, ma'am. He went on back home. Reckon he'll be sleeping it off most of the day."

Carl Atwood was my least favorite of all our tenants. He was a banty rooster of a man, spindly legged and sway backed, with little muddy eyes that crowded his nose on either side. His lips were dark red, like the gills of a bass, and his tongue was constantly darting out to moisten them. He was always polite to me, but there was a sly, avid quality about him that made me uneasy.

I looked in the direction of the Atwood place. Hap said, "You want me to stay here till Mist McAllan come back?"

As tempted as I was to say yes, I couldn't ask him to lose an entire day in the fields during planting season. "No, Hap," I said. "We'll be fine."

"Florence will be over in a little while. And I'll keep a sharp eye out for Carl."

"Thank you."

I spent the day pacing and looking anxiously out the windows. The Atwoods would have to go. As soon as Henry got home, I'd tell him so. I wouldn't have my children living near such a man.

Later that afternoon, I was at the pump getting water when I saw two figures coming up the road. They walked slowly and unsteadily, one leaning on the other. As they got closer I recognized Vera Atwood and one of her daughters. Vera was huge with child. Except for the jutting mound of her belly, she was little more than skin stretched over bone. One eye was swollen shut, and she had a split lip. The girl had the look of a frightened fawn. Her eyes were large, brown and wide-set, and her dark blonde hair wanted washing. I guessed her to be ten or eleven at most. This, then, wasn't the Atwood girl who'd had an out-of-wedlock baby in February. That child was fourteen, Florence had told me, and her baby had lived only a few days.

"Howdy, Miz McAllan," Vera called out. Her voice was soft and eerily childlike.

"Hello, Vera."

"This here's my youngest girl, Alma."

"How do you do, Alma," I said.

"How do," she replied, with a dip of her head. She had a long, elegant neck that looked incongruous sprouting from her ragged dress. Her face under the grime that covered it was fine-boned and sorrowful. I wondered if she ever smiled. If she ever had reason to.

"I come to speak with you woman to woman," Vera said. She swayed on her feet, and Alma staggered under the extra weight. The two of them looked ready to collapse right there in the yard.

I gestured to the chairs on the porch. "Please, come and sit."

As we made our way up the steps, Florence appeared in the doorway. "What you doing walking all this way, Miz Atwood?" she said. "I done told you, you got to stay off a your feet." Then Florence saw the state of Vera's face. She scowled and shook her head, but she held her tongue.

"Had to come," said Vera. "Got business with Miz McAllan."

I handed Florence the bucket. "Bring us a pitcher of water, will you?" I said. "And some of that shortbread I made yesterday. And keep an eye on Amanda Leigh for me."

"Yes'm."

Vera half sat, half lay in the chair with one hand curled over her upthrust belly. The faded fabric of her dress was stretched so taut I could see the nipple-like lump her navel made. I felt a wave of longing to have a child growing inside of me again. To be full to bursting with life.

"You wanna touch it?" she asked.

Embarrassed, I looked away. "No, thank you."

"You can if you want." When I hesitated, she said, "Go on. He's kicking now, you can feel it."

I went over to her. As I laid my palm against her belly, her scent enveloped me. Everyone smelled a little ripe on the farm, but Vera's odor was positively eye-watering. I stood there holding my breath and waited. For a long moment nothing happened. Then I felt two sharp kicks against my hand. I smiled, and Vera smiled back at me, and I saw the ghost of the girl she'd once been. A pretty girl, much like Alma.

"He's a feisty un," she said proudly.

"You think it's a boy?"

"I pray for it. I pray to God every day He's done sending me girls."

Florence brought out a tray with the food and drinks. Vera accepted a glass of water but waved the shortbread away. Alma looked to her mother for permission before taking a piece off the plate. I expected her to cram it in her mouth, but she nibbled at it delicately.

"Go on now," her mother said. "I need to have a word with Miz McAllan."

"There's a mockingbird's nest in that bush over there," I said.

Alma went obediently down the steps and over to the bush, and Florence went back in the house. Her footsteps didn't go far, though, and I knew she was listening.

"Your Alma's a good girl," I said.

"Thankee. You got two of your own, ain't you?"

"Yes. Isabelle's three and Amanda Leigh's five."

"I reckon they're good girls too. Reckon you'd do anything for em."

"Yes, of course I would."

Vera leaned forward. Her eyes seemed to leap out from her haggard face and grab hold of me. "Don't put us off then," she said.

"What?"

"I expect you're wanting to, on account of what Carl done last night."

"I don't know what you mean," I stammered.

"I seen that nigger walking this way earlier. I know he must a told you."

I nodded reluctantly.

"We ain't got nowhere to go if you put us off. Nobody'll hire us this late in the season."

"It's not up to me, Vera, it's up to my husband."

She laid a hand on her belly. "For this un's sake, and my other younguns', I'm asking you to keep us on."

"I'm telling you, it's not my decision."

"And if it was?"

If her eyes had accused me, I might have been able to look away from them, but they didn't. They just hoped, blindly and fiercely.

"I don't know, Vera," I said. "I have my own children to think about."

She stood up, stomach first, grunting with the effort. I stood too but didn't move to help her. I sensed she wouldn't have wanted it. "Carl never hurt nothing that weren't his own," she said. "It ain't his way. You tell that to your husband when you tell him the rest." She turned away. "Alma!" she called. "We got to be going now."

Alma came at once and helped her mother down the steps, and together they tottered across the yard to the road. I went inside. I needed to see my girls, badly. As I walked past Florence, she muttered, "That man gone burn in hell someday, but it won't be soon enough."

Amanda Leigh was reading quietly on the couch. I scooped her up and carried her into the bedroom where her sister was taking her nap. Isabelle's features looked blurred and insubstantial under the mosquito netting. I jerked it back, startling her awake, then sat down with Amanda on the bed and crushed them both to me, breathing in their little girl scent.

"What is it, Mama?" Amanda Leigh asked.

"Nothing, darling," I said. "Give your mother a kiss."

BAD NEWS IS about the only thing that travels fast in the country. I was giving Amanda Leigh her piano lesson when I heard the car pull up out front, followed by the sound of running feet. The door flew open and Henry came in, looking a little wild. "I stopped at the feed store and heard what happened," he said. "Are you all right?"

"We're fine, Henry."

The girls pelted over to him. "Daddy! Daddy!"

He knelt down and hugged them both so hard they squealed, then came over to me and took me in his arms. "I'm sorry, honey. I know you must have been scared. I'll go over there right now and tell the Atwoods they have to leave."

I hadn't known what I was going to say to him until that moment, when I found myself shaking my head. "Don't put them off," I said.

He stared at me as though I'd gone crazy. Which I undoubtedly had.

"Vera Atwood came by this morning, Henry. She's eight and a half months pregnant. If we put them off now, where would they go? How would they survive?"

A burst of harsh laughter came from the doorway. I looked up and saw Pappy standing there with a box of groceries. He came in and set them on the table. "Well ain't this a touching scene," he said. "Saint Laura, protector of women and children, begging her husband for mercy. Let me ask you this, gal. When Atwood decides to come after you, what are you gonna do then, huh?"

"He won't," I said.

"And how do you figure that?"

"Vera swore he wouldn't. She said he never hurt anything that wasn't his own."

The old man laughed again. Henry's jaw was tight as he looked at me. "This is farm business," he said.

"Honey, please. Just think it over."

"I'll go have a word with Carl tomorrow morning, see what he has to say for himself. That's all I'll promise."

"That's all I'm asking."

Henry walked toward the front door. "Next thing you know she'll be telling you what to plant," Pappy said.

"Shut up," Henry said.

I don't know who was more astonished, me or Pappy.

The next day at dinnertime, Henry told us about his meeting with Carl Atwood. Apparently the horse had gotten into the drying shed and had eaten all of Carl's tobacco. Which explained why the creature had gone so berserk, and why Carl had been so furious.

"I told him I'd keep him on through the harvest," Henry said. "But come October, they'll have to leave. A man who'll do that, who'll kill the hardworking creature that saves him from toil and puts food on his table, is a man who can't be trusted."

I thanked him and reached for his hand to give it a squeeze, but he pulled it away. "Now that Carl's got no plow horse," he said, "he'll have to use one of our mules and pay us a half share like the Cottrills. It'll mean extra money in our pocket. That's the main reason I'm keeping them on." His eyes met mine and held them. "There's no room for pity on a farm," he said.

"Yes, Henry. I understand."

I didn't understand, not at all, but I was about to go to school on the subject.

HAP

PRIDE GOETH BEFORE destruction, and a haughty spirit before a fall. Many's the time I'd sermoned on it. Many's the time I'd stood in front of a church or a tent full of people and praised the meek amongst em while warning the prideful their day of reckoning was coming sooner than they thought, oh yes, it was a-coming right quick and they would pay for their impudent ways. I should a been telling it to the mirror is what I should a been doing, if I'd a listened to my own preaching I wouldn't a ended up in such a mess. Ain't no doubt in my mind God had a hand in it. He was trying to instruct me whatall I'd been doing wrong and thinking wrong. He was saying, *Hap, you better humble down now, you been taking the blessings I've given you for granted. You been walking around thinking you better than some folks cause you ain't working on halves like they is. You been forgetting Who's in charge and who ain't. So here's what I'm gone do: I'm gone send a storm so big it rips the roof off the shed where you keep that mule you so proud of. Then I'm gone send hail big as walnuts down on that mule, making that mule crazy, making it break its leg trying to bust*

*out of there. Then, just so you know for sure it's Me you deal-
ing with, the next morning after you put that mule down and
buried it and you up on the ladder trying to nail the roof back
onto the shed I'm gone let that weak top rung, the one you ain't
got around to fixing yet, I'm gone let it rot all the way through so
you fall off and break your own leg, and I'm gone send Florence
and Lilly May to a birthing and the twins out to the far end of
the field so you laying there half the day. That'll give you time
to think real hard on what I been trying to tell you.*

A dead mule, a busted shed and a broke leg. That's what
pride'll get you.

I must a laid there two three hours, tried to drag myself to
the house but the pain was too bad. The sun climbed up in the
sky till it was right overhead. I closed my eyes against it and
when I opened em again there was a scowling red face hanging
over me with fire all around the edges of it, looked like a devil
face to me. I wondered if I was in hell. I must a said it out loud
cause the devil answered me.

"No, Hap," he said, "you're in Mississippi." He pulled back
some and I seen it was Henry McAllan. "I stopped by to see if
you had any storm damage."

If my leg hadn't a been hurting so bad I'd a laughed at that.
Yessuh, I guess you could say we had us a little damage.

He went and fetched Ruel and Marlon from the fields. When
they picked me up to carry me in the house I must a blacked
out cause the next thing I remember is waking up in the bed
with Florence leaning over me, tying something around my
neck.

"What you doing?" I said.

"Somebody must a worked a trick on you. We got to turn it back on em."

I looked down under my chin and seen one of her red flannel bags laying there full of God knew what, a lizard's tail or a fish eye or a nickel with a hole in it, no telling whatall she had in there. "You take that thing off a me," I told her, "I don't want none of your hoodoo devilment."

"You get well, you can take it off yourself."

"Damnit, woman!" I tried to lift myself up so I could get the bag off and pain lit out from my leg, felt like somebody taken a dull saw to it and was working it back and forth, back and forth.

"Hush now," Florence said. "You got to lay still till the doctor gets here."

"What doctor?"

"Doc Turpin. Mist McAllan went to town to fetch him."

"He won't come out here," I said. "You know that man don't like to treat colored folks."

"He will if Mist McAllan asks him to," Florence said. "Meantime I want you to drink some of this tea I made you, it'll help with the pain and the fever."

I swallowed a few spoonfuls but my belly wasn't having it and I brung it right back up again. The fellow sawing away at my leg picked up his pace and I went back out.

When I come to it was nighttime. Florence was sleeping in a chair next to the bed with a lit lantern by her feet. Her face looked beautiful and stern with the light shining up from underneath it. My wife ain't pretty in the average female way but

I like her looks just fine. Strong jaw, strong bones and a will to match em, oh yes, I seen that back when we was courting. My brothers Heck and Luther made fun of me for marrying her on account of her being taller than me and her skin being so dark. They was just like our daddy, never did think of nothing but nature affairs in choosing a woman. I tried to tell em, you don't wed a gal just to linger between her legs, there's a lot more to a married life than that, but they just laughed at me. Fools, both of em. A man can't prosper by hisself. Unless he can hold onto his wife and she holds onto him too, he won't never amount to nothing. Before I married Florence I told her, "I aim to make this a lifetime journey so if you ain't up for it just say so now and we'll stop right here."

And she said, "Let's go." So we went on and got married, that was back in '23.

She must a felt me thinking bout her cause her eyes opened. "You wasting kerosene," I said.

"I reckoned you was worth it." She reached over and felt my forehead. "You running a fever. Let's get a little food in you, then we'll try some more willowbark tea."

Her touch was gentle but I could tell by the hard set of her mouth she was vexed, and I could guess the reason for it.

"Doc Turpin never showed up, huh?" I said.

"No. Told Mist McAllan he'd try to come out tomorrow after he was done with his other patients."

I looked down at my leg. It was covered with a blanket and Florence had propped it up on a sack of cornmeal. I shifted a little and was sorry I had.

"He sent poppy juice for the pain," she said, holding up a

brown bottle. "I gave you some just before sundown. You want some more?"

"Not yet, we got to talk first. How bad is it?"

"The skin ain't broke, but still. It needs to be set by a doctor."

"I'd trust you to do it."

She shook her head. "If I did it wrong . . ." She didn't finish the thought but she didn't have to. A cripple can't make a crop, and a one-legged man ain't good for much of anything at all.

"What'd you tell Henry McAllan?" I said.

"Bout what?"

"Bout that mule."

"The truth. He could see for hisself it wasn't in the shed."

"And what did he say?"

"He asked if we'd be wanting to use one of his mules and I said what if we did for awhile. And he said then we'd have to pay him a half share instead of a quarter and I said but the fields is already broke. And he said but you still got to lay em off and fertilize and plant and if you using my mule to do it you got to pay me a full half. And I said we wouldn't be needing his mule, we'd get along just fine without it. And he said we'll see about that."

Meaning, if we couldn't get the seed in quick enough to suit him he'd make us use his mule anyway and charge us half our crop for it. Half a crop would hardly be enough to keep us all fed for a year, much less buy seed and fertilizer, much less buy us another mule. You got to have your own mule, elseways you lost. Working on halves there ain't nothing left over, end of the year come around and you got nothing in your pocket

and nothing put by for the lean times. Start getting into debt
with the boss, borrowing for this, borrowing for that, fore you
know it he owns you. You working just to pay him back, and
the harder you work the more you end up owing him.

"We ain't using Henry McAllan's mule," I said. Big words,
but they was just words and we both knew it. Ruel and Marlon couldn't make a twenty-five-acre crop by themselves, they
was strong hardworking boys but they was just twelve, hadn't
come into their full growth yet. If Ronsel was home the three
of em could a managed it, but it was too much work for two
boys with no mule and I didn't have nearly enough put by for
another one. Paid a hundred and thirty dollars for the one
that died, reckoned on having him another ten twelve years
at least.

"That's what I told him," Florence said. "I also told him I
couldn't keep house for his wife no more cause I'd need to be
out in the fields with the twins."

I opened my mouth to tell her no but she covered it up with
her hand. "Hap, there ain't no other way and you know it. It
won't kill me to do a little planting and chopping till you get
to feeling better."

"I promised you I'd never ask you to do field work again."

"You ain't asking, I'm offering," she said.

"If I'd a just fixed that ladder."

"Ain't your fault," she said.

But it was my fault, for holding my head so high I couldn't
see the rotted board right under my foot. Laying there in that
bed, I never felt so low. The tears started to rise up and I shut

my eyes to hold em in. Damned if I was gone let into eye-shedding in front of my wife.

BY THE TIME Doc Turpin finally showed up late the next day my leg was swole up bad. I'd been to him twice before, once when I got lockjaw from stepping on a rusty nail and the second time when Lilly May taken sick with lung fever. He wasn't from Marietta, he'd moved up from Florida bout five years ago, word was he was in the Klan down there. We didn't have the Klan in our part of Mississippi. They tried to come into Greenville back in '22 but Senator Percy ran em off. He was a real gentleman, Mr. Leroy Percy was, a good sort of white man. Doc Turpin was the other sort. He hated the colored race, just hated us for being alive on this earth. Problem was he was the only doctor anywhere around. You had to go all the way to Belzoni or Tchula for another doctor, either way it was a two-hour wagon ride. Sometimes you had to, depending on when you got sick. Doc Turpin only treated colored people on certain days of the week and it wasn't always the same. Time I had that lockjaw it was on a Monday and he said he couldn't see me till Wednesday, but when I took Lilly May to him it was a Friday and he told me it was my lucky day cause Friday was nigger day.

When Florence brung him in to me he told her to go wait in the other room. "Is there any way I can help you, doctor?" she asked.

"If I want something I'll tell you," he said.

I would a liked her to stay and I knew she wanted to but she went on and left. Doc Turpin shut the door behind her and came over to the bed. He was a fat fellow with yellow-brown eyes and a funny little tilted-up nose, looked like it belonged on a lady's face. "Well, boy," he said, "I heard you went and broke your leg."

"Yessuh, I did."

"Henry McAllan sure does want to see you get well, so I spose I'd better fix you up. You know how lucky you are to have a landlord like Mr. McAllan?"

Seemed like every time I seen that man he was telling me how lucky I was. I didn't feel too lucky right at that moment but I nodded my head. He pulled the cover off a my leg and whistled. "You sure did bust yourself up good. You been taking that pain medicine I sent you?"

"Yessuh."

He poked my leg and I jumped. "When was the last time you had some of it?" he said.

"Right after dinner, bout four five hours ago."

"Well, in that case, this is gonna hurt some." He reached down into his bag and pulled out some pieces of wood and some strips of cloth.

"Can't you give me some more medicine?" I said.

"Sure I can," he said, "but it won't take effect for another fifteen or twenty minutes. And I don't have time to sit here and wait on it. Mrs. Turpin's expecting me home for supper." He handed me one of the pieces of wood, smaller than the others. There were marks all over it in curved rows. "Put that between your teeth," he said.

I put it in my mouth and clamped down on it. Sweat broke out all over me and I could smell my own fear, and if I could smell it I knew Doc Turpin could too. Couldn't do nothing bout that but I told myself I wasn't gone cry out, no matter what. God would see me through this like He seen me through so much else, if I just had faith in Him.

What time I am afraid, I will trust in Thee.

"Now, boy," he said, "I'd shut my eyes if I was you. And don't you move. Not if you want to keep that leg a yours." He winked at me and grabbed my leg by the knee and the ankle.

In God I will praise His word, in God I have put my trust. I will not fear what flesh can do unto me.

He pulled up sharp on my ankle and the pain come, pain so bad it made whatall I had before seem like stubbing a toe. I screamed into the stick.

Then nothing.

LAURA

WHEN HENRY TOLD ME Florence wouldn't be coming back, I felt something close to panic. It wasn't just her help around the house I'd miss, it was her company, her calm, womanly presence in my house. Yes, I had the children, and Henry in the evenings, but all three of them were unspeakably happy on the farm. Without Florence, I would be all alone with my anger, doubt and fear.

"It's only till July," Henry said. "Once the cotton's laid by, she should be able to come back."

July was three months away—an eternity. I spoke without thinking. "Can't we lend them one of our mules?"

As soon as the words were out of my mouth I regretted them. "Lend" is a dirty word for Henry, akin to the foulest profanity. He distrusts banks and pays cash for absolutely everything. At Mudbound he kept our money in a strongbox under the floorboards of our bedroom. I had no idea how much was in there, but he'd shown me where it was and told me the combination of the lock: 8-30-62, the date Confederate forces under the command of Robert E. Lee crushed the Union Army in the Battle of Richmond.

"No, we can't 'lend' them a mule," he snapped. "You don't just 'lend' somebody a mule. And I'll tell you something else, if Florence and those boys don't get that seed in real quick, they'll be using our mule all right, and paying us for the privilege."

"What do you mean?"

"Well, it's just like with the Atwoods. If they don't have a mule and they can't get the work done on time, they'll have to use one of ours. Which means they'll have to pay us a half share in cotton. It's hard luck for them, but good for us."

"We can't take advantage of them like that, Henry!"

His face reddened with outrage. "Take advantage? I'm about to let Hap Jackson use my stock to make his crop. A mule I paid good money for, that I'm still paying to keep fed. And you think I ought to let him use it for free? Maybe you think I should just give him that mule outright, on account of Hap being sick and all. Why don't we give him our car while we're at it? Hell, why don't we just give him this whole place?"

Sounded like a fine plan to me.

"I just think we owe it to them to help them, honey," I said. "After all, Hap hurt himself working for us, trying to repair our property."

"No. Hap hurt himself working for Hap. If he didn't repair that shed, *his* tools would rust, and *his* income would suffer for it. Farming's a business, Laura. And like any business, it carries risks. Hap understands that, and you need to understand it too."

"I do, but—"

"Let me put it another way," he said. "I sank everything we had into this place. Everything. We need to make some money this year. If we don't, *our* family's in trouble. Do you understand that?"

Like the Union Army at Richmond, I was utterly defeated. "Yes, Henry," I said.

He softened a little, gracious in victory. "Honey, I know this has been hard on you. We'll see about finding you a new maid just as soon as the planting's done. In the meantime, why don't you go to Greenville tomorrow and do a little shopping. Buy yourself a new hat and some Easter dresses for the girls. Take Eboline to lunch. Pappy and I can fend for ourselves for a day."

I didn't want a new hat, I didn't want to see Eboline and I especially didn't want a new maid. "All right, Henry," I said. "That sounds nice."

THE GIRLS AND I set out early the next morning. On the way I stopped at the Jacksons' to check on Hap and drop off some more food for them. I hadn't seen Florence since the day of the accident, and her haggard, unkempt appearance alarmed me.

"Hap's terrible sickly," she said. "His leg ain't healing straight and he been running a fever for three days now. I've tried everything but I can't get it to come down."

"Do you want us to get Doc Turpin back?"

"That devil! Never should a let him lay a hand on Hap in the first place. Half the colored folks who go to him end up sicker than they was before. If Hap loses his leg on account of that man . . ." She trailed off, no doubt contemplating various gruesome ends for Doc Turpin. My mind was racing in a different direction: If Hap lost his leg, I'd never get Florence back.

And so I went shopping in Greenville—not for hats and Easter dresses, but for a doctor willing to drive two hours each way to treat a colored tenant. It would have been easier to find an elephant with wings. The first two doctors I saw acted like I'd asked them to do my laundry. The third, an old man in his seventies, told me he didn't drive anymore. But as I turned to leave, he said, "There's Dr. Pearlman over on Clay Street. He might do it, he's a foreigner and a Jew. Or you could go to niggertown, they've got a doctor there."

I decided to take my chances with the Jewish foreigner, though I was unsure what to expect. Would he be competent? Would he try to cheat me? Would he even agree to treat a Negro? But my fears proved foolish. Dr. Pearlman seemed kindly and learned, and his office, though empty of patients, was well-kept. I'd barely finished explaining the situation to him before he was getting his bag and hurrying out the door. He followed me and the girls to Hap and Florence's house, where I paid him the very reasonable fee he asked and left him.

By the time we got home it was almost dark. Henry was waiting on the porch. "You girls must have bought out half of Greenville," he called out.

"Oh, we didn't find much," I said.

He walked over to the car. When he saw there were no packages, his eyebrows went up. "Didn't you get anything?"

"We got a doctor," said Amanda Leigh. "He talked funny."

"A doctor? Is somebody sick?"

I felt a flutter of nervousness. "Yes, Henry, it's Hap. His leg's not healing. The doctor was for him."

"That's what you spent your whole day doing?" he said. "Looking for a doctor for Hap Jackson?"

"I didn't set out to look for one. But there was a doctor's office right next to the dress shop, and I thought—"

"Amanda Leigh, take your sister in the house," said Henry.

They knew that tone and obeyed with alacrity, leaving me alone with him. Well, not quite alone; I saw the old man at the window, lapping up every word.

"Why didn't you come to me?" Henry asked. "Hap is my tenant, my responsibility. If he's sick, I need to know about it."

"I just happened to stop by their place on my way to town. And Florence said he'd gotten much worse, so I—"

"Did you think I wouldn't have taken care of it? That I wouldn't have gone and fetched Doc Turpin?"

He wasn't so much angry as hurt; I saw that suddenly. "No, honey, of course not," I said. "But Florence doesn't trust Doc Turpin, and since I was already in Greenville . . ."

"What do you mean, she doesn't trust him?"

"She said he didn't set Hap's leg properly."

"And you just took her word for that. The word of a colored midwife with a fifth-grade education over a medical doctor's."

Put like that, it sounded ridiculous. I had taken her word, unquestioningly. And yet, as I stood withering under the heat of my husband's gaze, I knew I'd do it again.

"Yes, Henry. I did."

"Well, I need you to do the same thing for me, your husband. To take my word for it that I'm going to do what's best for the tenants, and for you and the children. I need you to trust me, Laura." In a thick voice he added, "I never thought I'd have to ask you that."

He left me standing by the car. The sun had slipped below the horizon, and the temperature had dropped. I shivered and leaned against the hood of the DeSoto, grateful for its warmth.

HAP

WHEN I COME TO, Doc Turpin was gone and I was still alive, that was the good news. The bad news was my leg hurt like the dickens. It was all bandaged up so I couldn't see it, but I could feel it all right. Heat was coming off it and the skin felt dry and tight. That was a bad sign, I knew that from tending to mules.

"Doctor said you should get to feeling better in a day or two," Florence said.

But I didn't feel better, I felt worse and worse. The throbbing got real bad and I was in and out of sense. I remember faces floating over me, Florence's, the children's. My mama's, and she'd been laying in the clay going on twenty years. Then come a strange white man bending over me, a settle-aged man with a gray beard and one long eyebrow thick as a mustache.

"This is Doc Pearlman," Florence said. "He gone fix your leg."

He picked up my wrist and held it while he looked at his pocket watch. Then he shined a light in my eyes and put his eyeball right up next to mine and looked in there. "Your husband is in shock," he said, in a funny accent. He started shaking his head like he seen something that disgusted him, I reckoned he was mad on account of having to doctor a nigger. I didn't want no angry white man doctoring me and I told him so but he went ahead anyway and started taking the bandages off a my leg. I let into thrashing.

"Hold him still," he said to Florence.

She came and held my shoulders down. I tried to push her off me but I was too weak. I couldn't see what the doctor was doing and I had a bad feeling.

"Has he got a saw?" I asked her.

"No, Hap."

"Don't you let him cut my leg off. I know he's mad but don't you let him."

"You got to lay still now," Florence said.

The doctor bent down to me again, so close I could smell the pipeweed on his breath. "Your leg wasn't set properly, and it's in flames," he said.

"What?" I started fighting Florence again, trying to get up, but I might as well to been wrestling Goliath.

"Shh," she said. "It's just swole up is all. That's what's causing your fever."

"I'm going to make you sleep now," said the doctor. He put a little basket over my nose and mouth and dribbled some liquid on there. It had a sickly sweet smell.

"Please, Doc, I need my leg."

"Rest now, Mr. Jackson. And don't worry."

I tried to stay awake, but sleep was tugging, tugging. The

last thing I remember is him bending down to get something
out of his bag. There was a little knitted cap on the back of his
bald head, looked like a doily, and I wondered how he got it
to stay on there. Then sleep took ahold of me and swallowed
me up.

WHEN I WOKE UP it was morning and my leg still hurt,
but less than before. This time I was glad of the pain till I remembered ole Waldo Murch and his arm that had to be took
off back in '29. Waldo swore that arm still ached even though
it wasn't there no more. I'd seen him myself plenty of times,
rubbing at the air, and I wondered if it was that kind of imagine pain I was feeling. But I guess God must a decided He'd
humbled me enough cause when I pulled the blanket off there
was my leg, all bandaged and splinted up. I'm here to tell you,
seeing you got two legs when you thought you was down to just
one is a mighty glad feeling.

I could hear Florence moving around in the other room and
I called out to her.

"I'm fixing your breakfast," she said. "Be right there."

She brung me a plate of brains and eggs. Soon as I smelled
it my stomach let into growling, felt like I hadn't et in a week.
"Take this first," she said, handing me a pill.

"What is it?"

"Pencil pills. They to keep away the infection. You got to
take em twice a day till they all gone."

I swallowed the pill and tucked into the food. Florence put

her hand on my forehead. "Fever's down," she said. "You was plumb out of your head yesterday. Sure is a good thing that doctor showed up. Miz McAllan brung him all the way from Greenville."

"She went and fetched him by herself?"

"Yeah. Drove up in the car with him following her."

"When you see her, tell her we're much obliged."

She snorted. "You lucky you still got your leg after the job that butcher done on it. Doc Pearlman was considerable mad about it, I mean to tell you. Said Doc Turpin didn't deserve to be called a doctor."

"Reckon Doc Pearlman ain't from around here," I said.

"No, he's from somewhere over to Europe. Australia, I think he said."

"You mean Austria. That's the place Ronsel was where it snowed all the time."

Florence shrugged. "Whatever it's called, I'm mighty glad he ended up here instead of there."

"How long am I gone be laid up?"

"Eight to ten weeks, if there's no infection."

"Eight weeks! I can't lay here till June!"

She went on like I hadn't said a word. "Doc said we got to keep a sharp eye out for it. And you got to keep that leg real still. He's coming back on Monday to check on you, said if the swelling was down he'd make you a cast."

"How am I gone chop cotton in a cast? How am I gone preach on Sundays?"

"You ain't," Florence said. "The children and me gone do the chopping, and Junius Lee gone drive over from Tchula and do the preaching, and you gone keep your weight off a that leg like the doctor told you to. If you don't, you could wind up a cripple, or worse."

"And if I do and we have to go back to sharecropping, we'll never get out from under Henry McAllan."

"Can't worry bout that now," Florence said. "God'll see to that, one way or another. Meantime you gone do what the doctor told you."

"The contentions of a wife are a continual dropping," I said. "Proverbs 19:13."

"And a prudent wife is straight from the Lord," she shot back. "Proverbs 19:14."

Woman knows her Scripture, I'll give her that. Got no book-learning but there ain't nothing wrong with her memory.

"I better get out to the fields," she said. "Lilly May will be here if you need anything. You rest now."

Lingered along, lingered along. Laid in that bed knowing my wife was out doing my work for me. Couldn't even do my business without one of em helping me. I tried to put it off till Florence and the boys got home but one day I couldn't wait and I had to ask Lilly May to come help me with the pan. There's some things a daughter should never have to do for her daddy. Made me wish I'd a just crapped myself and set in it till Florence got home.

Meantime she and the twins was just about done in from working in the fields. Florence's hands was all blistered up and I seen her rubbing her back when she thought I wasn't looking.

She didn't complain though, nary a word, just went on and did what had to be done. They worked straight through, even on Sunday, and Florence don't hold with working on the Sabbath. They had to do it though. Had to get them fields planted before Henry McAllan decided to bring in his mule.

Monday rolled around and Doc Pearlman come back just like he said he would. He took the bandages off a my leg and looked at it. "Goot," he said, which I took to mean good. "The swelling is gone. We must make the cast now. For that I will need boiled water."

Florence sent Lilly May to do it. Meantime, Doc Pearlman was checking me all over, looking in my eyes and listening to my heart and wiggling my toes. He didn't seem to mind touching me. I wondered if all the white people in his country were like him.

"Florence says you from over to Austria," I said.

"Ya," he said. "My wife and I came here eight years ago."

Fore I could think what I was saying I said, "Our son Ronsel was there. He's a tanker, fought under General Patton."

"Then I'm grateful to him."

I shot a glance at Florence. She looked as fuddled as I was. Speaking real slow to be sure he understood me, I said, "Ronsel fought against Austrian folks."

He got a kindling look in his eye, made all the hairs on my arms stand straight up. "I hope he killed a great many of them," he said. Then he left the room to go wash his hands.

"Well, what do you make of that?" I said to Florence.

She shook her head. "All kind a crazy white people in the world."

THE RAIN CAME the next day, a big hard rain that packed the fields down tight as wax. Nothing we could do but set there and watch it and fret for two days till it finally cleared up. Florence and the children went back out to the fields, even Lilly May. Field work was hard for her with her bad foot and all but there wasn't no help for it.

I laid in the bed with my leg propped up, itching and cussing. Felt like I had a bunch of ants crawling around under my cast, looking for their next meal. There was no way to scratch either, the cast went all the way from my ankle to the top of my thigh.

I was weaving a basket out of a river birch trunk, trying to take my mind off the itching, when I heard a infernal noise and I looked out the window and seen Henry McAllan driving up on that tractor. He turned it off and got down.

"Hap?" he called out.

"Over here," I called back.

He come to the bedroom window and looked in. We howdyed and he asked how I was feeling.

"Whole lot better, thanks to that doctor Miz McAllan brung me," I said. "Sure am grateful to her for fetching him."

"I expect you are," he said. He lit a cigarette. "How much longer you gonna be in that cast?"

Behind him off in the distance I could see Florence and the children out plowing. I mean to tell you, setting there jawing with Henry McAllan while my family was toiling in the hot sun hurt me a lot worse than my leg. "Another month or so is all," I said.

"Is that a fact."

"Yessuh."

"You know, I broke my leg in the Great War. As I recollect, it was a couple of months before the cast came off, and longer than that before I could do any real work."

"I'm a fast healer, always have been," I said.

He took a drag off his cigarette. I waited, knowing what was coming. "The thing is, Hap, it's the second week of April," he said. "Y'all ought to be well into planting by now but you haven't even gotten your fields laid off."

"Soil has to be rebroke first on account of the rain."

"I'm aware of that. But if they were using a mule they'd be done in no time. As it is it'll be the end of the week before they even start fertilizing, much less getting that seed in the ground. There's just the three of them, Hap. I can't afford to wait any longer. You're a farmer, you understand that."

"It won't take that long. We got Lilly May helping too."

"A crippled little girl's not going to make the difference and you know it." He flicked his cigarette into the dirt. "You tell one of your boys to come fetch that mule after dinner today."

Then I looked on all the works that my hands had wrought, and on the labor that I had labored to do: and behold, all was vanity and vexation of spirit, and there was no profit under the sun.

"Yessuh," I said. The word stuck in my throat, but wasn't nothing else I could say. *That's it, Hap,* I told myself, *you a sharecropper again now, might as well get used to it.*

When Florence come in for dinner with the children I didn't even have to tell her, she took one look at my face and said, "He sending that mule, ain't he."

"Yeah. Starting this afternoon."

"Well," she said, "it'll make the plowing go faster anyway."

We set down to eat. It wasn't much of a meal, just fatback and grits one of the sisters from church had brung by earlier, but I said the blessing like always. When I was through Florence kept her head bent for a good long while. I knew what she was praying for. It was the same thing I'd been asking Him for every day since I fell off a that ladder: for Ronsel to come home and deliver us.

II.

LAURA

HENRY STAYED MAD at me, and he showed it by ignoring me in our bed. My husband was never an especially passionate man, but he'd always made love to me at least twice a week. In the first months of our marriage I'd felt awkward and reluctant (though I never refused him—I wouldn't have dreamed of it). But eventually we settled into an intimacy that was sweet and familiar, if not entirely fulfilling. He liked to do it at night, with one lamp on. At Mudbound it was one candle. That was his signal: the sound of the match head rasping against the striker. Joined with Henry, his body shuddering against mine, I felt very close to him and miles distant from him at the same time. He was experiencing sensations I wasn't, that much was plain to me, but I didn't expect ecstasy. I had no idea it was even possible for a woman. I hadn't always enjoyed Henry's lovemaking, but it made me feel like a true wife. I never realized how much I needed that until he turned away from me.

If my bed that April was cold, my days were hot, sweaty and grueling without Florence to help me. Henry hired Kester Cottrill's daughter Mattie Jane to come and clean for me, but she was slovenly and a chatterbox to boot, so after the first day I restricted her to laundry and other outdoor tasks. I saw Florence mostly from a distance, bent over a hoe, chopping out the weeds that threatened the tender cotton plants. Once I ran into her in town and started to complain about Mattie Jane. Florence gave me a look of incredulous scorn—*This is your idea of a problem?*—that shamed me into silence. I knew I should be grateful I wasn't spending twelve or more hours a day in the cotton fields, but it was poor consolation.

One Saturday at the end of April, the five of us went into town to do errands and have dinner at Dex's Diner, famed for its fried catfish and the sign outside that read:

JESUS LOVES YOU
MONDAY - FRIDAY 6:00-2:00
SATURDAYS 6:00-8:00

After we ate we stopped at Tricklebank's to get the week's provisions. Henry and Pappy lingered on the front porch with Orris Stokes and some other men, and the girls and I went inside to visit with the ladies. While I chatted with Rose, Amanda Leigh and Isabelle ran off to play with her two girls. Alice Stokes was there, radiantly pregnant, buying a length of poplin for a maternity dress. Wretched as I was, I couldn't bring myself to begrudge her happiness. We'd been chatting for a few minutes when a Negro soldier came in the back door. He was a tall young man with skin the color of strong tea. There were sergeant's stripes on his sleeves and a great many medals on his chest. He had a duffel bag slung over one broad shoulder.

"Howdy, Miz Tricklebank," he said. "Been a long time." His voice was sonorous and full of music. It rang out loudly in the confines of the store, startling the ladies.

"Is that you, Ronsel?" Rose said wonderingly.

He grinned. "Yes, ma'am, last time I looked."

So this was Florence's son. She'd told me all about him, of course. How smart he was, how handsome and brave. How he'd taken to book-learning like a fish to water. How he drew people to him like bees to honey, and so on. "Ain't just me talking mama nonsense," she'd declared. "Ronsel's got a shine to him, you'll see it the minute you lay eyes on him. The gals all want to be with him, and the men all want to be like him. They can't help it, they drawn to that shine."

I had thought it was mama nonsense, though I hadn't said so. What mother doesn't believe her firstborn son has more than his fair share of God's gifts? But when I saw Ronsel standing there in Tricklebank's, I understood exactly what she meant.

He dipped his head politely to me and the other ladies. "Afternoon," he said.

"Well, I declare," said Rose. "Aren't you grown up."

"How you been doing, Miz Tricklebank?"

"Getting along fine. You seen your folks yet?"

"No, ma'am," he said. "Bus just got in. I stopped to buy a few things for em."

I studied him as Rose helped him with his purchases. He

looked more like Hap, but he had Florence's way of filling up a room, and then some. You couldn't help but watch him; he had that kind of force. He glanced over at me curiously, and I realized he'd caught me staring. "I'm Mrs. McAllan," I said, a little embarrassed. "Your parents work on our farm."

"How do," he said. His eyes only met mine briefly, but in those few seconds I had the feeling I'd been thoroughly assessed.

"Do Hap and Florence know you're coming home?" I said.

"No, ma'am. I wanted to surprise em."

"Well, I know they'll be mighty glad to see you."

His forehead wrinkled in concern. "Are they all right?"

He didn't miss much, this son of Florence's. I hesitated, then told him about Hap's accident, emphasizing the positive. "He's using crutches now, and the doctor said he should be walking again by June."

"Thank God for that. He can't stand to be idle. He's probably driving Mama crazy, being underfoot all day."

Uneasily, I looked away from him. "What is it?" he asked.

I realized suddenly that the other women had gone dead silent and were watching us, making no effort at discretion. Some looked shocked, others hostile. Rose looked concerned, and her eyes held a warning.

I turned back to Ronsel. "Your parents lost their mule," I said, "and then we had a spell of bad weather. They're using our stock now. And your mother's working in the fields with your brothers."

His jaw tightened and his eyes turned cold. "Thank you for

telling me," he said. The ironic emphasis on the first two words
was impossible to miss. I heard a sharp intake of breath from
Alice Stokes.

"Excuse me," I said to Ronsel. "I have shopping to do."

As I walked away from him, I heard him say, "I'll come
back for that cloth later, Miz Tricklebank. I better get on home
now."

He paid Rose hurriedly and headed for the front door with
his purchases and his duffel bag. Just before he reached the
door, it opened and Pappy came in, followed by Orris Stokes
and Doc Turpin. Ronsel stopped just short of running into
them.

"Beg pardon," he said.

He tried to step around them, but Orris moved to stand in
his way. "Well, looky here. A jig in uniform."

Ronsel's body went very still, and his eyes locked with
Orris's. But then he dropped his gaze and said, "Sorry, suh. I
wasn't paying attention."

"Where do you think you're going, boy?" said Doc Turpin.

"Just trying to get home to see my folks."

The door opened again, and Henry and a few other men
came inside, crowding behind Pappy, Orris and Doc Turpin.
All of them wore unfriendly expressions. I felt a flicker of
fear.

"Honey," I called out to Henry, "this is Hap and Florence's
son Ronsel, just returned from overseas."

"Well, that explains it then," drawled Pappy.

"Explains what?" said Ronsel.

"Why you're trying to leave by the front door. You must be confused as to your whereabouts."

"I ain't confused, suh."

"Oh, I think you are, boy," Pappy said. "I don't know what they let you do over there, but you're in Mississippi now. Niggers don't use the front here."

"Why don't you go out the back where you belong," said Orris.

"I think you'd better," said Henry. "Go on now."

It got very quiet. The air fairly crackled with hostility. I saw muscles tense and hands clench into fists. But if Ronsel was afraid, he didn't show it. He looked slowly around the store, meeting the eyes of every man and woman there, mine included. *Just go,* I pleaded with him silently. He let the moment drag out, waiting until just before the breaking point to speak.

"You know, suh, you're right," he said to Pappy. "We didn't go in the back over there, they put us right out in front. Right there on the front lines, face-to-face with the enemy. And that's where we stayed, the whole time we were there. The Jerries killed some of us, but in the end we kicked the hell out of em. Yessuh, we sure did."

With a nod to Rose, he turned and strode out the back door.

"Did you hear what he just said?" sputtered Pappy.

"Nigger like that ain't gonna last long around here," said Orris.

"Maybe we ought to teach him better manners," said Doc Turpin.

Things might have turned ugly, but Henry stepped forward and faced them, hands up and palms out. "No need for that. I'll have a word with his father."

For a moment I was afraid they wouldn't back down, but then Orris said, "See that you do, McAllan."

The men dispersed, and the tension lifted. I did my shopping and rounded up the girls, and we left Tricklebank's. On the way back to Mudbound, we came upon Ronsel walking down the middle of the road. He moved to one side to let us pass. As we went by him, I traded another glance with him through the open window of the car. His eyes were defiant, and they were shining.

RONSEL

HOME AGAIN, HOME AGAIN, jiggety-jig. Coon, spade, darky, nigger. Went off to fight for my country and came back to find it hadn't changed a bit. Black folks still riding in the back of the bus and coming in the back door, still picking the white folks' cotton and begging the white folks' pardon. Nevermind we'd answered their call and fought their war, to them we were still just niggers. And the black soldiers who'd died were just dead niggers.

Standing there in Tricklebank's, I knew exactly how much hot water I was in but I still couldn't shut my mouth long enough to keep myself from drowning. I was acting just like my buddy Jimmy back in our training days. I told him and told him he'd better humble down if he knew what was good for him, but Jimmy just shook his head and said he'd rather get beat up than act like a scared nigger. And he did get beat up, once in Louisiana and twice in Texas. The last time a bunch of local MPs roughed him up so bad he was in the infirmary for ten days, but Jimmy never did humble down. If we hadn't shipped out I think they might've killed him. When I told him that he just laughed and said, "I'd have liked to seen em try."

Jimmy would've been proud of me that day at Tricklebank's, but my daddy would've blistered my ears. All he knew was the Delta. He'd never walked down the street with his head held high, much less had folks lined up on either side cheering him and throwing flowers at him. The battles he'd fought were the kind nobody cheers you for winning, against sore feet and aching bones, too little rain or too much, heat and cotton worms and buried rocks that could break the blade of a plow. Ain't never a lull or a cease-fire. Win today, you got to get up tomorrow and fight the same battles all over again. Lose and you can lose everything. Only a fool fights a war with them kind of odds, or a man who ain't got no other choice.

Daddy had aged a considerable bit in the two years since I'd last seen him. There was white in his hair and new worry lines around his eyes. He'd lost weight he didn't need to lose too, Mama said that was since he broke his leg. But his voice was as strong and sure as ever. The day I got home I could hear it from way out in the yard, thanking God for the food they were about to eat and the sun He'd been sending lately to make the cotton grow, and for the health of all here present including the laying hens and the pregnant sow, and for watching over me wherever in creation I was. Which by that time was standing right in the doorway.

"Amen," I said.

For a minute nobody moved, they all just set there gawping at me like they didn't recognize me. "Well?" I said. "Ain't nobody gone offer me some supper?"

"Ronsel!" yelled Ruel, with Marlon a half second behind him like always.

Then they were up and hugging me, and Mama and Lilly May were kissing my face and carrying on about how big and handsome I was and asking me how was my trip and when did I get back to the States and how come I hadn't wrote to tell them I was on my way home. Finally Daddy hollered, "Quit fussing over him now and let him say hello to his father."

He was setting there with his leg propped up on a stool. He held out his arms and I went and gave him a big hug, then knelt down by him so he wouldn't have to look up at me.

"I knew you'd come," he said. "I prayed for it, and here you are."

"And here you are with your leg in a cast. How'd you manage to do that?"

"It's a long story. Why don't you set down and eat and I'll tell you all about it."

I couldn't help smiling. With my daddy, everything's a long story. I heaped my plate. There was salt pork and beans and pickled okra, with Mama's biscuits to sop up the juice.

"I used to daydream about these biscuits," I said. "I'd be setting on top of my tank eating my C rations—"

"What's a sea ration?" said Ruel.

"Is that some kind of fish?" said Marlon.

"C like the letter C, not like the ocean. It's Army food. I brought some home so you could try them. They're in my bag. Go on, you can look."

The twins ran over to my duffel bag, opening it and pulling everything out onto the floor. Still a couple of kids, though they were near as tall as me. Made me a little sad to watch them, so young and eager. I knew they wouldn't stay that way much longer.

"Anyway," I said to Mama, "I told all the guys about your biscuits. By the time the Jerries surrendered I had every man in the company dreaming of them, even the Yankee lieutenants."

"I dreamed about you," Mama said.

"What did you dream?"

She shook her head, running her hands up over her arms like she was cold.

"Tell me, Mama."

"It don't matter, none of it come true. You back with us now, safe and sound."

"Back where you belong," Daddy said.

AFTER DINNER THE two of us were having a jaw on the porch when we seen a truck coming down the road. It pulled up in our yard and Henry McAllan got out.

"Wonder what that man wants now?" said Daddy.

I got to my feet. "I reckon he wants to talk to me."

"Why in the world would Henry McAllan want to talk to you?" said Daddy.

I didn't answer. McAllan was already at the foot of the steps.

"Afternoon, Mist McAllan," said Daddy.

"Afternoon, Hap."

"Ronsel, this is our landlord. This here's my son Ronsel that I been telling you bout."

"We've met," said McAllan.

Daddy turned to me, worried now.

"I better speak with you alone, Hap," said McAllan.

"I ain't a child, sir," I said. "If you got something to say, you can say it to my face."

"All right then. Let me ask you a question. You planning on staying here and helping your father?"

"Yes, sir."

"Well, you're not helping him, acting like you did earlier at Tricklebank's. You're just helping yourself to a heap of trouble, and your family too."

"What'd you do?" asked Daddy.

"Nothing," I said. "Just tried to walk out the door is all."

"The front door," McAllan said, "and when my father and some other men objected to it he made a fine speech. Put us all in our place, didn't you?"

"Is that true?" said Daddy.

I nodded.

"Then I reckon you better apologize."

McAllan waited, his pale eyes fixed on me. I didn't have a choice and he knew it. He might as well to been God Almighty as far as we were concerned. I made myself say the words. "I'm sorry, Mr. McAllan."

"My father will want to hear it too."

"Ronsel will pay him a visit after church tomorrow," said Daddy. "Won't you, son?"

"Yes, Daddy."

"That's fine then," said McAllan. "Let me tell you something else, Ronsel. I don't hold with everything my father says, but he's right about one thing. You're back in Mississippi now, and you better start remembering it. I'm sure Hap would like to have you around here for a good long while."

"Yessuh, I would," said Daddy.

"Well then. Y'all enjoy your Saturday."

As he turned to leave, I said, "One more thing, sir."

"What?"

"We won't be needing that mule of yours much longer."

"How's that?"

"I aim to buy us one of our own just as soon as I can find a good one."

Daddy's jaw dropped. I heard a little gasp from inside the house and knew Mama was listening too. I'd wanted to buy it first and surprise them with it, but I wanted to knock Henry McAllan down a peg even more.

"Mules cost a lot of money," he said.

"I know what they cost."

McAllan looked at my father. "All right, Hap, you let me know when he finds one. In the meantime I'll rent you mine on a day-to-day basis. I'll just put it on your account and we can settle after the harvest."

"I'll settle with you in cash soon as I get that mule," I told him.

I could tell Henry McAllan didn't like that, not one bit. His voice had a sharp edge to it when he answered. "Like I said, Hap, I'll just put it on your account."

Daddy laid a hand on my arm. "Yessuh, that'll be fine," he said.

McAllan got in his truck and started up the engine. As he

was about to pull away, he called out, "Don't forget to stop by the house tomorrow, boy."

I watched the truck disappear into the falling dusk. The whippoorwills had started their pleading and the lightning bugs were winking in and out over the purpling fields. The land looked soft and welcoming, but I knew what a lie that was.

"No point in fighting em," said Daddy. "They just gone win every time."

"I ain't used to walking away from a fight. Not anymore."

"You better get used to it, son. For all our sakes."

WE FOUGHT FOR six months straight across France, Belgium, Luxembourg, Holland, Germany and Austria. With the different infantry battalions we were attached to, we killed thousands of German soldiers. It wasn't personal. The Jerries were the enemy, and while I tried to account for as many as I could, I didn't hate them. Not till the twenty-ninth of April 1945. That was the day we got to Dachau.

We didn't know what it was even, just that it was in our way. Nary one of us had ever heard of a concentration camp before. There'd been rumors floating around about Germans mistreating POWs, but we thought they were just tall tales meant to scare us into fighting harder.

By then I'd gotten my own tank command. Sam was my bow gunner. We were driving toward Munich a few miles ahead of the infantry when we caught the smell, a stink worse than anything I'd ever smelled in my life, and by that time I'd smelled plenty of corpses. About a mile later we came to a compound fenced all around by a concrete wall, looked like a regular military post from the outside. There was a big iron gate set in the wall with German writing on the top. Then we seen the people lined up in front of the gate, naked people with sticks for arms and legs. SS soldiers were walking up and down the lines, shooting them with machine guns. They were falling in waves, falling down dead right in front of us. Sam took out the soldiers while Captain Scott's tank busted down the gate.

Hundreds of people—if you can call skin scraped over a pile of bones a person—came staggering out of there. Their heads were shaved and they were filthy and covered with sores. Some of them ran off down the road but most of them were just walking around in a daze. Then they caught sight of this dead horse that'd been hit by a shell. It was like watching ants on a watermelon rind. They swarmed the carcass, ripping off pieces of it and eating them. It was horrible to see, horrible. I heard one of the guys retching behind me.

We followed the sound of gunshots to this big barnlike building. It was on fire and I could smell roasting flesh. We came around the corner and seen more SS soldiers shooting at people inside. The building was full of bodies stacked six foot high on top of one another, smoking and burning. Some of them were still alive and they were crawling over the dead ones, trying to get out. The SS soldiers were standing there just as calm as they could be, shooting anybody that moved.

We opened fire on those motherfuckers. Some of them ran and we got out of the tank and chased them down and shot them. I took out two myself, shooting them in the back as they were running away from me, and I felt nothing but glad.

I was walking back to my tank when a woman tottered over to me with her hands stretched out toward me. She had on a ragged striped shirt but she was naked from the waist down—that's the only way I could tell she was a woman. Her eyes were sunk way back in the sockets and she had sores all over her legs. She looked like a walking corpse. I started backing away from her but I stepped in a hole and fell and then she was on me, clutching me, jabbering nonstop in whatever language she spoke. I was pushing her away, yelling at her to get the fuck off me, when all the strength seemed to go out of her and she went limp. I laid there underneath her and stared up at the sky—such a pale pretty blue, like nothing bad had ever happened under it or ever could happen. Her weight on me was light as a blanket, so light she was hardly there at all. But then I felt the warmth of her body through my uniform. I ain't never been so ashamed of myself. It wasn't her fault if she seemed less than human, it was the fault of them that did this to her, and them that didn't raise a voice against it.

I sat up, trying to be careful. Her head was laying in my lap and she was looking up at me like I was her sweetheart, like the sight of me was everything she ever hoped for in this world. I rooted around in my pockets and found a chocolate bar. I unwrapped it and gave it to her. She sat up and crammed the whole thing in her mouth, like she was afraid I was going to change my mind and take it away from her. I felt a shadow on me and looked up and seen other prisoners surrounding us, dozens of them, ragged and stinking and pitiful. Some were talking and making eating motions with their hands and mouths, and some were just standing there quiet as ghosts. I was feeling around in my pockets to see what other food I had when the woman in my lap curled up into a ball, moaning and grabbing her stomach.

"What's the matter?" I said. "What's the matter with you?" But she just laid there jerking and moaning like she was gut-shot. It went on a long while and there wasn't nothing I could do. Finally she went still. I put my head on her chest and listened but I couldn't hear a heartbeat. Her eyes were wide and staring. They were blue, the same pale blue as the sky.

"Ronsel!"

I looked through the stick-thin legs of the prisoners and seen Sam walking toward me. Tears were running down his face. "Medic says not to feed em," he said. "Says it can kill em since they ain't eaten in so long."

I looked back down at her, the woman I'd just killed with a chocolate bar. I wondered what her name was and who her people were. I wondered whether anybody ever held her like I was doing, whether anybody ever stroked her hair. I hoped somebody did, before she came to this place.

I NEVER THOUGHT I'd miss it so much. I don't mean Nazi Germany, you'd have to be crazy to miss a place like that.

I mean who I was when I was over there. There I was a liberator, a hero. In Mississippi I was just another nigger pushing a plow. And the longer I stayed, the more that's all I was.

I was in town picking up some feed for the new mule when I ran into Josie Hayes. Well, she was Josie Dupock now—she'd gone and married Lem Dupock last September. Josie and me used to walk out together before the war. I was real sweet on her, even thought about marrying her. But when I joined up she was so vexed with me she wouldn't see me or speak to me, and I ended up leaving Marietta without saying goodbye to her. I sent her a few letters but she never wrote back, and after awhile I just let it go. So when I seen her there on Main Street, I wasn't sure what to expect.

"Heard you was back," she said.

"Yeah. Got home about two months ago. How you been?"

"Been fine. I'm married now."

"Yeah, Daddy wrote and told me."

A silence came down between us. Time I knew Josie we were always laughing and jollying. I used to tickle her till she squealed but she never tried to get away, just wriggled and giggled and if I stopped she'd tease me till I started up again. She didn't look like she did much laughing now. She was still a fine-looking gal but her eyes had hardened up, and I had a good idea of why. Lem and me went to school together. He was the kind always starting trouble and never ending up with the blame, just setting off to the side smiling while the rest of us were getting our butts switched. When we got older he was always slipping around at the gals, had him two or three at a time. Lem Dupock wouldn't never give a woman nothing but tears, I could've told Josie that a long time ago.

"Ain't seen you in church," I said.

"Ain't been there. Lem ain't the church-going kind."

I hesitated, then asked, "He treating you all right?"

"What's it to you, how he's treating me?"

Not a damn thing I could say to that. "Well," I said, "I'd best be getting on home, Josie. You take care of yourself."

I started to head back to the wagon but she grabbed ahold of my arm. "Don't go, Ronsel. I need to talk to you."

"What about?"

"Bout us."

"Ain't no us, Josie. You seen to that five years ago."

"Please. There's some things I want to say to you."

"I'm listening."

"Not here. Meet me tonight."

"Where?"

"My house. Lem's gone, he went down to Jackson. I ain't expecting him back till next week."

"I don't know, Josie," I said.

"Please."

I knew I shouldn't have gone over there but I went anyway. Ate the supper she fixed me and talked about old times. Let her tell me how sorry she was. Let her show me. Josie and me used to fool around some but we never laid down together. I'd imagined it plenty of times though, how it would feel to have her and to let her have me. Afterward we'd snuggle up and talk and laugh together, that was how I always pictured it.

It wasn't nothing like that. It was sad and lonesome during and stone quiet after. I thought Josie was asleep but then in a husky voice she said, "Where you gone to, Ronsel? Who you thinking bout?"

I didn't tell her the truth: that I was all the way to Germany, thinking about a white woman named Resl, and the man I was when I was with her.

HER FULL NAME was Theresia Huber, Resl was just a nickname. That surprised me at first, that the Germans would have nicknames like we did. Shows you how well the Army trained us not to think of them as human.

Resl's husband was a tanker too, he got killed at Strasbourg. That was one of the first things she asked me: "Vas you at Strasbourg?" I was glad I could tell her no. She had a six-year-old daughter, name of Maria, a shy little thing with dark blue eyes and hair white as cotton. That was how I met Resl in the first place, was through Maria. When we rolled into a town the women would send their children out to beg us for food. German or not, it was a hard thing watching hungry kids rooting around in garbage cans, so we always kept some extra rations in our mess kits. The day we got to Teisendorf there were more kids than usual swarming around our tanks. Maria was hanging back a little like she was afraid. I went over to her and asked her name. She didn't answer, I reckoned she didn't understand me, so I pointed at my chest and said "Ronsel" then pointed at hers. But she just stood there looking up at me

with eyes too big for her face. Child that age should've still had
baby fat in her cheeks but hers were hollowed out. I gave her
all my extra rations that day and the next. The third day she
took me by the hand and led me back to her house. Sam went
with me. We always went in pairs, just in case. Even though
the Jerries had surrendered, you could still run into trouble in
some of them little Bavarian towns—SS soldiers hiding out in
somebody's cellar, that kind of thing. But when we got to the
house all we found was Resl, waiting for us with hot soup and
a little old loaf of brown bread about the size of my hand. We
gave her our rations and told her we weren't hungry but she
kept on pushing the food at us. We could tell it was hurting her
feelings that we wouldn't eat so finally we had some. The soup
was mostly water with a few potatoes and onions floating in
it and the bread like to broke our teeth, but we made "mmm"
sounds and told her it was good.

"Goot!" she said. Then she smiled for the first time and my
breath caught. Resl was that sorrowful kind of pretty that's
even prettier than the happy kind. Some women get like that,
hard times just pares them down till all that's left is their
beauty. I'd seen it at home amongst my own people too but
somehow it was different over there, and not just because the
faces were white. Here was a woman who'd never wanted for a
thing in her life and now all of a sudden she had nothing—no
husband, no food, no hope. Well, not nothing, she had her
daughter and her pride, and those were the two things she
lived for.

Resl's English wasn't too good and I hardly spoke ten words

of German, but that don't matter between a man and a woman who understand each other. Up to that point I'd stayed away from the fräuleins—after whatall I seen at Dachau I just didn't want to mess with them—but plenty of the other guys had German sweethearts. Jimmy taken up with this gal, she wasn't even a fräulein, she was a frau, meaning a missus with a live husband. Jimmy met her up in Bissingen, the first town we occupied after the cease-fire, and when we left there to go to Teisendorf she followed after him. There were plenty of others like her too. I used to wonder what would make a woman want to transact herself that way, want to leave her husband and take up with a colored man who'd laid waste to her country and killed her people. But after knowing Resl awhile I started to understand it better. It wasn't just that she'd been without a man for two years and here I was giving her food and whatever else she wanted from me. That was part of it, sure, but there was more to it than that. The two of us had something in common. Her people were conquered and despised, just like mine were. And just like me, Resl was hungry to be treated like a human being.

I spent every spare minute I had at her house. With the money and provisions I gave her, she made dumplings and sauerkraut and rye bread, and sausage when we could get it. Every night after she put Maria to bed, Resl and me would set on the couch for a spell. Sometimes she'd talk in German in a low sad voice—remembering how things used to be, I guessed. Sometimes I'd tell her about the Delta: how the sky was so big it shrank you to nothing, and how in the summertime the lint from the cotton laid a fuzzy coat of white over everything in the house. Then after awhile I'd feel her tug at my hand and we'd go upstairs. I'd been with a fair number of women by that time, I never made a dog of myself like some of the guys but I'd had my share of romances. But I never felt nothing like I felt with Resl in the nights. She gave her whole self to me, didn't hold back, and before too long I didn't either. When I was on duty I'd be thinking about her the whole time, got to where I could smell her scent even when I wasn't with her. One time in the quiet after, she put her hand on my chest and whispered, "Mein Mann." I was happy to be her man and I told her so, but later I found out from Jimmy it also meant "my husband." That fretted me for a few days, till I made myself see the truth. The way we were together, we might as well to been man and wife.

So in September when most of the other guys took their discharges and headed home, I volunteered to stay in Teisendorf. Lot of greenhorns were coming over from the States to replace the guys who'd shipped out, and the Army needed seasoned men to show them the ropes. Jimmy and Sam told me I was crazy for staying, but I couldn't stand to leave Resl. First time I ever lied to my mama and daddy was when I wrote and told them the Army wasn't ready to let me go yet. I didn't like to do it but Daddy wouldn't have understood the truth. Me loving a white woman, he might've come around to that, though he would've told me I was a damn fool. But me not jumping at the first chance to come home—that, he never would've understood, not if he had a hundred years to think about it.

But then in March the Army gave me a choice: either re-enlist or ship out for the States. I wasn't about to sign up for four more years of soldiering so I took my discharge. Lot of tears over it but there wasn't nothing else I could do. I couldn't stay in Germany, and I damn sure couldn't bring Resl and Maria home with me. On the boat to New York I told myself it was just one of them things, just a wartime romance that was never meant to last, between two people who didn't have nobody else.

Till that night with Josie I even believed it.

FLORENCE

Every day I asked God, Please send him home to us. Send him home whole and right in his mind. And if that's too much to ask of You just let him be right in his mind and not like my uncle Zeb, who come back from the Great War with all his parts but touched in the head. One morning my mama and I went out to the yard and found all six of our hens laid out in a neat row with their necks wrung and Uncle Zeb laying sound asleep at the end of the row like he was number seven. Few weeks later he wandered off and we never laid eyes on him again.

Four years I prayed for my son to come home. The first two years we only seen him twice, that was when he was still in training in Louisiana and Texas. We was hoping he'd miss out on all the fighting but then in the summer of '44 they sent him over there, smack dab in the middle of it. Every now and then there'd be an article about his battalion in the *AFRO American* and Hap would read it out loud to me. Course by the time we got ahold of the paper it was usually a month old or more and Ronsel was long gone from wherever they was writing about.

Same with his letters, it took em forever to reach us. Whenever we got one I'd hold it in my hand and wonder if he was being shot at or lying somewhere bleeding or dead right at that moment, but the marks on the paper didn't tell me. And when the war was over and he didn't come home, them marks didn't tell me why. Ronsel was always after me to learn how to read but I don't see the point of it myself. Writing on a paper ain't flesh and blood under your roof.

But there's a old word that goes, "Be careful what you wish for or you might just get it." God answered all my prayers. He sent my son home safe and with enough money for a new mule too. We was back to working on a quarter share and I was keeping house again for Miz McAllan while Lilly May stayed home and looked after her father. (Well, I didn't exactly pray to keep Laura McAllan's house but I sure did like the extra money.) Hap was getting around good on his crutches, preaching again on Sundays and spinning his old dreams, talking bout getting a second mule and taking on more acres and saving up to buy his own land. Marlon and Ruel loved having their big brother back. They followed him around like puppies, pestering him for stories about the places he seen and the battles he was in. Oh yes, we all got our wishes, all on account of Ronsel, and all except for him.

What he wanted was to leave. He never said so—I didn't raise my children to be complainers—but I could tell he wasn't happy from the day he got home. At first I thought he was just vexed on account of that ugly business at Tricklebank's with ole Mist McAllan and them other no-count white men. Told myself he'd been away a long while and just needed to get hisself settled back in, but that didn't happen. He was jumpy and broody, and he twitched and moaned in his sleep. When he wasn't working in the fields he was writing letters to his Army friends or setting on the porch steps staring off at nothing. Didn't talk at mealtimes, wasn't chatting up the gals at church. That fretted me more than anything. What man don't want a woman's arms around him after he's just got done fighting a war?

Part of him was still fighting it, I knowed that from his sleep talk. I reckoned he seen some pretty terrible things over there and maybe done some too, things that wasn't setting easy with him. But I also knowed it wasn't just the war troubling him. It was the Delta, pressing in on him and squeezing the life right out of him. And we was too, by wanting him to stay.

Hap said that was hooey. Said I worried too much about Ronsel and always had. Maybe that was true and maybe not but I knowed my son and it wasn't like him to be so quiet. Four of my five children come peaceful into the world, but not Ronsel. When I was carrying him he squirmed all day and kicked all night. My aunt Sarah, she taught me midwifing, she said all that ruckus was a good sign, it meant the baby was healthy. "Well," I told her, "I sure am glad somebody's feeling good cause I'm plumb wore out." Then when I went into labor, Ronsel decided he was just gone stay put. I labored thirty-two hours with him. He like to tore me in two coming out and when he finally did he bout busted our ears with his squalling. Aunt Sarah didn't even have to turn him upside down and swat him, his lungs already knowed what to do.

After all that I thought I was gone have a devil baby on my hands but Ronsel was just as sweet as he could be. Strong too. Before he was even a year old he was walking. I'd set him on a pallet at the end of the row I was picking and here he'd come, toddling down that row, wanting my breast. He was always babbling and singing to hisself. His first word was *Ha!* and he said it fifty times a day, pointing at his foot or a cloud or a cotton worm, any little thing that caught his eye. By the time he was three he was talking up a storm, wanting to know everything bout everything. Come time to go to school he was always itching to go, and always hangdogging around during planting and picking time when school was closed. When he finished eighth grade his teacher come to see me, said Ronsel had a gift. Well, she wasn't telling me nothing I didn't already know. She said if we'd let him come in the afternoons she'd keep on teaching him. I had a wrangle with Hap over that, he wanted Ronsel helping him full-time in the fields. But I stood my ground, told Hap we had to let our son use whatall the Lord seen fit to give him, not just his strong back and his strong arms.

"You sure this is what you want?" Hap asked him.

"Yes, Daddy."

"You'll still have to help me till two o'clock every day and get all your chores done besides. Won't leave you no time for fishing or having fun."

"I don't mind," Ronsel said.

Hap just shook his head and let him go. And when the war come and Ronsel was hell-bent on joining the white man's army, Hap didn't understand that either but he let him.

When I looked at my children I could see me and Hap in all of em. And I loved my husband and myself too, and so I loved our children. But when I looked at Ronsel I seen something more, something me and Hap couldn't a gave him cause we ain't got it. A shine so bright it hurt your eyes sometimes but you still had to look at it.

I loved all my children, but I loved Ronsel the most. If that was a sin I reckoned God would forgive me for it, seeing as how He the one stacked the cards in the first place.

LAURA

THE COTTON BLOOMED at the end of May. It was magical, like being surrounded by thousands of little white fairies, shimmering in the sunlight. The blooms turned pink after a few days and fell off, revealing green bolls no bigger than my fingertip. They would ripen over the summer and burst open in August. My own time would come right around the new year. My morning sickness had started in early May, so I reckoned I was about two months pregnant.

I wanted to be certain before I told Henry. There was no obstetrician in Marietta, much less a hospital; most women had their babies at home with Doc Turpin. I had no intention of going that route if I could help it. I was about to ask Eboline for the name of her doctor in Greenville when I received a timely invitation from Pearce to attend Lucy's confirmation at Calvary at the end of June. Lucy was my goddaughter as well as my niece; of course I had to go. And while I was in Memphis, I would pay a visit to my old obstetrician, Dr. Brownlee.

Henry couldn't spare the time to accompany me, but he agreed to let me and the girls go for a week. Seven days in civi-

lization! Seven days with no mud, no outhouse and no Pappy.
It was a heady prospect. I would have a hot bath every day,
twice a day if I wanted to. I would call people on the telephone
and have afternoon tea at the Peabody and visit the Renoirs at
the museum. I might even lie awake in bed at night and read
a book by lamplight that didn't flicker.

Henry drove us to the train station. He went at his usual
leisurely pace, slowing often to look at the farms we passed
and compare the growth of their cotton, soybeans, and corn to
ours. I wanted to tell him to hurry up or we'd miss the train,
but I knew he couldn't help himself. Henry never had much
use for nature in its untouched state. Forests didn't move him,
nor mountains, nor even the sea, but show him a well-tended
farm and he was breathless with excitement.

We arrived at the station with ten whole minutes to spare.
Henry kissed the girls and exacted solemn promises from them
to be good and mind me. Then he turned to me. "I'll miss you,"
he said. Time and the daily sight of his cotton thriving had
thawed him considerably, though he was still touchy about his
authority and had only just resumed our intimate relations in
the last week.

"I wish you could come with us," I said.

As soon as the words were out of my mouth I realized they
weren't true. I wanted some time away from him, not just from
Pappy and the farm. I wondered if Henry suspected how I felt.

"You know I can't be away for that long, not this time of
year," he said. "Besides, you girls will have more fun without
me along."

"I'll write to you every day."

He bent and kissed me. "You just make sure and come back, hear? I couldn't do without you."

He said it lightly, with a smile, but I thought I detected a faint undercurrent of worry in his voice. I felt a twinge of guilt at that, but not nearly enough to make myself say, *I'm not going after all, not without you.*

The train ride seemed interminable to me. It was stiflingly hot, and the sooty air that blew through the open windows made me queasy. But to the children, who had never been on a train before, it was a grand adventure. My parents met us at the station, Daddy with a big hug and Mother with the expected flood of tears.

It was wonderful, after five months of exile, to be among my own people again. To stand in church and hear the voices of my family, young and old and in-between, ringing out on every side of me. To sit between my sisters on Etta's wicker glider and sip sweet tea while our children chased lightning bugs together in the slowgathering dusk. And best of all, to share my joyful news, once Dr. Brownlee had confirmed it, with all of them, and be the object of their tender fussing. At any other time, I might have padlocked myself to my old bed in my parents' house and thrown away the key rather than return to Mudbound. But within a few days, I began to want Henry: the groan of his weight settling onto the mattress beside me at night; the damp, heavy press of his arm across my waist; the rasp of his breathing as I fell asleep. I never felt more in love with my husband than when I was carrying his children.

I reckon that's the Lawd's doing—that's what Florence would have said.

The night before we were to return, just as I was about to turn off the bedside lamp, I heard a soft drumming of fingernails on my door. My mother came in and sat on the edge of the bed, bringing the familiar smell of Shalimar with her. It was Daddy's favorite scent and she never wore any other, just like she never cut her hair because he liked it long. During the day she wore it pinned up, but now it hung like a girl's in a long silver plait down her back. She was seventy-one years old, and to me, as lovely as ever. And as maddeningly indirect.

"I've been thinking about your brother," she said.

"Pearce?" Pearce was the one of us she worried the most about, because he was entirely too serious and had married into money.

"No, Teddy," she said. Teddy was her favorite, though she'd always tried valiantly to hide the fact. Teddy was everybody's favorite. He was a natural clown; he didn't hesitate to spend his dignity, and we all loved him for it, even Pearce.

"What about him?"

"I was just about your age when I was carrying him, you know."

I'd heard the story many times: How she'd conceived at thirty-eight, after the doctor had told her she'd never have another child. How it had been the most trouble-free pregnancy and shortest labor of them all.

"The last baby came the easiest," I said, quoting the familiar ending to the story. "I hope it'll be the same for me."

"Except Teddy wasn't the last baby," my mother said in a low voice.

"What do you mean?"

"He was a twin. His little sister was stillborn ten minutes after him. She barely weighed four pounds."

"Oh, Mother. Does Teddy know?"

"No, and don't you ever tell him," she said. "I don't want it haunting him like it has me. I should have listened to the doctor, he warned me not to get pregnant again. He said I was too old, that my body couldn't take the strain, but I thought I knew better. And so that poor little child, your sister—" She broke off and looked down at her hands.

"Is that why you're telling me this?" I asked. "Because you're afraid for me?" She nodded. "But Mother, if you hadn't gotten pregnant again, you wouldn't have had Teddy. And how could any of us bear it without him? We couldn't."

She gave my hand a hard squeeze. "You just be extra careful not to strain yourself," she said. "Let Henry and your colored girl do for you, and if you feel tired, rest. You rest even if you aren't tired, for a couple of hours every afternoon. Promise me."

"I will, Mother, I promise. But you're worrying for nothing. I feel fine."

She reached out and stroked my hair just as she had when I was a child. I closed my eyes and let sleep take me, feeling utterly safe.

• • •

THE NEXT DAY, I returned to the farm, if not quite eagerly, then at least willingly. Henry was thrilled by my news. "This one will be a boy," he said. "I feel it in my bones."

I hoped his bones were right. Not that I didn't adore my girls, but I wanted the fiercer, less complicated love, unsullied by judgment and comparisons to one's own self, that my sisters had for their sons, and my brothers for their daughters.

"Well, one thing's for sure," said Florence, the day I told her I was pregnant. "You definitely carrying a male child."

"What makes you say that?"

"I've knowed for almost two months now. The signs are all there, plain as the nose on your face."

I ignored the implication that she'd known I was pregnant before I had. "What signs?" I asked.

"Well, you ain't had much morning sickness, that's one way you can tell it's a boy. And you craving meat and cheese more than sweets."

"I always do."

"Besides," she said, with a decisive wave of her hand, "the pillows on your bed are to the north."

"What difference does that make?"

The lift of her eyebrows sent a clear message: How could I possibly be so ignorant of such a universally known fact? "You'll see, six months from now," she said.

Things between the two of us were much the same as they had been, but she was noticeably stiffer around Pappy and, to a lesser extent, Henry. That was because of the trouble with Ronsel, I knew. We hadn't seen much of him since the day he'd come to apologize to the old man, and for Ronsel's sake I was glad. He and Pappy weren't oil and water, they were oil and flame. Best for all concerned if they stayed far apart.

Unfortunately I had no such option with respect to my father-in-law. He was constantly underfoot and more cantankerous than ever once Henry put him to work helping me and Florence around the house. Henry was always protective of me when I was pregnant, but this time he was positively Draconian: under no circumstances was I to risk any sort of exertion. Florence could do only so much in a day, so it fell to Pappy to help with the hauling, milking, churning and so on.

"You'd think a man would be allowed to enjoy the fruits of his labor in his old age," he said. "You'd think his family wouldn't put him to work like a nigger."

"It's only for a little while, Pappy," I said. "Just to make sure you have a healthy grandchild."

He snorted. "Just what I need. Another granddaughter."

JULY SPED BY. The weather got hotter and the cotton grew. I wasn't showing much yet, but I could feel the baby's presence inside of me, a tiny spark I fed with prayers and whispered exhortations to grow and be well. My pregnancy had completely healed the breach between Henry and me, unraveling our anger and knitting us back together again. We began to talk about what we would do when the baby was born. There was no question of our staying on the farm with an infant. Henry promised we'd look for a house to rent right after the harvest. If necessary, he said, we'd live in one of the neighboring towns, Tchula or Belzoni, even though it would mean a longer drive for him. The thought of being in a real house again was exhilarating. I began to feel a certain wistful nostalgia for Mudbound—now that I knew I was leaving it—and even occasionally to enjoy its rustic charms.

It was on such a day, an unusually balmy Saturday toward the end of July, that disaster struck. As usual when anything bad happened, Henry was away. He and Pappy had gone to Lake Village to see about some hogs, so I was alone with the girls. They were making mud pies by the pump and I was sitting under the oak mending one of Henry's shirts. There was a nice breeze and a sweet smell of poison in the air; the crop dusters had flown over that morning. I must have nodded off, because I didn't see Vera Atwood come into the yard. I woke to the sound of her girlish voice, loud and shrill. "Where's your mama at?" she was saying. "Where is she?"

"I'm right here, Vera," I said.

She whirled and looked at me. Her breath was coming in whistling gasps, and her dress was drenched with sweat. She must have run all the way to our house.

"What's the matter?" I said.

"You got to take me to town," she said. "I'm gonna kill Carl."

It was then that I saw the butcher knife in her hand. I felt a surge of raw fear. The girls were standing just a few feet away from her. I stood and said, "Come here, Vera. Come and tell me what's happened."

She came, staggering a little. The girls started to follow, but I made a shooing motion with my fingers. Amanda Leigh took her sister's hand and held her back.

"He's started in on Alma," said Vera.

"What do you mean?"

"He's started in on her just like he done with Renie. I got to stop him. You got to take me."

"He beat her?"

"No."

When I took her meaning my body went cold despite the heat. Renie was the eldest Atwood girl, the one whose baby Florence had delivered in February, just two months before Vera's own. Both children had died within a few days of being born—crib death, Florence had told me.

"He ain't gonna have Alma too, not if I can help it," Vera said.

"Where is he now?"

"He went to town to get some shotgun shells. Said he's taking her hunting this afternoon."

Just keep her talking, I thought. Henry and Pappy were due back any time now. "Hunting?" I said.

"That's how he started with Renie, taking her out to the woods with him."

"How can you be sure? That he . . .?"

"Renie wouldn't eat nothing they brought back. Deer, rabbit, squirrel—didn't matter what it was, she wouldn't touch it. Said she wasn't hungry. But Carl sure was. Set there gobbling that food like he hadn't et in a week, gnawing on the bones and talking about how nothing tastes better than meat you hunted and brought down yourself. 'Ain't that right, Renie,' he says to her. And her setting there skinny as a rail, staring at that food like it was full of maggots."

Vera was rocking back and forth on the balls of her bare feet, the knife swinging at her side. Her head was tilted, and her eyes were wide and unfocused. She looked like a woman I'd seen once at a hypnotist's show at the state fair.

Just keep her talking. "Did you say anything to him about it?" I asked.

"No. He would have just denied it. When Renie started to show I asked her who done it but she wouldn't say, not even when I got after her with the switch. Just stood there real quiet and took it like she deserved a whupping. I knew right then but I didn't want to know. I told myself if it was a boy then it wasn't but if it was a girl then it was, that would be the proof cause Carl ain't got nothing in him but girls. And when that baby came out and I seen its parts, I knew it for his seed."

I stole a glance at Amanda Leigh and Isabelle. Their gingham dresses were spattered with mud. A streak of it ran across Isabelle's forehead where she'd brushed her bangs out of her eyes, and she was sucking on her thumb, watching us.

"Look at me," Vera demanded.

I obeyed instantly.

"You look at me," she said.

"I'm looking, Vera. I see you."

"A few days after it was born I came in the bedroom and found Carl holding it. He had his finger in its mouth and the baby was sucking on it, and Renie was laying there watching em. Right then I decided to do it."

"What?" I asked. But I knew.

"I waited till they was all asleep that night. And then I took a pillow and I sent that baby out of his reach, like I hadn't done for Renie."

"And your own baby?"

Her face contorted, and then she was standing right beside me and the knife was touching the side of my neck. I could hear my heart thundering in my ears. "You got to drive me to town *now*," she said.

Her breath smelled of rotting teeth. Fighting back nausea, I said, "Vera, listen to me. My husband will be back soon. When he gets here, we'll talk to him. Henry will know what to do."

"No," said Vera, "I can't wait. We got to go now. Come on."

She jerked me by the arm, pulling me toward the truck, but the key wasn't in it; it was hanging on a nail by the front door. Amanda Leigh and Isabelle were watching us with big frightened eyes. What would I do with them? I couldn't leave them alone on the farm—they were too little, anything might happen to them. But how could I take them with us? I didn't think Vera would harm them, but in the wild state she was in I couldn't be sure. I pictured Carl's red lips pressed to Alma's. Pictured Vera sitting next to my children in the truck with the butcher knife in her hand.

"I can't, Vera," I said.

"Why not?"

"Henry doesn't let me drive the truck. I'm not even sure where he keeps the key."

"You're lying."

"I swear it's true. The one time I tried to drive it I almost wrecked it. See that big dent there, on the front fender? I did that. Henry was so mad he took the key away."

Vera grabbed my shoulder hard. Her eyes bulged, the pupils dilated despite the brightness of the day. "I got to stop him!" she said, giving me a shake. "You got to help me stop him!"

I felt another swell of nausea. I sagged in her grip. "Vera, I can't. I don't have the key. For all I know Henry took it with him."

She let go of me, and I sank to the ground. She threw her head back and gave a keening cry. It was a sound of such desolation that I had to stop myself from running into the house and getting the key.

"Mama?" Amanda Leigh's voice, thin with fear. I glanced over at them, then back at Vera. I saw the madness drain from her face.

"Don't be scared," she said to the girls. "I ain't gonna hurt you or your mama." She turned to me. Her eyes were serene and terrible. "I'm going now," she said.

"I'll speak to Henry as soon as he gets home. He'll help you, I promise."

"It'll be too late then."

"Vera—"

"You look after them girls of yourn," she said.

She set off down the road toward town, moving at a steady lope, the knife glinting in the sun. As the girls ran over to me, I felt the first cramp hit—a mocking imitation of labor pains. I sank to my knees and pressed my hands to my stomach.

"What's the matter, Mama?" asked Amanda Leigh.

"I need you to be a big girl, and go and fetch Florence from her house. Do you know how to get there?"

She nodded solemnly.

"Hurry now," I said. "Run as fast as you can."

She went. I felt another cramp, like a fist grabbing my insides and squeezing hard, then wetness between my legs. Isabelle clung to me, sobbing. I lay in the dirt and curled my body around hers, letting her cry for both of us, and for the child who would never be her brother.

THEY FOUND CARL's body lying in the road halfway between the farm and town. Vera had stabbed him seventeen times, then gone on to Marietta and turned herself in to Sheriff Tacker. Rose and Bill saw her walking down Main Street. They said she was covered in blood, like she'd bathed in it.

I learned these details later. At the time, I was too lost in my own agony to care about anyone else's. I lay in the bed, sleeping as many hours a day as my body would permit, waking reluctantly to lie with my face turned to the wall. I got up only to use the outhouse. Florence nursed me, cajoling me to eat and pushing clean nightgowns over my head. The children brought me gifts: wildflowers, drawings they'd made, a molted rattlesnake skin that I feigned delight with, though it repelled me. Rose paid me a couple of visits, offering news from town between awkward throat-clearings. Henry tried to comfort me when he came to bed at night, but I lay stiff against him, and after a few days he kept to his side.

A week passed in this way, then two. The children grew fretful, and Henry's compassion turned to impatience. "What's the matter with her?" I overheard him say to Florence. "Why doesn't she get up?"

"You got to give her time, Mist McAllan. That baby left a hollow place that ain't been filled back up yet."

But Florence was wrong about that. It had been filled up, and to the bursting, with rage—toward Vera and Carl, toward Henry and God, and most of all, myself. It blazed inside of me, and I fed it just like I'd fed the baby, keeping it alive with what-ifs and recriminations. If it hadn't been Florence's day off. If Henry hadn't left me alone with the girls. If he hadn't brought me to this brutal place to begin with. If I'd just listened to him when he told me there was no room for pity on a farm. I played that phrase over and over in my head like a fugue, cudgeling myself with it. Thinking of Henry's face when he walked in and found me lying in the bed, empty of our child; of the way he'd schooled his features, packing away his sorrow so I wouldn't see it and be hurt by it, letting only his tenderness show. Tenderness for me, the woman who had just lost his baby through her own stubborn foolishness. Yes, I knew miscarriages were common, especially in women my age, but I still couldn't shake the idea that the stress of Vera's assault had caused mine; that if I'd let Henry put the Atwoods off like he'd wanted to, I wouldn't have lost the baby. It had been a boy, just as we'd hoped. Florence didn't tell me and she wouldn't let me look at it, but I saw it in her face, and in Henry's.

I resumed my life some three weeks after the miscarriage, on a Monday. There was no fanfare, no scene between me and Henry, or me and Florence, in which I was lectured on my responsibilities and dragged, flailing and cursing, from my sickbed. I simply got up and went on. I bathed my sour body, combed my hair, put on a clean dress and took up my roles of wife and mother again, though without really inhabiting them. After a time I realized that inhabiting them wasn't required. As long as I did what was expected of me—cooked the meals, kissed the cuts and scrapes and made them better, accepted Henry's renewed nocturnal attentions—my family was content. I hated them for that, a little. Sometimes, in the small hours of the night, I would wake in the stifling airless heat with Henry's skin hot as a brand against mine and imagine myself getting up, dressing swiftly, going into the girls' room and brushing my lips softly against their foreheads, then taking the car key from the nail by the door, walking across the muddy yard, getting in the DeSoto and driving off—down the dirt road, across the bridge, to the gravel road, to the highway, and then straight east until the road ran into the sand. It had been so long since I'd smelled the ocean and immersed myself in that cool bluegreen.

I didn't act on this impulse, of course. But I sometimes wonder if I might have, in another week or another month, if Jamie hadn't come to live with us.

WE WEREN'T EXPECTING him; the last we'd heard he was in Rome. We'd gotten a postcard back in May with a picture of the Colosseum on the front and a hastily scrawled message on the back about how the Italian girls were almost as beautiful as Southern girls. It had made me smile, but not Henry.

"It's not right," he said, "Jamie wandering all over and not coming home."

"I know you find this hard to believe, but not everybody longs to be in rural Mississippi," I said. "Besides, he's a young man, with no responsibilities. Why shouldn't he travel if he wants to?"

"I'm telling you, it's not right," Henry repeated. "I know my brother. Something's the matter with him."

I didn't want to believe it, and so I didn't. Nothing could ever be the matter with Jamie.

He came to us in late August, in the hot, slow days before the harvest. I was the first to see him: an indistinct form, shimmering slightly in the heat, striding up the dusty road with a suitcase in each hand. He wore a hat, so I couldn't see his red hair, but I knew it was Jamie by the way he walked—back straight, shoulders steady, hips absorbing all the motion. A movie star's walk.

"Who's that?" asked Pappy, squinting through the haze of smoke that surrounded him. The two of us were sitting on the porch, me churning butter and the old man back to doing his usual nothing. The girls were playing in the yard. Henry was out in the barn, feeding the livestock.

I shook my head in answer to Pappy's question, pretending ignorance for reasons I couldn't have explained, even to myself. As Jamie got closer I began to make out details: aviator sunglasses, oval patches darkening the armpits of his white shirt, baggy trousers sagging around his narrow hips. He spotted us and lifted one suitcase in greeting.

"It's Jamie!" said Pappy, waving his cane at his son. There was nothing wrong with the old man's legs; he was spry as a fox. The cane was purely for effect, a prop he used whenever he wanted to appear patriarchal or get out of working.

"Yes, I think you're right."

"Well don't just sit there, gal! Go and greet him!"

I stood, swallowing a tart response—for once, I wanted to obey him—and walked down the steps and across the yard. I was painfully conscious of the sweat staining my own dress, of my sun-browned skin and unwashed hair. I ran my hands through it, feeling it catch on the calluses on my palms. Farmwife's hands, that's what I had now.

I was about a hundred feet away from him when Pappy hollered, "Henry! Your brother's home! Henry!"

Henry emerged from the barn holding a feed bucket. "What?" he yelled. Then he saw Jamie. He whooped, dropped the bucket and broke into a run, and so did Jamie. Henry's bad leg made him awkward, but he seemed not to notice it. He pelted forward with the joyous abandon of a schoolboy. I realized I'd never seen my husband run before. It was like glimpsing another side of him, secret and unsuspected.

They came together ten feet in front of me. Clapped each other on the back, pulled apart, searched each other's faces: ritual. I stood outside of it and waited.

"You look good, brother," Jamie said. "You always did love farming."

"You look like hell," Henry replied.

"Don't sugarcoat it, now."

"You need to put some meat on those bones of yours, get some good Mississippi sun on your face."

"That's why I'm here."

"How'd you get out here?"

"I hitched my way from Greenville. I met one of your neighbors at the general store in town. He dropped me off at the bridge."

"Why didn't Eboline drive you?"

"One of the girls wasn't feeling well. Sick headache or some such thing. Eboline said they'd be down this weekend."

"I'm glad you didn't wait," Henry said.

Jamie turned to me then, looking at me in that way he had—as if he were really seeing me and taking me in whole. He held his hands out. "Laura," he said.

I went to him and gave him a hug. He felt light against me, insubstantial. His ribs protruded like the black keys of a piano. *I could pick him up*, I thought, and had a sudden irrational urge to do so. I stepped back hastily, flustered. Aware of his eyes on me.

"Welcome home, Jamie," I said. "It's good to see you."

"You too, sweet sister-in-law. How are you liking it here in Henry's version of paradise?"

I was spared from lying by the old man. "You'd think a son would see fit to greet his father," he bellowed from the porch.

"Ah, the dear, sweet voice of our pappy," said Jamie. "I'd forgotten how much I missed hearing it."

Henry picked up one of Jamie's suitcases and we headed

toward the house. "I think he's lonely here," Henry said. "He misses Mama, and Greenville."

"Oh, is that the excuse he's using these days?"

"No. He doesn't make excuses, you know that," Henry said. "He's missed you too, Jamie."

"I just bet he has. I bet he's quit smoking and joined the NAACP, too."

I laughed at that, but Henry's reply was serious. "I'm telling you, he's missed you. He'd never admit it, but it's true."

"If you say so, brother," Jamie said, throwing an arm around Henry's shoulder. "I'm not gonna argue with you today. But I have to say, it's mighty good of you to have taken him in and put up with him all these months."

Henry shrugged. "He's our father," he said.

I felt a ripple of envy, which I saw echoed on Jamie's face. How simple things were for Henry! How I wished sometimes that I could join him in his stark, right-angled world, where everything was either right or wrong and there was no doubt which was which. What unimaginable luxury, never to wrestle with whether or why, never to lie awake nights wondering what if.

AT SUPPER THAT NIGHT, Jamie regaled us with stories about his travels overseas. He'd been as far north as Norway and as far south as Portugal, mostly by train but sometimes by bicycle or on foot. He told us about snow-skiing in the Swiss Alps: how the mountains were so tall the tops of them pierced the clouds, and the snow so thick and soft that when you fell it was like sinking into a feather bed. He took us to the sidewalk cafés of Paris, where waiters in crisp white shirts and black aprons served pastries made of a hundred layers, each thinner than a fingernail; to the bullfights in Barcelona, where the matadors were hailed as gods by roaring crowds of thousands; to the casino in Monaco, where he'd won a hundred dollars on a single hand of baccarat and sent Rita Hayworth a bottle of champagne with the winnings. He made it all sound grand and marvelous, but I couldn't help noticing how drawn he looked, and how his hands shook each time he lit one of his Lucky Strikes. He ate little, preferring to smoke one cigarette after another until the room was so hazy the children's eyes were red and watery. They didn't complain, though. They were completely under their uncle's spell, especially Isabelle, who made eyes at him all through dinner and demanded to sit in his lap afterward. I'd never seen her so smitten with anyone.

Henry was the only one of us who seemed impatient with Jamie's stories. I could tell by the crease between his eyebrows, which got deeper and deeper as the evening wore on. Finally he blurted out, "And that's what you've been doing all these months, instead of coming home?"

"I needed some time," said Jamie.

"To play in the snow and eat fancy foreign bread."

"We all heal in our own ways, brother."

Henry made a gesture that took in Jamie's appearance. "Well, if this is what you call healing, I'd hate to see what hurting is."

Jamie sighed and passed a hand across his face. The veins on the back of his hand stood out like blue cords.

"Are you hurt, Uncle Jamie?" asked Isabelle worriedly.

"Everybody was hurt some in the war, little Bella. But I'll be all right. Do you know what *bella* means?" She shook her head. "It's Italian for 'beautiful one.' I think that's what I'll call you from now on. Would you like that, Bella?"

"Yes, Uncle Jamie!"

I would heal him, I thought. I would cook food to strengthen him, play music to soothe him, tell stories to make him smile. Not the weary smile he wore tonight, but the radiant, reckless grin he'd given me on the dance floor of the Peabody Hotel so many years before.

The war had dimmed him, but I would bring him back to himself.

HENRY

THE WAR BROKE my brother—in his head, where no one could see it. Never mind all his clever banter, his flirting with Laura and the girls. I could tell he wasn't right the second I saw him. He was thin and jittery, and his eyes had a haunted look I recognized from my own time in the Army. I knew too well what kind of sights they were seeing when he shut them at night.

Jamie was thin-skinned to begin with, had been all his life. He was always looking for praise, then getting his feelings hurt when he didn't get it, or enough of it. And he never knew his own worth, not in his guts where a man needs to know it. Our father was to blame for that. He was always whittling away at Jamie, trying to make him smaller. Pappy thought he had everybody fooled, but I knew why he did it. He did it because he loved my brother like he never loved anybody else in his whole life, not even Mama, and he wanted Jamie to be just like him. And when Jamie couldn't be or wouldn't be, which was most of the time, Pappy punished him. It was a hard thing to watch, but I learned not to get in the middle of it. We all did, even Mama. Defending Jamie just made Pappy whittle harder.

Once when I was home for Christmas, Jamie must have been six or seven, we were hauling wood and we flushed a copperhead out from under the woodpile. I grabbed the axe and chopped its head off, and Jamie screamed.

"Stop acting like a goddamn sissy," Pappy said, cuffing him on the head. "You'd think I had three daughters instead of two."

Jamie squared his shoulders and pretended he didn't care—even that young, he was good at acting—but I could tell how hurt he was.

"Why do you do that?" I asked Pappy when we were alone.

"Do what?"

"Cut him down like that."

"It's for his own good," Pappy said. "You and your mother and sisters have near to ruined him with your mollycoddling. Somebody needs to toughen him up."

"He's going to hate you if you're not careful," I said.

Pappy gave me a scornful look. "When he's a man, he'll understand. And he'll thank me, you wait and see."

My father died waiting for that thanks. It gives me no satisfaction to say so.

JAMIE DIDN'T TALK to me about the war. Most men don't, who've seen real combat. It's the ones who spent their tours well behind the lines who want to tell you all about it, and the ones who never served who want to know. Our father didn't waste any time before he started in with the questions. Jamie's first night home, as soon as Laura and the girls had gone to bed, Pappy said, "So what's it like, being a big hero?"

"I wouldn't know," Jamie said.

Pappy snorted. "Don't give me that. They wrote me about your fancy medals."

Jamie's "fancy medals" included the Silver Star and the Distinguished Flying Cross, two of the highest honors an airman can receive. He never mentioned them in his letters. If the Army hadn't notified Pappy, we wouldn't have known about them.

"I was lucky," Jamie said. "A lot of guys weren't."

"Bet you got plenty of tail out of it too."

My brother just shrugged.

"Jamie never needed medals to get girls," I said.

"Damn right, he don't," Pappy said. "Takes after me that way. I didn't have two cents to rub together when your mama married me. Prettiest girl in Greenville, could've had any fellow in town, but it was me she wanted."

That was true, as far as I knew. At least, Mama had never contradicted his version of their courtship. I believe they married each other almost entirely for their looks.

"She wasn't the only one either," Pappy went on. "I had em all sniffing after me, just like you do, son."

Jamie shifted in his chair. He hated being compared to our father.

"Well one thing's for sure," Pappy said. "You must've killed a whole lot of Krauts to get all them medals."

Jamie ignored him and looked at me. "You got anything to drink around here?"

"I think I've got some whiskey somewhere."

"That'll do just fine."

I found the bottle and poured two fingers all around. Jamie downed his and refilled his glass again, twice as full as before. That surprised me. I'd never known my brother to be a drinker.

"Well?" Pappy asked. "How many'd you take out?"

"I don't know."

"Take a guess."

"I don't know," Jamie repeated. "What does it matter?"

"A man ought to know how many men he's killed."

Jamie took a hefty swig of his whiskey, then smiled unpleasantly. "I can tell you this," he said. "It was more than one."

Pappy's eyes narrowed, and I swore under my breath. Back in '34, when he was still working for the railroad, Pappy had killed a man, an escaped convict from Parchman who'd tried to rob some passengers at gunpoint. Pappy pulled his own pistol and shot him right in the eyeball. A single shot, delivered with deadeye accuracy—at least, that was how he always told it. Over the years the elements of the story had hardened into myth. The terrified women and children, and the cool-headed conductor who never felt a moment's fear. The onlookers who cheered as he carried the body off the train and dumped it at the feet of the grateful sheriff. Killing that convict was the proudest moment of our father's life. Jamie knew better than to belittle it.

"Well," Pappy said with a smirk, "at least I looked my *one* in the eye before I shot him. Not like dropping bombs from a mile up in the air."

Jamie stared tight-jawed into his glass.

"Well," I said, "time to hit the hay. We've got an early day tomorrow."

"I'll just finish my drink," Jamie said.

Pappy got up with a grunt and took one of the lanterns. "Don't wake me up when you come in," he said to Jamie.

I sat with my brother while he finished his whiskey. It didn't take him long, and when he was done his eyes flickered to the bottle like he wanted more. I took it and put it back in the cupboard. "What you need is a good night's sleep," I said. "Come on, Laura made up your bed for you."

I took the other lantern and walked him out to the lean-to. At the door I gave him a quick hug. "Welcome home, little brother."

"Thanks, Henry. I'm grateful to you and Laura for having me."

"Don't talk nonsense. We're your family, and this is your home for as long as you want, hear?"

"I can't stay long," he said.

"Why not? Where else have you got to go?"

He shook his head again and looked up at the sky. It was a cloudless night, which I was glad to see. I wanted the cotton to stay nice and dry till after the harvest. Then it could rain all it wanted to.

"Actually," Jamie said, "it was more like four miles up in the air."

"What was?"

"The altitude we dropped the bombs from."

"How can you even see anything from that high up?"

"You can see more than you'd think," he said. "Roads, cities, factories. Just not the people. From twenty thousand feet, they're not even ants." He let out a harsh laugh. It sounded exactly like our father. "How many did you kill, Henry? In the Great War?"

"I don't know exactly. Fifty, maybe sixty men."

"That's all?"

"I was only in France for six weeks before I got wounded. I was lucky, I guess."

For a long time Jamie was silent. "Pappy's right," he said finally. "A man ought to know."

After he'd gone in I shuttered the lantern and sat on the porch awhile, listening to the cotton plants rustle in the night wind. Jamie needed more than a good night's sleep, I thought. He needed a home of his own, and a sweet Southern gal to give him children and coax his roots back down into his native soil. All of that would come in good time, I had no doubt of it. But right now he needed hard work to draw the poison from his wounds. Hard work and quiet nights at home with a loving family. Laura and the girls and I would give him that. We'd help him get better.

When I went in to bed I thought she was asleep, but as soon as I was settled under the covers, her voice came soft in the dark. "How long is he planning to stay?" she asked.

"Not for long, is what he says. But I aim to change his mind."

Laura sighed, a warm gust on the back of my neck.

• • •

THE HARVEST STARTED two weeks later. The cotton plants were so heavy with bolls they could barely stand up. There must have been a hundred bolls per plant, fat and bursting with lint. The air prickled with the smell of it. Looking out over the fields, breathing that dusty cotton smell, I felt a sense of rightness I hadn't known in years, and maybe not ever. This was my land, my crop, that I'd drawn forth from the earth with my wits and labor. There's no knowledge in the world as satisfying to a man as that.

I hired eight colored families to pick for me, which was as many as I could find. Orris Stokes had been right—field labor was hard to come by, though why anybody, colored or white, would prefer the infernal stink of a factory and the squalor of a city slum to a life lived under the sun, I will never understand. The talk at Tricklebank's was all about these new picking machines they were using on some of the big plantations, but even if I could have afforded one I wouldn't have wanted it. Give me a colored picker every time. There's nothing and no one can harvest a cotton crop better. Cotton picking's been bred into the Southern Negro, bred right into his bones. You just have to watch the colored children in the fields to see that. Before they're even knee-high their fingers know what to do. Of course, picking's like any other task you give one of them, you've got to keep a close eye on them, make sure they're not snapping on you, taking the boll along with the lint to increase the weight of their haul. You take that trash to the gin, you'll get your crop downgraded right quick. Any picker we caught snapping got his pay docked by half. You better believe we had them all picking clean cotton before long.

Jamie was a big help to me. He threw himself into every task I gave him, never once complaining about the work or the heat. He pushed himself hard, too hard sometimes, but I didn't try to stop him. Moodwise, he was up and down. He'd go along fine for three or four days, then he'd have one of his nightmares and wake us all with his shouting. I'd go out there and calm him down while our father grumbled about being kept awake. Pappy thought it was a weakness of character, something Jamie could fix if he just put his mind to it. I tried to explain to Pappy what it was like, reminding him how I'd once had those same kind of nightmares myself, and I was in combat for a lot less time than Jamie.

"Your brother needs to toughen up," Pappy said. "You wouldn't see me quaking and screaming like a girl."

On the weekends Jamie would take the car and disappear for a night, sometimes two. I was pretty sure he was going to Greenville to drink and mess around with cheap women. I didn't try to stop that either. I figured he was old enough to make his own decisions. He didn't need his big brother telling him what to do anymore.

But I figured wrong. One Monday in October I was on the tractor in the south field harvesting the last of the soybeans when I saw Bill Tricklebank's truck coming up the road in a hurry. Jamie had been gone since Saturday, and I was starting to worry. When I saw Bill's truck I knew something must have happened. We didn't have a phone, so when somebody needed to reach us they called Tricklebank's.

I got down off the tractor and ran across the field to the

road. I was out of breath by the time I reached Bill. "What is it?" I said. "What's the matter?"

"The Greenville sheriff's office called," Bill said. "Your brother's been arrested. They got him in the county jail."

"What for?"

He looked away from me and mumbled something.

"Speak up, Bill!"

"Driving drunk. He hit a cow."

"A *cow*?"

"That's what they said."

"Is he hurt?"

"Just a bump on the head and some bruises, is what the deputy told me."

Relief flooded me. I gripped Bill by the shoulder and saw him wince a little. The man was thin as a dandelion stalk and about as sturdy. "Thank you, Bill. Thank you for coming out and telling me."

"That ain't all," he said. "There was a . . . young lady in the car with him."

"Was she hurt?"

"Concussion and a broke arm. Deputy said she'd be all right though."

"I'd be obliged if you and Rose would keep this to yourselves," I said.

"Sure thing, Henry. But you ought to know, Mercy's the one who placed the call."

"Damn." Mercy Ivers was the nosiest of the town's operators, with the biggest mouth. If everybody in Marietta didn't already know Jamie was in jail, I had no doubt they would by nightfall.

Bill dropped me at the house and went on his way. Laura and Pappy were waiting on the porch. I filled them in, leaving out the part about the young lady. I was sorry my wife had to know about any of it, but with the Tricklebanks and Mercy Ivers involved there was no help for it. I figured Laura would be angry, and she was—just not in the way I expected.

"After all he's done for his country," she said, "to throw him in jail like a common criminal! They ought to be ashamed."

"Well, honey, he was blind drunk."

"We don't know that," she said. "And even if he was, I'm sure he had reason to be, after all he's been through."

"What if he'd hit another car instead of a cow? Somebody could have been badly hurt."

"But nobody was," she said.

Her defending him like that nettled me. My wife was a sensible woman, but where Jamie was concerned she was as blind as every other female who ever breathed. If it had been me out driving drunk and killing livestock, you can bet she wouldn't have been nearly so forgiving.

"Henry? Was someone else hurt?"

It was on the tip of my tongue to tell her and knock him off the pedestal she'd built for him—I was that mad at both of them. Lucky for Jamie I'm no rat. "No, just him," I said.

"Well then," Laura said, "let me get some supper for you to take to him. I'm sure they haven't fed him properly." She went inside.

"You want me to come with you?" Pappy asked.

"No," I said. "I'll take care of it."

"You'll need money for bail."

"I've got enough in the strongbox."

Pappy pulled his wallet out of his pants pocket, took out a worn hundred-dollar bill and held it out to me. I gaped at it, then at him. My father was a Scot to the marrow. Parting him from money was like trying to get milk out of a mule.

"Go on, take it," he said gruffly. "But don't you tell him I gave it to you."

"Why not?"

"I don't want him expecting more."

"Whatever you say, Pappy."

AT THE GREENVILLE jail I asked to see Sheriff Partain. I knew him slightly. He and my sister Thalia had been high school sweethearts. He'd wanted to marry her, but she had her sights set higher. Caught herself a rich tobacco planter from Virginia and moved up north with him. Told everybody she'd broken Charlie Partain's heart beyond repair. For Jamie's sake, I hoped she'd been wrong. Thalia always did have an exaggerated idea of her own importance.

When the deputy led me into Charlie's office he came out from behind his desk and shook my hand, a little too hard. "Henry McAllan. How long's it been?"

"About fifteen years, give or take."

Charlie hadn't changed much in that time. He had a little

belly on him, but he was still a good-looking fellow, big and affable, with an aw-shucks smile that couldn't quite hide the ambition underneath it. A born politician.

"How you been?" he asked.

"Just fine. I'm living over to Marietta now. Got me a cotton farm there."

"So I heard."

"You've done well for yourself," I said, gesturing at the badge on his shirt. "Congratulations on winning sheriff."

"Thanks. I was an MP in the war, guess I just got a taste for the law."

"About my brother," I said.

He shook his head gravely. "Yeah, it's a bad business."

"How is he?"

"He's all right, but he's got one helluva headache. Course, drinking a whole fifth of bourbon'll do that to you."

"Can you tell me what happened, Charlie? I got the story secondhand."

He walked back behind his desk, taking his time about it, and sat down. "You know," he said, "I like to be called sheriff when I'm working. Helps me keep the job separate. You understand." His face stayed friendly, but I didn't miss the sharp glint in his eye.

"Of course. Sheriff."

"Have a seat."

I sat in the chair he gestured to, facing the desk.

"Seems your brother and a female companion were parked out east of town on Saturday night. Watching the moon is what she said." Charlie's tone indicated how much he believed that.

"Who is this gal?"

"Her name's Dottie Tipton. She's a waitress over at the Levee Hotel. Her husband Joe was a friend of mine. He died at Bastogne."

"Sorry to hear it. Jamie fought in the Battle of the Bulge too. It's where he won his Silver Star. He was a bomber pilot, you know."

"You don't say," Charlie said, crossing his arms over his chest.

So much for my efforts to impress him. I decided I'd better stick to the business at hand. "So the two of them were parked, and then what happened?"

"Well, that's where it gets kinda fuzzy. Your brother don't remember a thing, or so he claims."

"And the woman?"

"Dottie says he ran into that cow by accident when they were driving back to town. Which I might believe if we'd found it laying in the road instead of smack-dab in the middle of Tom Easterly's pasture."

"You said yourself Jamie was drunk. He probably just lost track of the road."

Charlie leaned back in his chair, putting his feet up on the desk. Enjoying himself. "Uh-huh. There's just two problems with that."

"What?"

"One, he busted through a split-rail fence. And two, he hit

that cow dead on, like he was aiming for it. Had to been going fast too. That was some mighty tenderized beef."

I shook my head, unable to imagine why Jamie would deliberately run into a cow. It made no sense at all.

"Your brother got something against livestock?" Charlie asked, with a lift of his eyebrow.

I decided to level with him. "Jamie isn't well. He hasn't been himself since he got home from the war."

"That may be," Charlie said. "But it don't give him the right to do whatever the hell he wants. To just *take* whatever he wants. He ain't in the almighty Air Corps anymore." He ground out his cigarette. "All those flyboys, thought they were such hot stuff. Strutting around in their leather jackets like they owned the world and everything in it. The way the girls chased after em, you'd have thought they were the only ones putting their necks on the line. But if you ask me, it was the men on the ground who were the real heroes. Men like Joe Tipton. Course they didn't give Joe a Silver Star. He was just an ordinary soldier."

"There's honor in that too," I said.

Charlie's lip curled. "Mighty big of you to say so, McAllan."

I wanted to punch the sneer right off his face. What stopped me was the thought of Jamie in that cell on the other side of the wall. I locked eyes with Charlie Partain. "My brother flew sixty missions into German territory," I said. "Risked his life sixty times so more of our boys could come home in one piece. Maybe not your friend Joe, but Jamie saved a whole lot of others. And now—now he's messed up in the head and he needs some time to get himself straightened out. I think he deserves that, don't you?"

"I think Joe Tipton's widow deserves better than to be treated like a whore."

Then she shouldn't act like one, I thought. "I'm sure my brother never meant her any disrespect," I said. "Like I told you, he isn't himself. But I give you my word, sheriff, if you'll drop the charges and send him home with me, you won't have any more trouble from him."

"What about Dottie's hospital bills and Tom's cow?"

"I'll take care of it. I'll do it today."

Charlie shook out a cigarette from the pack on his desk and lit it. He took three leisurely drags without saying a word. Finally he got up and walked to the door. "Dobbs!" he yelled. "Go fetch Jamie McAllan. We're releasing him."

I got up and held my hand out to him. "Thank you, sheriff. I'm much obliged."

He ignored my hand and my thanks both. "Tell your brother to stay away from Dottie, and from Greenville," he said. "If I catch him making trouble here again, he'll be the one who needs saving."

WHEN THEY BROUGHT him out to me he wouldn't meet my eyes, just stammered an apology while Charlie Partain and his deputy watched. He reeked of whiskey and vomit. He looked like hell too. There was a bad gash on his forehead and one eye was swollen nearly shut.

Still, he was in better shape than the DeSoto, which they'd taken to the municipal pound. We went there first, intending to pick it up, but I didn't need a mechanic to tell me it was undrivable. The front end was collapsed like an overripe pumpkin, and the engine was a mangled mess. Jamie's face went white when he saw it.

"Jesus, did I do that?"

"Yeah, you did," I said. "What the hell happened?"

"I don't know. The last thing I remember is Dolly telling me to slow down."

"Her name's Dottie. And you put her in the hospital."

"I know, they told me," he said in a low voice. "But I'm gonna make it up to her, and to you. I swear it."

"You can make it up to me all you want, but you're never to see her again."

"Says who?"

"Charlie Partain. Her husband was a friend of his."

"I wondered why he was so pissed off. He gave me this shiner, you know."

"He hit you? That son of a bitch."

"I reckon I deserved it."

He looked so hunched and miserable. "Next time, do me a favor," I said.

"What?"

"Go after a rabbit, will you?"

It took him a few seconds but then he started laughing, and so did I. The two of us laughed till tears ran down our faces, like we hadn't done in years. And if Jamie's face stayed wet for a time after we were done, I pretended not to notice.

I dropped him at the Levee Hotel, where he'd been staying. While he was getting cleaned up I drove over to the hospital and paid Dottie Tipton's bill. They were sending her home that afternoon, which I was glad to hear. I didn't visit her—what in the world would I have said?—but I asked one of the nurses to tell her Jamie was sorry and hoped she'd get better soon.

When I picked him up he looked and smelled a little better. We stopped at Tom Easterly's place on the way out of town. Bastard wanted two hundred dollars for his cow, which was a good fifty dollars more than it or any other cow was worth, but I thought of Charlie Partain and paid it. The whole thing ended up costing me close to three hundred dollars, not counting the car. Figured I was looking at another four hundred minimum to fix it, and double that if I had to replace it. I'd planned on spending that money on a rent house for Laura and the girls, but now that wouldn't be possible.

All the way home I dreaded telling her, dreaded seeing that disappointed look on her face.

"We're tapped out," I said, when we were alone in bed. "Even with a good harvest, there won't be enough for a house in town this year. I'm sorry, honey."

She didn't say a word, and I couldn't see her expression in the dark.

"The good news is, Jamie's promised to stay another six months to make it up to us. With his help, I should be able to put enough by that we can get a house next year."

She sighed and got out of bed. I heard her bare feet scuffing on the floor, down to the foot of the bed and around to my side. Then I heard a familiar scraping sound and saw a match flare. She lit the candle, parted the mosquito netting and got in, squeezing in next to me. Her arm went around me.

"It's all right, Henry," she whispered. "I don't mind it so much."

I felt her lips on my neck, and her hand slip down into my pajamas.

JAMIE

BECAUSE OF HENRY. Somehow it always comes back to that.

There I was again, indebted to him for pulling my ass out of the sling I'd custom-made to hold it. He wouldn't tell me how much he was out on my account, but I figured it was close to a thousand bucks.

Henry wasn't the only one I owed. Thanks to me, Laura didn't get her house in town, her indoor toilet and grass lawn. Instead she got another year of stink and muck. She never reproached me for it, though, never even raised an eyebrow at me. She welcomed me home as sweetly as if I were returning from church and not the county jail. A lot of women act sweet, but with most of them that's all it is, an act they learn young and hone to perfection by the time they're twenty-one. My sisters were both masters of the craft, but Laura was something else altogether. She was sweet to the core.

Then there was Dottie Tipton. I snuck into Greenville to see her a week after the accident. (That's how everybody except my father referred to it—"the accident." Pappy referred to it as "your drunken rampage" and took to calling me "the cow-slayer.") Dottie was tickled pink to see me. Nothing was too good for the man who'd given her a concussion and put her arm in a cast. She changed her dress and put on lipstick, one-handedly fixed me a drink in a crystal highball, fussed over my bruises. Was I sure I wasn't hungry? She'd be happy to whip up a little something, it would be no trouble at all. I pictured us sitting at her dining room table eating supper off her wedding china, no doubt with dessert afterward in her bedroom. The urge to leap up and run out the door was as powerful as anything I'd ever felt before battle. It was Dottie's dead husband who stopped me. Joe Tipton stared out at me from his silver frame on the mantel, his expression stern under the cap of his uniform. *Don't you do it, you craven son of a bitch*, that expression said. So I stayed awhile and had a few drinks and laughs with her. The drinks made the laughs come easier, and the lies too. When it was time to say goodbye, I was tender and rueful—Antony to her Cleopatra. *Bravo*, said Joe. *Now get the fuck out.* Dottie clung to me a little when I told her I could never see her again, but she didn't cry. Another thing I owed her for.

All those people whose lives I'd careened into—just like that, they let me off the hook. All that was left was for me to do the same, and that wasn't hard. Booze helped, and remembering: Flaming planes trailing black smoke, falling from the sky. Men falling from the planes, falling with their chutes on fire, falling with no chutes at all, throwing themselves out of the planes rather than be burned alive. The *wuff wuff wuff* of enemy flak, ripping them all to pieces, the falling planes and falling men and pieces of men.

They say you have to hate to be in the infantry, but that wasn't true in the Air Corps. We never saw the faces of our enemies. When I thought of them at all, I pictured blank white ovals framed by blond crew cuts — never bangs or curls or pigtails, though I knew our bombs fell on plenty of women and kids too. Sometimes we just picked a big city and blasted the hell out of it. Other times, if we couldn't get to our primary target, usually a military installation or factory, we went after a "target of opportunity" instead. We called them AWMs, short for "Auf Wiedersehen, Motherfuckers." There was an unspoken rule never to bring the bombs back home. My last run, thunderstorms kept us from reaching the munitions depot we were supposed to hit, so we ended up dumping our full load on a big park full of refugees. We knew from our intelligence briefing that there were SS soldiers there, seeking cover among the civilians. Still, we killed thousands of innocent people along with them. When we got back to base and made our strike report to the CO, he congratulated us on a job well done.

A few seconds before I hit that cow it turned its head and looked straight at me. It could have moved, but it didn't. It just stood there watching me as I bore down on it.

I GUESS I COULD have talked to Henry about the war, but whenever I started to bring it up I found myself cracking a joke or making up a story instead. He wouldn't have understood what I felt. The horror, yes, but not the guilt, and certainly not the urge I'd sometimes had to drive my plane into an enemy fighter and turn us both into a small sun. Henry, longing for oblivion—the very idea of it was laughable. What my brother longed for was right under his feet. He scraped it from his boots every night with tender care. The farm was his element, just as the sky had once been mine. That was the other reason I didn't confide in him: I didn't want to muddy his happiness.

Whiskey was the only thing that kept the nightmares at bay. After the accident I knew Henry, Laura and Pappy were all keeping a close eye on me, so I was careful never to have more than a couple of beers in front of them. I did my real drinking in secret. I had bottles stashed everywhere—on top of the outhouse, out in the barn, under a floorboard on the front porch—and I always carried a tin of lemon drops to hide the smell on my breath. I never got falling-down drunk, just maintained a nice steady infusion throughout the day. A lot of it I sweated out. The rest I put to use. I was the designated charmer of the household, the one responsible for keeping everybody else's spirits up. To play my part I needed booze.

I played it brilliantly, if I do say so myself. None of them guessed my secret, except for Florence Jackson. Her sharp eyes didn't miss much. One time I discovered a half-full bottle of Jack Daniel's tucked underneath my pillow, like a gift from the Bourbon Fairy. I knew it was Florence who'd put it there because it was washing day and the sheets had been changed. I must have left it somewhere, and she'd found it and returned it to me. This one act of kindness aside, she didn't much like me.

I tried to win her over, but she was immune to my charm—one of the only women I'd ever met who was. I think she must have sensed the part I would play in the events to come. Henry would scoff at me for saying so, but I believe Negroes have an innate ability that us white people lack to sense things, a kind of bone-sense. It's different from head-sense, which we have more of than they do, and it comes from an older, darker place.

Florence may have sensed something, but I had no idea of what I was setting in motion the day I gave Ronsel Jackson a lift from town. It was just after the new year. I'd been back in Mississippi for four months, but it felt more like four years. I drove into Marietta to get my hair cut and pick up some groceries for Laura, and some bourbon for me. Usually I bought my liquor in Tchula or Belzoni, but that day I didn't have time. I was coming out of Tricklebank's with my purchases when I heard a loud explosion off to my left. I hit the ground, covering my head with my hands and dropping the box of groceries, which spilled out into the street.

"It's all right," said a deep voice behind me. "It was just a car." A tall Negro in overalls stepped out from behind a parked truck. He pointed at an old Ford Model A moving away from us down the street. "It backfired, is all," he said. "Must've had a stuck intake valve." Belatedly I recognized Ronsel Jackson. I'd only spoken to him a couple of times and only about farm business, but I knew from Henry that he'd fought in one of the colored battalions.

Somebody chuckled, and I looked up to see a dozen pairs of

eyes staring at us from under hat brims. All the Saturday afternoon regulars were on the porch at Tricklebank's, exchang-
ing opinions on whatever passed for news in Marietta—at the
moment, no doubt, that crazy brother of Henry McAllan's, the
one who killed that cow over to Greenville. Hot-faced, I bent
down and started putting the groceries back in the box. Ronsel
helped me, handing me some oranges that had rolled his way.
The flour sack had come untied, spilling half its contents onto
the dirt, but the whiskey was mercifully intact. When I picked
it up, my hands were shaking so hard I dropped it again.

If Ronsel had said anything, if he'd even made a sound that
was meant to be sympathetic or soothing, I might have hauled
off and hit him—God knows I wanted to hit somebody. He
didn't give me the excuse, though. He just held his own hand
out, palm down, so I could see it was shaking every bit as bad
as mine. I saw the same frustration in his face that I was feeling, and the same rage, maybe more.

"Reckon it'll ever stop?" he asked, looking down at his
hand.

"They say it does eventually," I said. "Did you walk here?"

"Yessuh. Daddy's using the mule to break the fields."

"Come on, I'll give you a lift."

He headed for the bed of the truck. I was about to tell him
he could ride up front with me—it was cold out and starting
to drizzle—but then I saw the men on the porch watching us,
and I remembered Henry mentioning that Ronsel had gotten
into some trouble here awhile back. I waited till we were out
of town, then I pulled over, stuck my head out the window and
called out, "Why don't you come on up front?"

"I'm doing just fine back here," he called back.

The drizzle had turned into a steady rain. I couldn't see him, but he had to be cold and wet, and getting more so by the minute. "Get in, soldier!" I yelled. "That's an order!"

I felt the truck rock as he jumped off, then the passenger door opened and he got in, smelling of wet wool and sweat. I expected him to thank me. What he said was, "How do you know you outranked me?"

I laughed. "You obeyed my order, didn't you? Besides, I was a captain."

His chin came up. "There were Negro captains," he said. "I served under plenty of em."

"Let me guess. You were a sergeant."

"That's right," he said.

I reached into the box sitting between us, uncorked the whiskey and took a good long swallow. "Well, sergeant, how do you like being back here in the Delta?"

He didn't answer, just turned his head and stared out the side window. At first I thought I'd ruffled his feathers, but then I realized he was giving me privacy in which to drink. *A fine fellow, this Ronsel Jackson,* I thought, taking another swig. Then I had a second, more accurate realization: He wasn't looking at me because he figured I wasn't going to offer him any. He was protecting his dignity and giving me the leeway to be a son of a bitch at the same time. Annoyed, I thrust the bottle at him. "Here, have a snort."

"No thanks," he said.

"Are you always this stubborn, or is it just around white people who are trying to be nice to you?"

He accepted the bottle and took a quick sip, his eyes never leaving my face. The truth was, not that long ago I wouldn't have offered him any, not unless it was the last swig in the bottle. I wasn't sure whether it was a good or a bad thing that I didn't care anymore.

"What kind of an NCO are you?" I said, when he tried to hand the bottle back to me after that one little sip. This time he took a big snort, so big he choked and spilled some on his overalls. "Don't waste it, now," I said. "That's my medicine, I need every drop."

When I took the bottle back from him, I saw him notice my missing finger. "You get that in the war?" he asked.

"Yeah. Frostbite."

"How does a pilot manage to get frostbite?"

"You got any idea how cold it is at twenty thousand feet, with the wind blowing through like fury? I'm talking fifty, sixty below zero."

"Why'd you leave the window open?"

"Had to. There were no wipers. When it rained, you had to stick your head out the window to see."

He shook his head. "And I thought I had it bad, being stuck inside a rolling tin can."

"You were a tanker?"

"Sure was. Spearheaded for Patton."

"You ever piss in your helmet?"

"Yeah, plenty of times."

"We had relief tubes in the cockpit but sometimes it was easier just to use our flak helmets. And at twenty thousand

feet that piss freezes solid in less than a minute. One time I
went in my helmet and forgot all about it. It was a long haul.
When we got close to the target I put the helmet back on. We
did the bombing run and were dodging enemy flak when I felt
something wet running down my face. And then I smelled it
and realized what it was."

Ronsel gave a big booming laugh. "You must a caught hell
back at the Officers' Club."

"My buddies never let me hear the end of it. The ones who
survived, that is."

"Yeah. I hear you."

It was nearing dark and cold enough that I could see his
breath and mine, mingling in the air. I put the truck in gear
and we drove the rest of the way to the farm in silence, letting the bourbon be our conversation, back and forth. When
we pulled up to the Jackson place, Hap was outside filling a
bucket at the pump. The look of alarm on his face when he
saw his son in the cab of the truck was so exaggerated it was
comical.

I rolled down my window. "Evening, Hap."

"Everything all right, Mist Jamie?"

"Everything's fine. I just gave Ronsel here a lift from town."

Ronsel opened the door and got out, a bit unsteadily.
"Thanks for the ride," he said.

"You're welcome." As he was about to shut the door, I said,
"I expect I'll be heading into town again next Saturday afternoon. If you like I'll stop by here, see if you want a ride."

Ronsel glanced at his father, then back at me. He nodded

his head once, as solemnly as a judge. And in that moment, sealed his fate.

Maybe that's cowardly of me, making Ronsel's the trigger finger. There are other ways to look at it, other turning points I could pick, eeny, meeny, miny, moe: When that car backfired. When he got in the cab of the truck. When I handed him the whiskey. But I think it was right then, when he stood half-drunk in the rain and nodded his head. And I believe Ronsel would tell you the same thing, if you could ask him, and he could answer.

III.

LAURA

I FELL IN LOVE with my brother-in-law the way you fall asleep in the car when someone you trust is driving—gradually, by imperceptible degrees, letting the motion lull your eyes closed. *Letting,* that's the key word. I could have stopped myself. I could have shoved those feelings into some dark corner of my mind and locked them away, as I'd done with so many other feelings I'd found troubling. I tried to, for a time, but it was a halfhearted effort at best, doomed to failure.

Jamie set about making me love him from the first day he arrived. Complimenting me on my cooking and doing little things for me around the house. Things that said, *I see you. I think about what might please you.* I was starved for that kind of attention, and I soaked it up like a biscuit soaks up gravy. Henry was never a thoughtful man, not in the small, everyday ways that mean so much to a woman. In Memphis, surrounded by dozens of doting Chappells and Fairbairns, I hadn't minded so much, but at Mudbound I'd felt the lack of attention keenly. Henry was wholly preoccupied with the farm. I would have gotten more notice from him if I'd grown a tail and started to bray.

I want to make one thing clear: When I say that Jamie set about making me love him, I don't mean that he seduced me. Oh, he flirted with me plenty, but he flirted with everybody, even the men. He liked to win people. That makes it sound like a game, and perhaps to a certain type of man it is, but Jamie was no rake. He *needed* to win them. I didn't see that then. I saw only the way he leaned forward whenever I spoke, his head cocked slightly to one side as if to better catch my words. I saw the wildflowers he left for me in a milk bottle on the kitchen table, and the happy smiles of my children when he teased them.

Isabelle was his pet, and I was glad of it. I could never love her enough or give her enough attention. Jamie saw her need and met it with extravagant affection, which she returned in full measure. When he was in the room, none of the rest of us existed for her. He'd come in dirty and worn out from the fields, and she'd hold her chubby arms up to him like a Baptist preacher calling on the Almighty. Jamie would shake his head and say, "I'm too tired to hold you tonight, little Bella." She'd stamp her foot imperiously and reach for him, knowing better, and he'd swoop down and gather her into his arms, twirling her around and around while she squealed with delight. It wasn't just that he loved her; it was that he loved *her*, in particular. That was everything to her. Before long, she was insisting we all call her Bella. She refused to answer to Isabelle, even after Henry spanked her bottom for it. But she's his child as well as mine, at least in stubbornness, and eventually she got her way.

Even dimmed as he was, Jamie charmed and leavened us all. Pappy carped less, and Henry laughed more often and slept more soundly. I came alive again, like I hadn't been since before the miscarriage. I was less resentful of Henry and less mindful of the privations of the farm. He must have known Jamie was the cause of my improved spirits, but if it bothered him he didn't let on. He seemed to accept that Jamie "made the girls sparkle," as he'd told me all those years ago. It would have been unthinkable to Henry that his wife would have sexual feelings for his little brother.

And that's exactly what I was having: sexual feelings, of an intensity I'd never experienced in my life. Anything could bring them on: slicing a tomato, pulling weeds in the garden, running a comb through my hair. My senses were acute. Food was more succulent and smells more pungent. I was hungrier than usual and perspired more often. Not even pregnancy had made my body so strange to me.

Even so, it all might have come to nothing if Jamie hadn't built the shower for me. That shower became the crucible of my feelings for him. To understand why, you have to imagine life without running water or bathrooms. It was an all-day undertaking to get the whole family clean, so we bathed only on Saturdays. During the summer months I filled the tub and let the morning sun warm the water. I bathed the girls first, then myself, praying nobody would come calling while I was naked. For privacy we hung sheets from two clotheslines, placing the tub between them—an arrangement that left the bather exposed on two sides and gave the whole country an eyeful on windy days. After my bath I refilled the tub for Pappy. When he was done, I emptied and refilled it again—sometimes with the old man's grudging help, but more often by myself—for when Henry and Jamie came in from the fields. In the winter, the tub had to be dragged into the kitchen and the water hauled in and heated on the stove. Still, for all the work involved, Saturday was my favorite day of the week. It was the only day I felt truly clean.

The rest of the time, we stank. You can say all you want about honest sweat, but it smells just as bad as any other kind. Henry didn't seem to mind, but I never got used to it. I remembered my little bathroom on Evergreen Street with swooning nostalgia. I'd taken it completely for granted, even grumbled occasionally about the poor water pressure and the chips in the porcelain tub. Now, as I took my hasty spit baths from a pail of cold water in the kitchen, that little bathroom seemed a place of impossible luxury.

The worst time for me was during my menses. The musky-sweet reek of my blood on the cloths I wore seemed to fill the house until I could hardly breathe. I'd wait each night for the others to fall asleep, then tiptoe to the kitchen to wash the cloths and myself. One night, as I squatted over the basin with my nightgown bunched around my waist and my hand moving awkwardly between my legs, Henry walked in on me. He turned quickly and left, but oh, how ashamed I was!

Jamie must have guessed how I felt. One day in March, I returned from an overnight shopping trip to Greenville to dis-

cover a narrow wooden stall in back of the house, with a large
bucket attached to a pulley contraption mounted on top. Jamie
was just finishing it when the girls and I pulled up in the car.

"What is it, Uncle Jamie?" asked Amanda Leigh.

"It's a shower, little petunia."

"I don't like showers, I like baths!" cried Bella.

"I didn't build it for you, honey. I built it for your mama."

Bella frowned at that. Jamie tousled her hair, but his eyes
were on me. "Well," he said, "what do you think?"

"I think it's the most marvelous thing I've ever seen."

And it was. Of course, like everything at Mudbound, the
shower required some effort. You still had to heat water on the
stove and haul it outside—two or three bucketfuls, depending
on whether or not you were washing your hair. You lowered
the big shower bucket, poured the hot water in, then raised
it again by pulling on a rope attached to the pulley. Then you
went in the stall and got undressed, draping your clothes over
the walls. When you were ready, you tugged gently on a second
rope attached to the bucket's lip, tilting it and releasing just
enough water so you could soap yourself. Finally, you pulled on
the rope again and rinsed until all the water was gone.

I had my first shower that very evening. It was one of those
warm soft nights in early spring when the air itself seems like
a living being, surrounding and gently supporting you. As soon
as I stepped into the stall and closed the door, I was in a private universe. On the other side of the walls, I could hear the
deep thrumming of insects and frogs, the constant music of the

Delta, and more distantly, the men's voices interwoven with the sound of Amanda Leigh practicing her piano scales. I took off my clothes and just stood there for several minutes in that warm, embracing air. Overhead floated large clouds, stained fantastic hues of pink and gold by the setting sun. I pulled the rope and felt the water stream down my body and thought of my brother-in-law, of his hands sawing the planks, fitting them together, nailing them down. He'd even made me a soap dish, I saw. It was slatted at the bottom and held a small bar of embossed purple soap, the kind they had in fancy stores in Memphis. When I brought it to my nose I smelled the dusky, pungent sweetness of lavender. It was my favorite scent; I'd mentioned it to Jamie once, years ago. And he had remembered.

I ran the soap across my body and wondered: as he was building the shower, had he imagined me in it like this, naked and free under the darkening sky? I don't know what shocked me more, the thought itself, or the heavy ripple of pleasure it sent through me.

HENRY WAS THE beneficiary of all this newfound ardor. He'd almost always been the one to initiate our lovemaking, but now I found myself seeking him out in our bed, to his surprise and my own. Sometimes he would refuse me. He never gave an explanation, just took my exploring hand and returned it to my own side of the bed, patting it dismissively before he turned away. The anger that filled me on those nights was so hot and raw I was surprised it didn't set the bed ablaze. I'd never refused him, not once in all the years of our marriage. How dared he push me aside like an unwanted pet?

I tried to keep my feelings for Jamie secret, but I've never been good at subterfuge; my father used to call me his little trumpeter for the way my face proclaimed my every emotion. One day Florence and I were working in the house together, me cooking and her sorting laundry, and she said, "Mist Jamie doing some better."

"Yes," I said, "I think he is."

Seven months on the farm had done him good. I had no illusions that he was completely healed, but he was having fewer nightmares, and physically he seemed stronger. My cooking had put some meat on him; I was especially proud of that.

"He got hisself a woman, that's why," Florence said, with a sly smile.

I felt a constriction in my throat, like a stone was lodged there. "What are you talking about?"

"See here?" She held up one of his shirts. There was a smudge of red on the collar.

"That's blood," I said. "He probably cut himself shaving." But I knew better. Dried blood would have been brown.

"Well, it sure is some mighty sweet-smelling blood then," said Florence.

The stone in my throat seemed to swell until I could hardly swallow.

"Ain't good for a man to be without a woman," she went on

conversationally. "Now a woman, she likes a man, but she can get along just fine without him. The Almighty seen to that. But a man ain't never gone thrive without a woman by his side. He be looking high and low till he find one. Course Mist Jamie, he the kind come by em easy. They be lined up like daisies on the side of the road, just waiting for him to pluck em. He just got to reach out his hand and—"

"Shut your mouth," I said. "I won't listen to another word of such low talk."

We stared at each other for a moment, then Florence dropped her gaze, but not before I saw the knowing look in her dark eyes. "Now go and fetch some water," I said. "I want to make some coffee."

She obeyed, moving with an unhurriedness that bordered on insolent. When the front door closed behind her, I went to the table and picked up the shirt. I raised it to my nose and smelled the cloying scent of lily-of-the-valley perfume. I tried to imagine the type of woman who would wear that scent. Her dresses would be low-cut and her fingernails would be painted the same shade of carmine as her lipstick. She'd have a throaty laugh and smoke cigarettes from a long holder and let her slip show on purpose when she crossed her legs. She'd be nothing but a cheap little tramp, I thought.

"Smell something you like, gal?" I turned and saw Pappy framed in the front window. I felt my cheeks flame. How long had he been standing there, and how much had he overheard? Long enough and plenty, judging by the smirk on his face.

Nonchalantly, or so I hoped, I dropped the shirt into the

basket. "Just sweat," I said. "You know, the odor that comes from a person's body when they do work of some kind? Perhaps you've heard of it."

I left the room before he could reply.

THE TROUBLE STARTED the first Saturday in April. I was driving the old man to town when we encountered Jamie coming the other way in the truck. As we drew closer I could see Ronsel Jackson in the passenger seat. He'd wisely kept his head down in the year since he'd been home. We rarely saw him, except as a distant figure in the fields, hunched over his plow. That view of him seemed to have appeased Pappy; at least, he'd stopped ranting about "that smart-mouthed nigger" on a daily basis.

"Who's that with Jamie?" Pappy said, squinting at them.

The old man was too vain to wear glasses in public, so he often depended on us to be his eyes. For once, I was glad. "I don't know," I said. "I can't make him out."

The road was too narrow for two vehicles to pass. Jamie pulled the truck over to let us by, and I was forced to slow to a crawl. As we passed them, Jamie raised his hand in greeting. Ronsel sat beside him, looking straight ahead.

"Stop the car!" Pappy ordered. I braked, but Jamie drove on. Pappy's head whipped around to follow the truck through the rear window. "Did you see that? I think he had that nigger with him."

"Who do you mean?"

"The Jackson boy, the one with the big mouth. You didn't see him?"

"No. The sun was in my eyes."

Pappy turned to me, fixing me with his basilisk stare. "You lying to me, gal?"

"Of course not, Pappy," I replied, with all the innocence I could muster.

He grunted and faced forward, crossing his arms over his chest. "I'll tell you one thing, it better not have been that nigger."

We ran our errands and returned to the farm several hours later. I was hoping for a word alone with Jamie before Pappy could speak to him, but as luck would have it, he and Henry were out front working on the truck when we pulled up. The children ran to meet us, clamoring for the candy I'd promised them.

"I'll give it to you inside," I said. "Jamie, would you help me carry these groceries in the house?"

"Wait just a goddamn minute," Pappy said to Jamie. "Who was that you had with you in the truck?"

Jamie's eyes flickered to me. I shook my head slightly, hoping he'd catch on and make something up.

"Well? Are you gonna answer me or not?" Pappy said.

"Girls, go inside," I said. "I'll be right there."

Reluctantly, they went. Jamie waited until they were out of earshot before answering Pappy. "As a matter of fact, it was Ronsel Jackson. What's it to you?" His voice was steady, but his cheeks had a hectic look. I wondered if he'd been drinking again.

"What's this?" asked Henry.

"I gave Ronsel a lift from town. Evidently our pappy doesn't approve."

"Not when he's sitting in the cab with you, I don't, and I bet your brother don't either," Pappy said.

Henry's expression was incredulous. "You let him sit inside the truck all the way from town?"

"What if I did?" Jamie said. "What does it matter?"

"Did anybody see you?"

"No, but I wouldn't care if they had."

They glared at each other, Jamie defiantly, Henry with a familiar mixture of anger, hurt and bewilderment that I'd last seen directed at me. Henry shook his head. "I don't know who you are anymore," he said. "I wonder if you do." He turned and walked toward the house. Jamie looked after him like he wanted to stop him, but he didn't move.

"Don't ever let me catch you giving that jigaboo a ride again," Pappy said.

"Or what?" Jamie said. "You gonna come after me with your cane?"

The old man grinned, revealing his long yellow teeth. He rarely smiled; when he did, the effect was both bizarre and repellent. "Oh, it ain't what I'll do to *you*."

Pappy followed Henry inside, leaving me alone with Jamie. His body looked tensed, poised for violence or flight. I was torn between wanting to soothe and chide him.

"I can't stay here," he said. "I'm going to town."

To his woman, I thought. "I wish you'd change your mind," I said. "I'm making rabbit stew for supper."

He reached out and lightly brushed my cheek with one finger. I swear I felt that touch in every nerve of my body. "Sweet Laura," he said.

I watched him go. As the truck and its wake of dust got smaller and smaller and finally disappeared, I thought, *Rabbit stew. That's what I'd been able to offer him.* It was all I would ever be able to offer him. The knowledge was as bitter as bile.

FLORENCE

I RAN THE BROOM over his foot three times. Said, "Sorry, Mist Jamie, ain't I clumsy today." The third time Miz McAllan gave me a scolding and sent me out of the house, finished the sweeping her own self. I didn't care what she thought, or him either. I just wanted him gone. But he didn't go, not even after I threw salt in his tracks and put a mojo of jimsonweed and gumelastin under his bed. He kept right on coming back, turning up like the bad penny he was.

He was a shiny penny though, with his handsome face and his littleboy smile. Folks just took to him natural, they couldn't help themselves, like the way a child hankers for a holly berry. He don't know it's poison, he just sees something pretty and red and he wants it in his mouth. And when you take it away from him he cries like you taking away his own heart. There's a whole lot of evil in the world looks pretty on the outside.

Jamie McAllan wasn't evil, not like his pappy was, but he did the Dark Man's business just the same. He was a weak vessel. Whiskey on his breath at noon and womansmell all over his clothes every Monday. Now a man can like his nature

activity and even his drink and still be the Lord's, but Jamie
McAllan had a hole in his soul, the kind the devil loves to find.
It's like a open doorway for him, lets him enter in and do his
wicked work. I thought maybe he got it in the war and it would
close on up in time but it just kept on getting bigger and bigger.
None of em seen it but me. Jamie McAllan geehawsed em all,
specially Miz McAllan. The way she looked at him you would
a thought he was her husband and not his brother. But Henry
McAllan didn't seem to mind, that's if he even noticed. Tell
you one thing, if my sister ever stretched her eyes at Hap like
that, I'd claw em right out.

Even my son was took in by him. I knowed about their Saturday afternoon drives and them other times too when Ronsel
went out walking after dark. Only place colored folks round
here go walking after dark is to and from the outhouse, if they
know what's good for em anyway. No, I knowed exactly where
he was. He was out in that ole falling-down sawmill by the
river, getting drunk with Jamie McAllan. I seen Ronsel heading off that way plenty of times and heard him stumbling in
late at night. I tried to tell him to keep away from that man
but he wouldn't listen.

"What you doing, hanging around with that white man?" I
asked him.

"Nothing. Just talking."

"You asking for trouble is what you doing."

Ronsel shook his head. "He ain't like the rest of em."

"You right about that," I said. "Jamie McAllan's got a snake
in his pocket and he carries it along with him wherever he

goes. But when that snake gets ready to bite, it ain't gone bite
him, oh no. It's gone sink them fangs into whoever else is with
him. You just better make sure it ain't you."

"You don't know him," Ronsel said.

"I know he's drinking whiskey every day and hiding it from
his family."

Ronsel looked away. "He's just chasing off his ghosts," he
said.

My son had plenty of em too, I knowed that, but he wouldn't
talk to me bout em. He was like a boarded-up house since he
come back from that war, nothing going into him or coming
out of him—at least, nothing from or to us. Jamie McAllan
had more of Ronsel than we did.

I didn't tell Hap about the two of em drinking together. I
don't like to keep things from my husband but him and Ronsel
was already butting heads all the time. That was Hap's doing,
he was pushing Ronsel to talk to Henry McAllan bout taking
over the Atwoods' old acres. There was a new cropper family
in there but Mist McAllan wasn't happy with em, he'd said so
to Hap. Ronsel told his daddy he'd think it over, but he wanted
them acres like a cat wants a pond to swim in. And Hap just
kept on pushing him and pushing him, that was the landsick-
ness talking is what that was.

"You don't stop, you gone push him right out the door," I
told him.

"He's a man grown," Hap said. "He needs to get his own
place, start his own family. Might as well be here. One of the
twins can help him. With the four of us working fifty acres,

and if cotton prices stay above thirty cents a pound, in three four years we'll have enough to buy our own land."

Ronsel couldn't a cared less about having his own land, but there wasn't no point in telling that to my husband. Might as well to been singing songs to a dead hog. Once Hap gets a notion a something, he's deaf and blind to everything that don't mesh with it. It's what makes him a good preacher, his faith never wobbles. Folks see that in him and it bucks em up. But what works in the pulpit ain't always good at your own kitchen table. All Ronsel seen was his daddy not caring bout what he wanted. And what he wanted was to leave. I hated the thought of him going but I knowed he had to do it soon, just like I had to set back and let him.

By springtime he was getting drunk with Jamie McAllan every couple days. So when ole Mist McAllan seen the two of em together in the truck, I was glad. I thought it would put a stop to the whole business.

Ronsel didn't mention it to us. Just like the last time, we had to find out what happened from Henry McAllan. He come by one afternoon, all het up, wanting a word with Hap and Ronsel. And just like the last time, I listened in. Reckoned I had a right to know what was being said on my own front porch, whether the men thought so or not.

"I expect you know why I'm here, Ronsel," Mist McAllan said.

"No suh, I don't."

"My brother tells me he gave you a lift from town today."

"Yessuh."

"I reckon it wasn't the first time."

"No, not the first."

"Exactly how long has this been going on?"

"I can't rightly say."

"Hap, do you know what I'm talking about?"

"No, Mist McAllan."

"Well, let me tell you then," Henry McAllan said. "Apparently your son here and my brother have been riding around the countryside in my truck for God knows how long, sitting in the cab together like two peas in a pod. My father saw them today, coming back from town. You telling me you knew nothing about this?"

"No suh," Hap said. "Well, I knew Mist Jamie given Ronsel a ride every once in awhile, but I didn't know he was setting up in front with him."

But Hap did know, cause he'd seen em together that first time. You better believe he gave Ronsel a talking-to that day, told him never to sit in the front seat of a white man's car again unless he was the driver and wearing a black cap to prove it.

"And now that you do know," Mist McAllan said, "what have you got to say about it?"

A silence come down amongst em. I could feel Hap struggling, trying to decide how to answer. It wasn't right, Henry McAllan asking him to take sides against his own son like that. If Mist McAllan wanted Ronsel humbled down he should a done it his own self, instead of expecting Hap to do it for him. *Don't you do it, Hap,* I thought.

But before he could answer, Ronsel spoke up. "I don't reckon my father's got anything to say about it, seeing as how he didn't know nothing about it. It's me you should be asking."

"Well then?" Henry McAllan said. "What in the world were you thinking?"

"White man tells me to get in his truck, I get in." Ronsel's voice was pretend-humble though, even I could hear it.

"You mocking me, boy?" Henry McAllan said.

"No suh, course not," Hap said. "He just trying to explicate hisself."

"Well let me explicate something to you, Ronsel. If I catch you riding in the car with my brother again, you're going to be in a heap of trouble, and I don't mean a nice little talk like we're having right now. My pappy isn't much of a talker when he gets riled up, if you take my meaning. So the next time Jamie offers you a ride, you tell him you need the exercise, hear?"

"Yessuh," Ronsel said.

"You know, Hap," Henry McAllan said, "I expected better sense from a son of yours." In a louder voice he said, "And that goes for you too, Florence."

After he was gone I went to the front door and looked out. Ronsel was standing on the edge of the porch staring after Henry McAllan's truck, and Hap was setting in his rocking chair staring at Ronsel's back.

"Well, Daddy," Ronsel said, "ain't you gone say I told you so?"

"Got no need to say it."

"Come on, I know you're itching to. So say it."

"Got no need."

For a long while the only sound was the crickets and the tree frogs and the squeak of Hap's rocker. Then Ronsel cleared his throat. *Here it comes,* I thought.

"I'll stay till the cotton's laid by," he said. "Then I'm leaving."

"Where you gone go, son?" Hap said. "Some big city up north, where you got no home and no people? That ain't no way to live."

"Wherever I go and however I live," Ronsel said, "I reckon it'll be better than here."

HENRY

By PLANTING TIME I was about ready to kill my brother, messed up in the head or not. It wasn't just that he was drinking again and lying about it after he swore to me he'd stop. It was his selfishness that really got my goat. Jamie did whatever he damn well pleased without a thought for how it might affect anybody else. There I was, working hard to make a place for myself and my family in Marietta, and having a drunk brother who consorted with whores and niggers sure wasn't helping me. And on top of everything I had to listen to Laura make excuses for him while my father sat there smirking. Pappy thought I was blind to it but he was wrong. Even if I hadn't had two perfectly good eyes in my head, my ears would have told me.

Whenever Jamie was around she sang. And when it was just me, she hummed.

STILL, I DIDN'T MEAN to say what I said, not like that. But Jamie pushed me too far and the words just spilled out, and once they were out I couldn't take them back.

The two of us were in the barn. Jamie had just milked the cow and was taking the pail to the house when he tripped and fell, spilling the milk all over the floor and himself. He started laughing, acted like it was nothing. And I guess in the scheme of things it wasn't but right at that moment it rankled me.

"You think it's funny, spilling good milk," I said.

"Well, you know what they say, no use crying over it."

By the way he ran the words together and lurched to his feet I could tell he'd been drinking. That rankled me even more. I said, "No, especially when it's somebody else's."

That wiped the grin off his face. "I see," he said, in a sarcastic tone. "What do I owe you, Henry?" He reached in his pocket and pulled out a handful of change. "Let's see, there must have been three gallons there, that'd run what, about two dollars? Let's say two and a quarter to be on the safe side. I wouldn't want to gyp you." He started to count out the money.

"Don't be an ass," I said.

"Oh no, brother, I insist." He held out the money. When I wouldn't take it, he reached over and tried to shove it in my shirt pocket. I batted his hand away, and the coins fell to the floor.

"For Christ's sake," I said. "This isn't about money and you know it."

"What's it about then? What would you have me do, Henry?"

"Sober up, for one thing," I said. "Take some responsibility for yourself and start acting like a grown man."

"One pail of spilled milk and I'm not a man?" he said.

"You're sure not acting like one lately."

His eyes got small and mean, just like our father's did when anybody crossed him. "And how should I act, brother—like you?" Jamie said. "Walking around here like God Almighty in his creation, laying down the law, so wrapped up in myself I can't see my wife is miserable? Is that the kind of man I should be? Huh?"

I'd never hit my brother before but right then I was mighty close to it. "Be whatever kind of man you want," I said. "Just do it someplace else."

"Fine. I'll go to town." He started to walk out.

"I don't mean for the night," I said.

I saw it in his face then, that look like he used to get as a boy when one of Pappy's gibes cut deep. Then it was gone, pasted over with indifference. He shrugged. "Yeah, well," he said. "I was getting tired of this place anyway."

He's got nothing, I thought. *No wife or kids, no home to call his own. No idea of himself he can shape his life around.* "Look," I said, "that didn't come out like I meant it to."

"Didn't it?" Jamie said. "Seemed to me it came out pretty easy, like you've been thinking it for a good long while."

"I just think you need a fresh start somewhere," I said. "We both know you're no farmer."

"I'll leave tomorrow, if that's soon enough for you."

I didn't want him going off mad and half-cocked. "There's no need for that," I said. "Besides, I'm counting on your help with the planting."

He acted like he hadn't heard me. "I'll catch the first bus out of here in the morning," he said.

"I'm asking you to stay a little longer," I said. "Just till we get the seed in."

He considered me for a long moment, then gave me a bitter smile. "Anything for my big brother," he said. He walked out then, back straight and rigid as a soldier's. Jamie would deny it but he's just like our pappy in one respect. He never forgets a slight, or forgives one.

LAURA

IF HENRY HADN'T been so stubborn.

If there hadn't been a ball game on.

If Eboline had taken better care of her trees.

It was the twelfth of April, a week after the incident with Ronsel. Henry, Jamie, Pappy and I were having dinner at Dex's. The girls were at Rose's, celebrating Ruth Ann's seventh birthday with a much-anticipated tea and slumber party.

Halfway through the meal, Bill Tricklebank came in looking for us. Eboline had called the store, frantic. A dead limb had cracked off her elm tree that morning and caved in her roof. No one was hurt, but the living room was exposed and there was a big storm headed our way. It was expected to hit Greenville sometime Monday.

"Damn," said Henry after Bill had left. "Wouldn't you know it'd be right in the middle of planting season."

"I'll go," Jamie offered.

"No," said Henry. "That's not a good idea."

Jamie's mouth tightened. "Why not?" he said.

Things were still tense between him and Henry. I was staying out of it; the two times I'd tried to talk to Henry about it he'd practically taken my head off.

"You know why," Henry said.

"Come on, it's been six months. Charlie Partain's not gonna do anything even if he does happen to see me. Which he won't."

"That's right," said Henry, "because you're not going."

"Who's Charlie Partain?" I asked.

"The sheriff of Greenville," said Pappy. "He ain't too fond of our family."

"After the accident, he told me to keep Jamie out of town," said Henry, "and that's exactly what I aim to do."

"This isn't about Charlie Partain," said Jamie. "You don't trust me to go. Do you, brother?"

Henry stood, took a ten-dollar bill out of his wallet and set it on the table. To me he said, "Telephone Eboline and let her know I'm on my way. Then get somebody at Tricklebank's to take you all home. I'll be back in a few days."

He bent and gave me a swift kiss. When he turned to leave, Jamie grabbed his arm. "Do you?" he asked again.

Henry looked down at the hand on his arm, then at Jamie. "Let the tenants know there's a storm coming," he said. "Get the tractor inside the barn and fix that loose shutter in the girls' bedroom. And you better check the roof of the house, nail down any loose edges."

Jamie gave him a curt nod, and Henry left. We finished eating and walked over to Tricklebank's. Jamie and Pappy stayed on the porch while I went inside and called Eboline. Afterward

I bought a few groceries from Bill. When I came out with them, Pappy was at one end of the porch, listening to a ball game on the radio with some other men. Jamie was sitting alone at the opposite end, smoking and staring moodily out at the street. I went over to him and asked if he'd found us a ride.

He nodded. "Tom Rossi's going to take us. He went to the feed store, said to meet him over there."

Tom owned the farm to the west of ours. He was also the part-time deputy sheriff of Marietta. I found it oddly dispiriting, living in a place whose citizens only misbehaved enough to warrant a police force of one and a half.

"You about ready to leave?" I called to Pappy.

"Do I look like I'm ready, gal? The game just started."

"I'll bring him," said one of the other men.

"Supper's at six," I said.

Pappy waved us off, and Jamie and I left to go find Tom.

I sat between them on the ride to the farm, making awkward small talk with Tom while Jamie brooded beside me. As soon as Tom dropped us off, Jamie took the truck and drove off to warn the tenants about the storm. When I heard him return, I went outside. He was striding angrily toward the barn, his hair ablaze in the sun. I called out to him.

He kept going, calling back, "I need to fetch the ladder and see to the roof."

"That can wait a little while," I said. "I want to talk to you."

He stopped but didn't turn around. His body was rigid, his hands balled into fists. I went and stood directly in front of him.

"You're wrong about Henry not trusting you," I said.

"You think so, huh?"

"Don't you see, that's what he was trying to tell you, when he asked you to warn the tenants and all the rest of it. That he trusts you."

"Yeah," Jamie said, with a harsh laugh, "he trusts me so much he wants me gone."

"Don't be silly. He's just sore at you over the Ronsel business. He'll get over it."

Jamie cocked his head. "So, he hasn't told you yet," he said. "I didn't think he had."

"Told me what?"

"He kicked me out."

"What are you talking about?"

"He asked me to leave yesterday. I'm going as soon as we're done planting. Next week, most likely."

I felt a sharp pain somewhere near the center of my body, followed by a draining sensation that made me a little dizzy. It reminded me of how I'd felt when I used to give blood for the war effort. Only now it was all going, all the life and color in me, seeping out into the dirt at my feet. When Jamie left and I was emptied, I would be invisible again, just like I'd been before he came. I couldn't go back to being that dutiful unseen woman, the one who played her roles without really inhabiting them. I wouldn't go back. *No.*

I realized I'd spoken the word out loud when Jamie said, "I have to, Laura. Henry's right about one thing, I need to make a new start. And I sure as hell can't do it here." He waved his hand to take it all in—the shabby house and outbuildings, the ugly brown fields. And me, of course, I was part of that dreary landscape too. Henry's landscape. Fury gathered in my belly, rising up, scalding my throat. I truly hated my husband at that moment.

"I'd better get busy on those chores," Jamie said.

I watched him walk to the barn. At the door, he stopped and looked back at me. "I never thought my brother would turn against me like this," he said. "I never thought he was capable of it."

I could think of nothing to say in answer. Nothing that would comfort him. Nothing that would keep him here.

I LISTENED TO HIM move the tractor, hammer the shutter, climb up on the ladder to check the roof. Mundane sounds, but they filled me with sadness. All I could think of was the silence to come.

When he was finished he popped his head in the front window. "The roof looks fine," he said. "I've taken care of the rest."

"You want some coffee?"

"No, thanks. I think I'll take a nap."

He'd been asleep for maybe twenty minutes when I heard him moaning and shouting. I hurried out to the lean-to, but at the door I found myself hesitating. I looked at my hand on the latch and thought of all the things it had proven capable of since I'd been at Mudbound, things that would have frightened

or shocked me once. I looked at the ragged nails, the swollen
red knuckles, the slender strip of gold across the fourth finger.
I watched my hand lift the latch.

Jamie was sprawled on his back, his arms flung wide. He was
still dressed, except for his shoes and socks. His feet were long,
pale and slender, with a blue tracery of veins in the arches. I
had the urge to press my mouth to them. He cried out and one
arm flailed upward, as if he were warding something off. I sat
on the edge of the bed and took hold of his arm, pushing it
down against the sheet. With my other hand I smoothed his
hair back from his damp forehead. "Jamie, wake up," I said.

He tore his arm from my grasp and grabbed my shoulders,
his fingers digging into my skin. I said his name again and his
eyes opened, darting around wildly before settling on my face.
I watched sense come into them, then awareness of who I was,
and where we were.

"Laura," he said.

I could have looked away then, but I didn't. I held myself
very still, knowing he could see everything I felt and letting
him see it. It was the most intimate act of my life, more intimate even than the acts that followed. Jamie didn't move, but
I felt the change in the way his hands gripped me. His eyes
dropped to my mouth and my heart lurched, slamming against
the bone. I waited for him to pull me down to him, but he
didn't, and I realized finally that he wouldn't; that it was up
to me. I remembered the first time Henry had kissed me, how
he'd taken my face in his hands as though it were something
he had a right to. That was the difference between men and

women, I thought: Men take for themselves the things they want, while women wait to be given them. I would not wait any longer. I bent down and touched my lips to Jamie's, tasting whiskey and cigarettes, anger and longing that I knew was not just for me. I didn't care. I took it all, no questions asked, either of him or myself. His hands pulled me on top of him, undid the buttons of my blouse, unsnapped my garters. Urgent, impatient, speeding us past whether and why. I went willingly, following the path of his desire.

And then, suddenly, he stopped. He rolled me to one side and got up out of the bed, and I thought, *He's changed his mind. Of course he has.* He took my hand and drew me up to stand in front of him. Mortified, I looked down and started to button my blouse back up. His hand reached out, raised my chin. "Look at me," he said.

I made myself look. His gaze was steady and fierce. He ran his thumb across my mouth, stroking the bottom lip open, then his hand dropped lower. He brushed the backs of his fingers across my breast, once, and then again in the opposite direction. My nipples stiffened and my legs trembled. My body felt dense and heavy, an unwieldy liquid mass. I would have fallen but his eyes held me up. There was a demand in them, and a gravity I'd never seen before. I understood then: We wouldn't be swept away by passion, as I'd always imagined. Jamie wouldn't let us be. This would be a deliberate act. A choosing.

Without looking away from him, I reached out with my hand, found his belt buckle and pulled the leather from it. When I released the catch he let out a long breath. His arms went around me and his mouth came down on mine.

When he was poised above me I didn't think of Henry or my children, of words like *adultery, sin, consequences*. I thought only of Jamie and myself. And when I drew him into me I thought of nothing at all.

HE FELL ASLEEP on top of me, as Henry sometimes did when he was tired, but I felt none of my usual irritation or restiveness. Jamie's weight on me was sweet. I closed my eyes, wanting to shut out every other sensation, wanting his weight to imprint the shape of him into my flesh.

It was the thought of Pappy that got me to move. By the golden tint of the light coming in the window, it was late afternoon; he'd be home any time now. Carefully, trying not to wake Jamie, I extricated myself from beneath him. He stirred and moaned but his eyes stayed closed. I picked up my clothes from the floor, dusted them off and got dressed. I went to the mirror. My hair was disheveled, but apart from that I looked like myself: Laura McAllan on a normal Saturday afternoon. Everything had changed; nothing had changed. Astonishing.

I heard the cot springs creak slightly behind me and knew that Jamie was awake and watching me. *I should turn around and face him,* I thought, but my body refused to do it. I left the room quickly, without looking at him or speaking. Afraid I would find shame in his eyes, or hear regret in his voice.

About half an hour later I heard the truck start up and pull away.

HAP

THAT MONDAY AFTERNOON I was out by the shed hitching the mule to the guano cart when Ronsel finally come back from town. By that point I was mighty vexed with him. He'd went in to run an errand for his mama but he was gone way too long for that. Mooning around again, I reckoned, thinking bout going off to New York or Chicago or one a them other faraway places he was always talking bout, meantime here I was trying to get the fields fertilized and needing every bit of help I could get.

"Where you been?" I said. "Half the day's gone."

He didn't answer, it was like he didn't hear me or even see me. He was just staring off with this funny look on his face, like he'd had the stuffing knocked out of him.

"Ronsel!" I hollered. "What's the matter with you?"

He jumped and looked at me. "Sorry, Daddy. I guess I was off somewhere else."

"Come help me load this fertilizer."

"I'll be right there," he said.

He went in the house. Bout a minute later he come charging

out onto the porch, looking all around like he'd lost something. "You seen a piece of paper anywhere?" he said.

"What kind of paper?"

"An envelope, with writing on the front."

"No, I ain't seen nothing like that," I said.

He looked all around the yard, getting more and more worked up every second. "It must a fell out of my pocket on the road from town. Goddamnit!"

"Ronsel! What's in this envelope?"

But he didn't answer me. His eyes lit on the road. "I bet it fell out in that ditch," he said. "I got to go fetch it."

"I thought you were gone help me with this fertilizer."

"This can't wait, Daddy," he said. He took off running down the road. That was the last time I ever heard my son's voice.

RONSEL

THE ENVELOPE HAD a German stamp in the corner of it. It was dirty and beat up from traveling so many miles and passing through so many hands. The writing was a woman's, fancy and slanted. Soon as I seen it I knew it had to been from Resl. The censors had opened it and taped it back up again. I hated the thought of them knowing what she'd wrote me before I did.

When I pulled out the letter a photograph fell out, right onto the floor of the post office. I picked it up and looked at it. Amazing, how a little piece of shiny paper can change your whole life forever. My mouth went dry and my heart sped up. I opened the letter, hoping the censors hadn't blacked anything out, but for once it was all there.

Lieber Ronsel,
    This Letter I am writing with the Help of my Friend Berta on who you may remember. I do not know if it is arriving to you but I am hoping that it will. May be you are surprised to hearing from me. At first I am thinking I am not writing to you but then I have decided that I must do it, because it is

not right that a Mann does not know he is having a Son. That is what I want to say you—you have a Son. I name him after my Father und his Father, Franz Ronsel. He is born in the Nacht of the 14 November at 22:00, in the Hospital of Teisendorf. I ask myself what you is doing at that Moment. I am trying to imagine you in your flat Missippi but I can not make such a Picture in my Mind, only of your Face which I see everyday when I look at the little Franz. I am sending you a Foto so that you can see him. He have your Eyes und your Smile.

At your Leaving I did not know that I am carrying your Child in me and when I learned to know it my Proud did not let me write you. But now I have this beautiful Son and I am thinking on the Day on which he know he has no Father and his smiling will die. Compared to that my Proud is not important. For Franzl I ask you please, will you come back and stay with us hier, with me und Maria und your Son. I know it is not being easy but I have this Haus und I believe that together we are making a gut Life. Please answer quick and say me that you are coming back to us.

In Love,

Your Resl

The letter was dated 2 February 1947, more than two months ago. My heart was sore thinking of her waiting all that time for an answer and not getting one. I lifted the paper to my nose but if her scent had ever been on it, it was long gone. I looked at the photo again. There was Resl, looking as sweet and pretty as ever, with the baby bundled up in her arms. In

the picture his skin was a medium gray, lighter than mine
would've been, so I guessed he was gingercake-colored like my
daddy. She was holding up one of his little hands and waving
it at the camera.

My Resl. My son.

A SON, I HAVE A SON. That was the only thought in my
head, walking back from town with that letter in my pocket.
Knowing I was a father made the world sharper edged to my
eye. The sky looked bluer and the shacks that squatted underneath it looked shabbier. The newly planted fields on either side
of me seemed to stretch on and on like a brown ocean between
me and him. But how in the hell could I get to Germany? And
what would I do once I got there? I didn't speak the language,
had no way to support a family there. But I couldn't just abandon them. Maybe I could bring the three of them back, not
to Mississippi but someplace else where they wouldn't care
that she was white and I was colored. Had to be a place like
that somewhere, maybe in California or up north. I could ask
Jimmy, he might know. Too damn many mights and maybes,
that was the problem. I needed to think it through and make a
plan. In the meantime I'd help them however I could. I didn't
have much money left, maybe a few hundred dollars stuffed
into the toes of my boots at the bottom of my duffel bag. I'd
write to Captain Scott at Camp Hood, he'd know how to get it
to Resl. But first I'd write and tell her I still loved her and was
working on a plan, so she could whisper it to my son.

I was so busy thinking I didn't even hear the truck till it was almost on top of me. Turned around and there it was, coming straight at me. Soldier's instincts is all that saved me. I dived into the ditch on the side of the road and landed in mud. The truck passed so close to my head it like to gave me a crew cut, then it went off into the ditch right in front of me. I recognized it then, it was the McAllans' truck. For a minute I thought Old Man McAllan had tried to run me over but when the door opened Jamie got out. Well, fell out is more like it, he was drunker than I'd ever seen him, and that was saying something. He had a bottle in one hand and a cigarette in the other. He staggered over to where I was.

"That you, Ronshel?"

"Yeah, it's me."

"You all right?"

"I'm as muddy as a pig in a wallow, but other than that I'm fine."

"Shouldn't be walking in the middle of the road like that, you're liable to get yourself killed."

"It'll take more than a drunk white flyboy to kill me," I said.

He laughed and plopped down on the edge of the ditch, and I got up and sat beside him. He looked terrible sickly. Red-eyed, unshaven, skin all sweaty. He took a swig from the bottle and offered it to me. It was more than three-quarters empty already.

"No thanks, I better not," I said. "Maybe you better not either."

Jamie wagged his finger at me. "Do not think, gentlemen, I am drunk." He raised his left hand and said, "This is my ancient, this is my right hand." Then he raised the hand holding the bottle. A little whiskey sloshed out onto his pants leg but he didn't seem to notice. "And this is my left. Oh God, that men should put an enemy in their mouths to steal away their brains! That we should with joy, pleasure, revel and . . . revel and . . . what's the fourth thing, damnit?"

He looked at me like I was supposed to know. I just shrugged.

"With joy, pleasure, revel and . . . applause—that's it, applause!—transform ourselves into beasts!" He twirled his left hand in the air and bowed from the waist. He would've fell over into the ditch if I hadn't grabbed his shirt collar and yanked him back up.

"Hey," I said, "is something the matter?"

He shook his head and stared at the bottle, picking at the label with his fingernail. He was quiet a good long while, then he said, "What's the worst thing you ever did?"

"Killing Hollis, I guess." I'd told him about it one night at the sawmill: how I'd shot my buddy Hollis in the head after his legs got blown off by a grenade and he begged me to do it.

"No, I mean something that hurt somebody bad. Something you never forgave yourself for. You ever do anything like that?"

Yeah, I thought, *leaving Resl.* I was that close to telling him about her. I wanted to say the words out loud: *I'm a father, I have a son.* I'd already told him plenty of things, like about shooting Hollis and refusing to let the crackers in our tanks and the time me and Jimmy went to a cabaret in Paris where the dancing girls were all stark naked. But there was a mighty big difference between that and me having a child by a white woman. Jamie McAllan was born and bred in Mississippi. If he got fired up and decided to turn me in, I could get ten years in Parchman—that's if I didn't get lynched on the way there.

"No," I said, "nothing I can think of."

"Well I have. I've belied a lady, the princess of this country."

"What you talking bout? What princess?"

"And she, sweet lady, dotes, devoutly dotes, dotes in idolatry upon this spotted and inconstant man. Idolatry, idultery—ha!"

So that's what was troubling him. Thinking of Josie, I said, "Ain't good to mess with the married gals, you just looking for heartache there. Best thing to do is put it behind you, never see her again."

He nodded. "Yeah. I'm leaving here next week."

"Where you going?"

"I don't know. Maybe California. I always wanted to see it."

"I've got a buddy lives in Los Angeles. According to Jimmy, it never gets too hot or too cold there and it hardly ever rains. Course he could've been pulling my leg."

Jamie looked at me, a hard clear look like you get sometimes from somebody who's drunk, it's like they sober up just long enough to really see you. "You ought to leave here too, Ronsel," he said. "Hap can manage without you now."

"I am leaving, just as soon as the crop's laid by."

"Good. This is no place for you."

He finished the whiskey and tossed the bottle into the ditch.

When he tried to stand up his legs gave out. I got up and helped him to his feet. "Reckon you better let me drive you home," I said.

"Reckon I better."

Somehow we managed to push the truck out of the ditch, then I drove him as far as the bridge and got out. I figured he could make it from there, and I didn't want Henry McAllan or that old man seeing us.

"You drive careful the rest of the way," I told him. "Try not to run any more colored people off the road."

He smiled and held out his hand. We shook. "Doubt I'll see you again before I go," he said. "You take care of yourself, hear?"

"You too."

"You've been a friend. I want you to know that."

He didn't wait for me to say anything back, just waved and drove off. I followed the truck down the road toward home, watching it weave back and forth, thinking of how surprising a place the world could be sometimes.

MUST'VE BEEN HALF an hour later that I found the letter gone. The first thing I thought was it fell out in that ditch. Ran all the way back there and looked but all I found was Jamie's whiskey bottle. I kept on going all the way to town and still didn't find it. The post office was closed but I was sure I hadn't left it in there. Only two places it could be: in somebody's pocket who'd picked it up or in the McAllans' truck. I made myself keep calm. If I'd left it in the truck Jamie might've found it. He wouldn't show it to nobody, he'd keep it for me. Maybe he was over at my house right now looking to give it back to me. And if not and it was still in the truck, I could sneak over there after dark and get it before anybody saw it.

By the time I headed back home it was coming on to dark and raining hard. I'd left without my hat so I was soaking wet. I was about halfway there when I heard the sound of a vehicle bearing down on me for the second time that day. I turned around and seen two sets of headlights. I jumped down into the ditch but instead of passing me they stopped right beside me. I didn't recognize the car in front but I knew the truck behind it. There were white figures inside, four in the car and maybe another three in the truck. Seemed like they practically glowed in the dark. When they got out I seen why.

LAURA

JAMIE DIDN'T COME back on Saturday, or on Sunday. When Rose brought the girls home Sunday morning I asked if she'd seen him in town, and she said no. It was a long couple of days, waiting. The sweet ache between my legs was a constant reminder of what Jamie and I had done. I had a few pricks of conscience—seeing Henry's pajama bottoms hanging forlornly from a peg in our bedroom, his comb on the dresser, a stray white hair on his pillow—but real shame and regret were absent. In their place was a riotous sense of wonder. I'd never imagined myself capable of either great boldness or great passion, and the discovery that I had reservoirs of both astounded me. I couldn't stop picturing myself with Jamie. I burned the grits, forgot to feed the animals, scalded my arm on the stove.

Pappy was in a fouler mood than usual. He was low on cigarettes and furious at Jamie for leaving us with no transportation. He smoked his last one early Monday morning and spent the entire day punishing me for it. My biscuits were too dry, was I trying to choke him to death? My floors were so dirty they weren't fit for a nigger to walk on. My brats were making too much racket. My coffee was too weak, how many times had he told me he liked it strong?

Short of walking, there was no way to get to town until Henry or Jamie got home.

"Goddamnit, where is he?" Pappy called out for the tenth time.

"Mind your language," I said. "The children are right here."

He was out on the porch watching the road, which was preferable to having him in the house with us. Florence had gone home for the day. I was sewing new dresses for the girls, and they were making paper dolls. We could hear Pappy's boots clomping back and forth outside the window.

"It's just like him," said the old man, "pulling a stunt like this. Thinking only of himself, the hell with everybody else."

The irony of Pappy complaining about Jamie or any other person being selfish was too much, and I laughed out loud. The shutters banged open, revealing Pappy's scowling face at the window. I was reminded of a malevolent cuckoo clock.

"What are you snickering at?" he demanded.

"Something Bella just did."

"You think it's funny, an old man being without his cigarettes. Just you wait and see how you feel when you get old, and you have to do without your comforts because nobody cares enough to look after you."

"You could always ride one of the mules to town," I suggested, deadpan.

Pappy couldn't stand animals, especially large ones. I think he was afraid of them, though he never admitted as much. It was the reason we didn't have any pets on the farm; he wouldn't tolerate them.

"I ain't doing any such thing," he said. "Why don't you go ask that nigger gal if she'll go? Tell her I'll pay her two bits."

"I'm sure Florence has better things to do than fetch your cigarettes for you."

His face retreated as abruptly as it had appeared. "Never mind," he said. "I see the truck coming."

The girls ran out to the porch to wait for their uncle. I took a deep breath and followed them. I would need to be very careful around Jamie to avoid raising Pappy's suspicions.

"Drunk again," Pappy said scornfully.

The car was weaving all over the road. At one point it went off entirely and into the newly planted fields. I was glad Henry wasn't home to see that; he would have been apoplectic. Jamie pulled up in front of the house and got out of the truck. Bella started to run to him but I held her back. He was rumpled and unshaven. One shirt tail hung out of the front of his pants. "Afternoon Laura, Pappy, little petunias," he said, swaying on his feet.

"You got any cigarettes?" said the old man.

"Hello, son," said Jamie, slurring the words together. "I'm so glad to see you, how are you today? Why Pappy, thank you for asking, I'm fine, and how are you?"

"You can talk to yourself all you want, just give me a smoke first."

Jamie reached in his shirt pocket and pulled out a pack of

Lucky Strikes, tossing them to his father. The throw fell short, forcing Pappy to bend down and pick them up off the ground. "There's only one cigarette here," said the old man.

"Guess I smoked the rest."

"You ain't worth a damn, you know that?"

"Well, I'm worth one cigarette. That's something. Unless you don't want it."

"Just give me the truck keys."

Jamie held them up, dangling them. "Ask nice and maybe I will."

Pappy walked toward Jamie, his steps slow and menacing. "You trying to mess with me? Huh, mister big hero?" The old man's cane was in his left hand, but he wasn't leaning on it; he was gripping it like a club. "Just keep talking, and we'll find out which one of us is a man and which one ain't. See, I know the answer already, but I don't think you do. I think you're confused on the subject. That's why you keep giving me lip, is because you want to be straightened out. Ain't that right, boy?"

When he reached Jamie he stopped and leaned forward until their faces were inches apart. How strongly they resembled each other! I'd never seen it before—I'd always thought of Pappy as ugly—but their features were essentially the same: the arched sardonic brows, the slanting cheekbones, the full, slightly petulant mouth.

"Ain't that right?" said the old man again.

My muscles tensed; the urge to step between them was almost overwhelming. Suddenly Pappy raised his cane, thrusting it toward Jamie's face—a feint, but Jamie flinched and took a step back.

"That's what I thought," Pappy said. "Now give me the goddamn keys."

Jamie dropped them into his outstretched hand. The old man shook the cigarette out of the pack, lit it and blew the smoke in Jamie's face. Jamie crumpled to his knees and retched. Liquid gushed out, not a solid thing in it. I wondered when he'd last eaten. I went and knelt beside him, helpless to do anything but pat him gingerly on the back as his body convulsed. His shirt was soaked through with sweat.

I heard a bark of laughter and looked up. The old man was watching us from the cab of the truck. "Well, ain't you a pretty pair," he said.

"Just go," I said.

"Can't wait to have him all to yourself, eh gal? Too bad he's too liquored up to be any good to you."

"What are you talking about?"

"You know exactly what I mean."

"No, I don't."

"Then why's your face so red, huh?" Pappy started the truck. "Don't let him fall asleep on his back," he said. "If he throws up again he could choke to death."

He drove off. I looked down at Jamie. He'd stopped retching and was lying limp on his side in the dirt. "When he is best, he is a little worse than a man," Jamie said in a hoarse voice, "and when he is worst he is little better than a beast."

"What's the matter with Uncle Jamie?" Amanda Leigh called out.

I turned and saw the girls watching. I'd forgotten all about them. "He just has an upset tummy is all," I said. "Do me a favor, darling, fetch me a clean washrag. Dip it in the bucket, wring it out, then bring it here. And a glass of water too."

"Yes, Mama."

Somehow I got him to his bed in the lean-to. He fell onto it and lay on his back without moving. I took off his shoes. His socks were missing. A vivid and unwelcome picture of them lying abandoned under some woman's bed flashed into my mind. With some difficulty, I rolled him onto his side. When I'd gotten him settled I looked down to find him watching me with an unreadable expression.

"Sweet Laura," he said. "My angel of mercy." His hand lifted and cupped my breast, possessively, familiarly. I felt a stab of desire. His eyes fluttered closed and his hand fell to the bed. I heard a familiar tapping sound on the roof; gentle at first, then sharper and more insistent. It had begun to rain.

It MUST HAVE been about two hours later that the front door flew open and Florence came bursting in. The girls and I had just sat down to a late supper. Pappy still hadn't come home, and I wasn't going to wait on him any longer. The children were hungry and so was I.

"Where's Mist Jamie?" Florence said, without preamble. She was soaked to the skin and breathing harshly, like she'd been running.

"Taking a nap in the lean-to. What's the matter?"

"Where's the truck then?"

"Pappy took it to town. Now what in the world's gotten into you?"

"Ronsel went to town earlier and he ain't come back. What time did Mist Jamie get home?"

Her high-handed attitude was beginning to annoy me. "Shortly after you left," I said. "Not that it's any of your business."

"Something's happened to my son," Florence said, "and Mist Jamie's caught up in it somehow, I know it."

"You're talking nonsense. How long has Ronsel been gone?"

"Since bout five o'clock. He should a been home by now."

"Well, it's nothing to do with Jamie. Like I said, he's been here since around three-thirty. Ronsel probably ran into a friend in town and lost track of the time. You know how young men are."

Florence shook her head, just once, but I felt the weight of that negation as strongly as if she'd shoved me. "No. He ain't got no friends here, cept for Mist Jamie."

"What do you mean, they're friends?"

"You got to wake him up and ask him."

I stood up. "I'll do no such thing. Jamie's worn out, and he needs his rest."

Her nostrils flared, and her eyes flickered to the front door. *She means to force her way past me and go wake him,* I thought. I wouldn't be able to stop her; she was a foot taller than me and outweighed me by a good forty pounds. For the first time since I'd known her, I felt afraid of her.

"Best if you go on home," I said. "I bet Ronsel's there right now, wondering where you are."

There was real animosity in Florence's eyes, and it woke an answering flare in me. How dared she threaten me, and under my own roof? I remembered Pappy telling the girls one time that Lilly May wasn't their friend and never would be; that if it came down to a war between the niggers and the whites, she'd be on the side of the niggers and wouldn't hesitate to kill them both. It had angered me at the time, but now I wondered if there wasn't a brutal kernel of truth in what he'd said.

Bella started coughing; she'd swallowed her milk the wrong way. I went and whacked her on the back, then looked at Florence. I thought back to the first time we'd met; how crazy with worry I'd been for my children. The memory was like a clean blast of air, clearing my head of foolishness. This wasn't a murderous Negro in front of me, but an anxious mother.

"Watch the girls," I said. "I'll go and ask him."

I knocked on the door of the lean-to, but there was no answer, and when I opened it the lantern light revealed two empty beds. Jamie's pillowcase was cool to my hand. I checked the outhouse, but he wasn't there either, and there was no light in the barn. Where could he have gone, on foot and in such pitiful condition? He couldn't possibly have sobered up; it had been less than three hours since he got home. And where was Pappy? Tricklebank's was long closed, and it wasn't like the old man to miss supper and a chance to complain about my cooking.

It was with a growing feeling of dread that I went back to the house. "Jamie's not here," I told Florence. "He must have gone for a walk to clear his head. He sometimes does that in the evenings. I'm sure it's nothing to do with Ronsel."

Florence headed swiftly out the door. I followed her to the edge of the porch. "I'll send Jamie to your house as soon as he gets back," I called, "just to set your mind at ease. I'm sure you're worrying for nothing."

But I was talking to the air. The darkness had swallowed her up.

JAMIE

THE RAIN STARTLED me awake. The din of a Delta thunderstorm hitting a tin roof is about as close as you can get to the sound of battle without actually being in it. For a heart-pounding minute I was back in the skies over Germany, surrounded by enemy Messerschmitts. Then I realized where I was, and why.

I lay in the dark of the lean-to and took stock of my condition. My head hurt and my mouth was full of cotton. I was still a little tipsy, but not nearly lit enough to face Pappy and Laura. There'd been a bad scene earlier, that much I remembered, but the details were vague and that was just fine by me. Amnesia is one of the great gifts of alcohol, and I'm not one to refuse it. I groped under the bed for the bottle I kept stashed there, but when I picked it up it felt light in my hand. There were only a couple of swigs left and I took them both, then I shut my eyes and waited for the whiskey to kindle me. My stomach was empty so it didn't take long. I might have gone back to sleep, but I had to piss too bad. I fumbled for the lantern on the bedside table and lit it. Pappy's bed was empty. There was a pitcher of water sitting on the table, along with a basin, a neatly folded towel and some cornbread wrapped in a napkin. Laura must have left them there for me.

Laura. It came back to me then, in a rush of images: Her hair falling down around my face. Her breasts filling my hands. The dusky sweet scent of her. My brother's wife.

I went outside. It was full dark, but the lights were on in the house. I stood at the edge of the porch and added my own stream to the downpour, wondering what time it was. A flash of lightning lit up the yard, and I saw that both the truck and the car were gone. We didn't expect Henry till tomorrow, but why wasn't Pappy back? Maybe the old goat had gotten stuck in the rain. Maybe he was sitting in the truck in a ditch at this very moment, cussing the weather and me both. The thought cheered me.

As I was zipping up my pants I saw a light moving near the old sawmill. At first I thought it was Pappy coming home, but no headlights approached the house. The light bobbed along the river, winking in and out like somebody was walking through the trees with a lantern, then it went out. Whoever it was must have gone inside the sawmill. Ronsel, probably, or a drifter seeking shelter from the storm. They were welcome to it. I wasn't about to go investigate, not in that downpour.

I went back inside and got myself cleaned up. I didn't want to face Laura and the girls stinking of sweat and vomit and whiskey. I was half-dressed when I remembered the fifth I had stashed out in the sawmill. As soon as I pictured it, I wanted it. Without that bottle, I'd be on my own with Laura, and then with my father and Henry whenever they showed up. I knew Ronsel wouldn't drink my whiskey without invitation, but a drifter sure would, if he found it. The thought of some bum sucking down my Jack overcame my aversion to getting wet. I stuffed some cornbread in my mouth and put on my jacket and my hat. At the last second I grabbed my .38 and stuck it in my pocket.

I was wet through within seconds of leaving the porch. The wind tore my hat from my head, and the mud tried to pull my boots off with every step. It was so dark that if it hadn't been for the occasional bursts of lightning, I wouldn't have been able to see a thing. As it was I almost ran straight into a vehicle parked off to one side of the sawmill. The hood was warm. When the lightning came again I recognized Henry's truck. And there was another car parked beside it. *What the hell?*

I went around back of the building. Strips of light showed between the planks, and I put my eye up to one of the gaps. At first all I saw was white. Then it moved and I realized I was looking at the back of somebody's head, and that he was wearing a white hood. He wasn't the only one. There were maybe eight of them standing in a loose circle.

"How many times did you fuck her?" I heard a voice say.

One of the figures shifted, and I saw Ronsel kneeling in the center of them. His hands and feet were tied behind his back, and there was a noose around his neck. The rope was slung over a beam in the ceiling. The man holding the other end gave it a vicious yank. Ronsel gagged, and his head came up.

"Answer him, nigger!" said my father.

RONSEL

I STARTED TO RUN but then I heard the sound of a shotgun round being chambered. I froze and held my hands up. A high tight voice said, "If I was you, boy, I'd stay right where I was." It sounded like Doc Turpin, the sonofabitch who'd messed up my daddy's leg. He'd talked through his nose like that, that day at Tricklebank's. And Daddy had told me he used to be in the Klan.

"Get him in the car." That voice I recognized straightaway—it was Old Man McAllan. I wondered if Henry McAllan was there too underneath one of them hoods. Somebody came up behind me and threw a burlap sack over my head. I flailed out and he punched me in the kidneys, then somebody else grabbed my arms and tied them behind my back. They drug me to the car and threw me in. One of them got in on either side of me, then we started moving.

The wet sack on my head smelled like coffee, I reckoned they got it at Tricklebank's. They must've met up there before they set out to find me. That gave me a little hope. If Mrs. Tricklebank had been there and heard them talking she would've called Sheriff Tacker as soon as they left. He wasn't no great friend to Negroes but surely he wouldn't stand by and let one of us be lynched. Surely he wouldn't.

"Listen," I said, "I'll leave town."

"Shut up, nigger," said the man I thought was Turpin.

"I'll leave tonight, and I won't ever—"

"He said, shut up," snarled the man on my other side.

Something hard slammed into my ribs and all the breath went out of me. The pain was fierce, felt like some of my ribs were cracked. I kept quiet after that and so did they. Somebody lit a cigarette. I'd never been much of a smoker but when my nose caught the smell of it I wanted one bad. Funny how the body keeps right on wanting what it wants even when it thinks it's about to die.

The car made a turn and the ride got rough, I figured we'd gone off the road. A couple minutes later we stopped. They jerked me out of the car and marched me a ways into a building. The rain on the roof sounded like a thousand people clapping, cheering them on. I was shoved to my knees and I felt a rope go around my neck. They tightened it, not quite enough to choke me but one more hard tug and it would. It was hot under the sack and hard to breathe. Sweat and coffee stung my eyes and the burlap was itching my face. How long did it take to choke to death? If I was lucky my neck would break and I'd go quick, but if it didn't . . . I felt panic take ahold of me and I fought it down, slowing my breathing like they'd taught us in survival training. I would keep calm and wait for a chance to escape. And if I couldn't, if they meant to kill me, I'd show these fuckers how a man died. I was an NCO of the 761st Tank Battalion, a Black Panther. I wouldn't let them turn me into a scared nigger.

One of them jerked the sack off my head. At first all I seen was legs but then they stepped back some and I realized where I was: the old sawmill, where I'd spent so many nights drinking whiskey with Jamie McAllan. Seven or eight men stood in a circle around me. Most of them were just wearing white pillowcases but two of them had on real Klan robes with pointed hoods and round badges on the chest. The badges had square black crosses on them with red dots in the middle like drops of blood. I looked up to where the rope was slung over a beam, then followed it down to the hands of one of the men in robes. He was tall, maybe six foot five, and built like a bear. Had to be Orris Stokes, he was the biggest fellow in town. I'd helped his pregnant wife carry her groceries home from Tricklebank's one time.

"Do you know why you're here, nigger?" he said.

"No sir, Mr. Stokes."

He handed the rope to one of the others, then reached out with one of his huge arms and backhanded me. My head snapped back and I felt one of my teeth come loose.

"You say that name again or any other name and we'll make you even sorrier than you're already gonna be, hear?"

"Yes, sir."

The other man in Klan robes stepped forward. It was Doc Turpin, I was sure of it now. I could see his paunch pushing his robe out and his little beer-colored eyes glinting through the holes in his hood. It was plain he and Stokes were in charge.

"Bring forth the evidence," Turpin said.

One of the others held something out to him. Soon as I seen that old yellow hand I knew what had to be in it. Turpin took the letter and the photograph from Old Man McAllan and held them up in front of my face. Resl and Franz smiled out at me. I wished I could climb into that picture with them, into that other world.

"Did you rut with this woman?" Turpin asked.

I didn't answer, even though he had the letter right there in his hand. There were worse things they could do to me than hang me.

"We know you did it, nigger," said McAllan. "We just want to hear you say it."

Another one jerked on the rope and the noose dug into my windpipe. "Go on, say it!" he ordered. His voice was deep and raspy from chain-smoking. No doubt who that was: Dex Deweese, the owner of the town diner.

"Yes," I said.

"Yes, what?" said Turpin.

"Yes, I . . . was with her."

"You defiled a white woman. Say it."

I shook my head. Stokes hit me again, this time with his fist, knocking the tooth he'd loosened earlier out of its socket. I spat it out onto the floor.

"I defiled a white woman."

"How many times did you fuck her?" said Turpin.

I shook my head again. Truth was, I *had* fucked Resl at first. I'd taken what she offered thinking of nothing but my own pleasure, knowing I'd soon be moving on to another post.

When had it gotten to be more than that? I closed my eyes, trying to remember, trying to smell her scent. But all I could smell was my own sweat and their hate. The animal stench of it filled the room.

Deweese gave the rope a hard yank and I gagged.

"Answer him, nigger!" said old man McAllan.

"I don't know," I choked out.

Turpin waved the photo in the air. "Enough times to get her with this—I won't call it a child—this . . . abomination! A foul pollution of the white race!" The men shifted and muttered. Turpin was working them up good. "And what's the penalty for abomination?"

"Death!" shouted Stokes.

"I say we geld him," one of them said.

The fear that took ahold of me then was like nothing I ever felt in my whole life. My guts were churning and it was all I could do not to shit myself.

Turpin said, "And if a woman approach any beast and lie down with it, thou shalt kill the woman and the beast. They shall surely be put to death, and their blood shall be upon them."

"String him up," said Old Man McAllan.

Right then the door banged open and we all turned toward it. Jamie McAllan stood there dripping water all over the floor. He had a pistol in his hand and it was pointed at Deweese.

"Let go of the rope," Jamie said.

JAMIE

"LET IT GO," I said.

One of the others moved, a shotgun in his hands, rising. I pointed the pistol at him. "Drop it!" I said.

He hesitated. For a few seconds everybody froze. Then my father spoke up. "He's bluffing," said Pappy, "and he's half-drunk besides. Point the gun at the nigger. Go on, he won't shoot you. My son don't have the balls to kill a man up close." He stepped in front of the man with the shotgun, blocking my aim. I found myself staring down the sight of the pistol into my father's pale eyes, framed in white cotton. "Do you, son?" he said.

Behind him I could see the barrel of the shotgun, now pointed at Ronsel's head. Pappy took a step toward me, then another. There was a roaring in my ears, and the hand holding the pistol was shaking. I put my other hand under the butt to steady it.

"Stop right there," I said.

He took another step toward me. "You gonna betray your own blood over a nigger?"

"Don't come any closer. I'm warning you."

"Kill me, and the jig still dies."

Hate rose up in me—for him, for myself. I'd lost, and we both knew it. I only had one play left to make. "If you kill him, you better kill me too," I said. "Because if Ronsel dies, I'm going straight to the sheriff. I swear I'll do it."

"What are you gonna tell him, boy?" said the fat one in Klan robes. "You can't identify nary one of us, except for your father."

Without taking my eyes off Pappy, I said, "You know, Doc, white's not your color. Makes you look a little hefty. Now Dex here can wear it because he's so skinny, and Orris, well, he's gonna look big no matter what he has on. But if I were you, Doc, I'd stick to brown and black."

"Shit," said Deweese.

"Shut up," said Stokes. "He can't prove nothing."

"And I don't want to," I said. "I'm leaving here in a few days. Just let Ronsel go, and he'll leave town and I'll leave town and neither one of us will ever say a word about this to anybody. Isn't that right, Ronsel?"

He nodded frantically.

"Let go of the rope, Dex," I said. "Come on now, just let it go."

It might have worked. Ronsel Jackson and I might have walked out of there, if my father hadn't laughed. I'd always hated his laugh. Harsh and pitiless as the cawing of a crow, it broke the spell I'd been trying to weave. Stokes and one of the others rushed me. I could have shot one of them, but I hesitated. They barreled into me and we crashed to the floor. Stokes punched me in the face. My arms were wrenched behind me, and somebody kicked me in the stomach. At some point I lost the gun.

"Nigger lover!" Turpin shouted. "Judas!"

The punches and kicks were coming from all sides now. I could hear Pappy yelling, "Stop it! That's enough!"

Finally a boot connected with the back of my head, and that was all. *Goodnight, Pappy. Goodnight, Ronsel. Goodnight.*

HAP

"PLEASE JESUS," I SAID, "shepherd Your son Ronsel, keep him from harm and light his way home to us." I was praying loud on account of the storm, hollering at the Lord like He couldn't a heard me elseways. So when we heard that knocking we all just about jumped out of our skins, all of us cept for Florence. It was like she'd been waiting for it to come. She didn't even open her eyes, just kept right on praying. But when I got up to answer the door she grabbed ahold of my leg and held onto it so tight I couldn't move.

"Don't answer it," she said.

I could feel her shivering against me, quaking like a spent mule. I'd never seen my wife brung so low and afraid, not in all the years we'd been married. It hurt my heart to see that. Lilly May let into crying and the twins was hugging themselves, rocking back and forth on their knees.

"Come on now," I said. "Ain't the time for weakness now. We got to be strong."

The knocking come again, harder this time, and Florence let go of me. Ruel and Marlon gave each other a look like twins do when they talking without words, then they helped their mother to her feet and stood on either side of her. Drew themselves up tall, like men, and put their arms around her and Lilly May.

I went and opened the door. There was a fellow standing on the porch, I couldn't tell who it was at first on account of his head was bent, but then he looked up and I seen it was Sheriff Tacker and I thought, *He's dead. My boy is dead.*

"I've got bad news, Hap," the sheriff said. "It's about Ronsel." He looked behind me to where Florence and the children were standing. "You better step outside with me," he said.

"No," Florence said. "Whatever you got to say, you say it to all of us."

The sheriff shifted on his feet and looked down at the hat in his hands. "Seems your son ran afoul of an angry bunch of men tonight. He's alive, but he's hurt bad. They were pretty riled."

"Where is he?" I said.

"How bad?" Florence said.

He answered me and not her. "My deputy's taken him to the doctor in Belzoni. I'll drive you there now if you want."

Florence came over and stood beside me. She took ahold of my hand and gripped it hard. "How bad?" she asked the sheriff again.

He fumbled in his pocket and pulled out a piece of paper. "We found this laying on the ground next to him." Sheriff Tacker handed it to me. It was a letter and it had blood all over it, at first I thought it was just spilled on there but then I turned it sideways and seen the word and the numbers written in it, Ezekiel 7:4, written in blood by somebody's finger.

"What does it say?" Florence asked me.

But I couldn't answer her, fear had closed up my throat like a noose.

"Apparently your son was having relations with a white woman," the sheriff said.

"What? What white woman?" Florence said.

"Some German gal. That letter's from her, telling him he's the father of her son."

"It ain't true," Florence said. "Ronsel wouldn't do that."

I didn't want to believe it either but it was right there on the paper, I could read it through the blood. *You have a son,* it said. *Franz Ronsel.*

"Says there's a photograph with it but we didn't find it," the sheriff said.

"What did they do to him?" Florence said. I couldn't feel my hand, she was squeezing it so hard.

"They could've hanged him," the sheriff said. "He's lucky to be alive."

"You tell me what they done," Florence said.

And mine eye shall not spare thee, neither will I have pity: but I will recompense thy ways upon thee, and thine abominations shall be in the midst of thee: and ye shall know that I am the Lord. Ezekiel 7:4.

"They cut out his tongue," the sheriff said.

FLORENCE

MY SON'S TONGUE.

"Dear God," Hap said. "Dear God, how can this be true?"

They cut out his tongue.

"They could've hanged him," the sheriff said again.

They.

"Who did it?" I said.

"We don't know. They were gone by the time we got there," he said. He was lying though, a five-year-old could a told that.

"Where?" I said.

"The old sawmill."

I knowed right then who was behind this business. "How'd you know to go looking for him there in the first place?" I said.

"We got a tip there might be trouble," the sheriff said.

"Who from?"

"That ain't important. What matters is, your boy's alive and he's on his way to the doctor. If you want to get to him, we need to leave now."

"Why'd you send him all the way to Belzoni? Why not take him to Doc Turpin in town?"

The sheriff's eyes slid away from mine, and I knowed something else too. "He was one of em, wasn't he?" I said. "Who else was there besides him and Ole Man McAllan?"

The sheriff's face hardened up and his eyes got squinty. "Now you listen to me," he said. "I understand you're mighty upset, but you got no call to be pointing fingers at Doc Turpin or anybody else. If I was you, I'd be more careful what I said."

"Or what? You gone cut my tongue out?"

His Adam's apple gave a jerk. I stared him down. He was a scrawny little fellow, no more meat on him than a starving quail. I could a snapped his neck in about two seconds.

"You're lucky we followed up on that tip," he said. "Lucky we found him before he bled to death." His face was like a child's, I could see everything in it. His fear of us. His anger at my son for laying hand to a white woman. His disgust at what they done to Ronsel, and his sympathy for the devils who done it. The little bit of shame he felt for covering up for em. His impatience to be done with nigger business and get home to his wife and his supper.

"Yessuh, sheriff," I said, "we're one lucky family."

He put on his hat. "I'm leaving now. You want me to take you to Belzoni or not?"

Hap nodded and said, "Yessuh. My wife'll come with you."

"No, Hap," I said. "You go. I'll stay here with the children."

"You sure?" he asked, surprised. "Ronsel will be wanting his mother."

"It's better if you go."

My husband gave me a stern sharp look and said, "You keep that door locked, now." Meaning, *You just stay put and don't do nothing foolish.*

And I looked right back at him and said, "Don't you worry bout us, you just take care of Ronsel." Meaning, *And I'll take care of what else needs taking care of.*

I would use Hap's skinning knife. It wasn't the biggest knife we owned but it had the thinnest blade. I reckoned it would go in the easiest.

LAURA

I WOKE TO CURSING and pounding: Pappy's voice, punctuated by his fists hitting the front door. "Wake up, goddamnit! Let me in!"

I'd fallen asleep on the couch. The room was pitch dark; the lantern must have burned out. I'd barred the door earlier, something I seldom did anymore, but after Florence left I'd felt unaccountably afraid. The night had seemed full of terrible possibility waiting to coalesce, to shape itself into monstrous form and come for me. As if a flimsy wooden door and an old two-by-four could have kept it out.

"Just a minute, I'm coming," I said.

Either the old man didn't hear me or he was enjoying himself too much to stop, because the racket continued while I got the lantern lit and went to the door.

"About time," he snapped, when I opened it. "I've been standing out here for five minutes." He pushed past me, tracking mud all over the floor, and looked around the room. "Jamie hasn't come home yet?"

"No, unless he's asleep in the lean-to."

"I checked already. He ain't there." Pappy's voice had an edge to it I'd never heard before. He removed his dripping hat, hung it on a peg then went back to the doorway and peered out into the night. "Maybe he missed the place in the dark," he said. "He was on foot, and you didn't leave a light on."

As they were meant to do, his words let loose a storm of guilt in me. Then their meaning penetrated. "How do you know he was on foot? Did you see him?"

"He ain't got a car, that's how I know," said Pappy. "So if he left here, he had to been walking."

The old man's back was to me, but I didn't have to see his yellow teeth to know he was lying through them. "You asked me if he'd come home *yet*," I said. "If you haven't seen him, how'd you know he left in the first place?"

He reached into his shirt pocket and pulled out a pack of cigarettes. He shook one out, then crumpled the pack in his fist and threw it out onto the porch. "Shit!" he said. "They're soaking wet."

I went to him and gripped his shoulder, turning him toward me. It was the first time I'd touched him on purpose since my wedding day, when I'd given him a dutiful, and obviously un-welcome, kiss on the cheek.

"What's wrong? Has something happened to him?"

He jerked his shoulder out of my hand. "Let me alone, woman. I'm sure he's fine." But he didn't sound sure, he sounded guilty and oddly defiant at the same time, like a wicked boy who's done some longed-for forbidden thing: hit his sister, or drowned a cat. A dark suspicion bloomed in me.

"Has this got something to do with Ronsel Jackson being missing?" I said, watching his face.

"Who says he's missing?"

"His mother. She came by here looking for him around seven."

He shrugged. "Niggers go missing all the time."

"If you've harmed that boy, or Jamie—"

The old man's features contorted, and his eyes lit with hate. "You'll what? Tell me what you'll do." His spittle flecked my face. "You think you can threaten me, gal? You better think again. I've seen the way you sniff after Jamie like a sow in rut. Henry may be too thick to notice but I ain't, and I ain't afraid to tell him either."

I could feel my face reddening, but I brazened it out. "My husband would never believe that."

He cocked his head to one side, calculating. "Well maybe he will and maybe he won't, but I bet it sure will stick in his craw. Henry ain't got much of an imagination but with a thing like that you don't need one. A thing like that, a man will always wonder about. There'll always be a little bit of doubt."

"You're despicable."

"I'm wet," he said. "Fetch me a towel."

He sauntered to the kitchen table, planted himself in one of the chairs and waited. For a moment I just stood there, paralyzed by the emotions tearing through me—shame, anger, fear, all battling for dominance. Then my limbs seemed to move of their own accord: walking to the linen cupboard, taking out a clean towel, walking back to him. He snatched it from my hand. "Now fix me something to eat. I'm hungry."

As mechanically as a windup toy, I went to the stove, took

cornbread from the oven and spooned chili onto a plate. Thinking of Henry, and how he would feel if Pappy carried out his threat and said something to him. I set the plate down in front of the old man and started to leave the room.

"If you hear Jamie come in," he said, around a mouth full of cornbread, "you come wake me up. And if Henry or anybody else asks you where I was tonight, you tell em I was right here at home with you, hear?"

I pictured those pale hateful eyes closed, the mouth shut, the skin waxen. Pictured it melting away until there was nothing but smooth white bone, crumbling slowly into dust. "Yes, Pappy," I said.

He gave me a malicious smile, knowing he'd won. Still, I thought, there were plenty of ways for an old man to die on a farm. You never knew when tragedy might strike out of the blue.

I LAY ON MY BED with my eyes open, waiting for Pappy to finish eating and turn in. When I heard the front door open and close, I got up and checked on the children. They were sleeping, with an untroubled abandon I envied. I set about cleaning up the mess the old man had left, grateful for work to keep my hands busy while I waited for Jamie and whatever else would come that night. But imposing order on the house did nothing to ease the turmoil in my mind. *A sow in rut*. Had I really been so transparent? Was that how Jamie thought of me? *A thing like that, a man will always wonder about*. I couldn't bear the thought of causing Henry such pain, even if it meant lying for Pappy. But if he'd harmed Jamie . . .

Suddenly remembering what the old man had said about Jamie being lost in the dark, I took one of the lanterns out to the front porch with the intention of leaving it there as a beacon. It was then that I saw the light in the barn. Jamie—it had to be.

I didn't even stop to change into my boots or put on my coat. I simply walked into the storm, my one thought to reach him. The night was wild: lashing rain, furious gusts of wind that whipped my hair and my clothes. The barn door was shut, and it took all my strength to get it open. Jamie was curled on the dirt floor of the barn, sobbing. The sounds that came from him were so anguished they were nearly inhuman. They mingled with the plaintive lowing of our cow, who was moving restlessly in her stall.

I ran and knelt beside him. He'd been beaten. There was a cut above his eyebrow, and one cheek was red and swollen. I pulled his head into my lap and when I did, felt a large lump on the back of it. Hot rage surged through me. Pappy had done this to him, I had no doubt of it.

"I'll go fetch some water and a clean cloth," I said.

"No," he said, wrapping his arms around my waist. "Don't leave me." He clung to me, shuddering. I murmured soothing nonsense to him and dabbed at the cut on his forehead with my sleeve. When his sobbing quieted I asked him what had happened, but he just shook his head and squeezed his eyes shut. I lay down behind him and curled my body around his, stroking his hair, listening to the droning patter of the rain on the roof. Time passed, ten minutes or twenty. One of the mules whickered, and I felt rather than heard movement, a displacement of air. I opened my eyes. Saw Florence standing in the open doorway of the barn. Her dress was soaked through, and her legs were muddy to the knee. Her face was a blasted ruin. The hairs on my arms rose up and I shivered, knowing something terrible must have happened to Ronsel. Then I saw the knife in her hand. *Ronsel is dead,* I thought, with absolute certainty, *and she means to kill us for it.* I was strangely unafraid. What I felt most keenly was pity—for Florence and her son, and for Henry and the girls, who would find our bodies in the barn and grieve and wonder. There was no way I could stop her; I didn't even think to try. I closed my eyes, pressing myself against Jamie's back, waiting for what would come. I felt a stirring of air, heard a whisper of bare feet on dirt. When I opened my eyes she was gone. The whole incident had taken perhaps fifteen seconds.

For a long while I just lay there, feeling my heart trip and gradually slow down until it kept pace with Jamie's again. A boom of thunder sounded, and I thought of the children. They'd be frightened if they woke and I wasn't there. Then I thought of Pappy, sleeping alone in the lean-to. And I knew where Florence had been headed.

I sat up. Jamie made a whimpering sound and drew his knees up to his chest. Before I left the barn I got a horse blanket and covered him with it. Then I knelt beside him and kissed him on the forehead.

"Sweet Jamie," I whispered.

He slept, oblivious, his breath whistling softly with each exhalation.

I DREAMED OF HONEY, golden and viscous. I floated in it like an embryo. It filled my eyes, nose and ears, shutting out the world. It was so pleasant, to do nothing but float in all that sweetness.

"Mama, wake up!" The voices were piercing, insistent. I tried to ignore them—I didn't want to leave the honeyed place—but they kept tugging at me, pulling me out. "Mama, please! Wake up!"

I opened my eyes to find Amanda Leigh and Bella hovering over me. Their mouths and chins were smeared in honey speckled with cornbread crumbs, and their hands on me were sticky. I looked at the clock on the bedside table; it was after nine. They must have gotten hungry and helped themselves to breakfast.

"Pappy won't wake up," said Amanda Leigh, "and he's not in his eyes anymore."

"What?"

"He's in his bed but he isn't in his eyes."

"We can't find Uncle Jamie," said Bella.

Uncle Jamie. I pictured him above me, mouth open, head thrown back in pleasure. Pictured him as I'd left him last night, curled in a ball on the floor of the barn.

I got up and put on my robe and slippers, then led the girls out to the lean-to. The rain had stopped, but it was a temporary respite; the clouds were dark gray for as far as I could see. The door creaked loudly when I pushed it open. I knew what I would find inside, but even so I wasn't prepared for the feeling of elation that shot through me when I saw Pappy's body lying stiff on the cot, vacant of malice and of life.

"Is he dead?" asked Amanda Leigh.

"Yes, darling," I said.

"Then how come his eyes are open?"

Her mouth was pursed, and there was a familiar vertical furrow between her eyebrows, a miniature version of the one that creased Henry's face when he was perplexed. I kissed her there, then said, "They must have been open when he died. We'll shut them for him."

I pushed down on his eyelids with the very tips of my fingers, trying not to touch the eyeballs, but the lids wouldn't budge—the old man was contrary even in death. I rubbed my fingers against my robe, wanting to rid them of the feel of that cold, hard flesh.

"Does he not want you to shut them?" Bella whispered.

"No, honey. His body is just too stiff right now. It's a natural part of dying. We'll be able to shut them tomorrow."

There was no blood and no knife wound, but Jamie's pillow was on the floor. She must have decided to suffocate him instead. I was glad; a wound would have raised unwelcome questions. I bent down to pick up the pillow and put it back on the bed. There was a piece of white fabric on the floor beneath it—a pillowcase, I saw when I picked it up. It wasn't one of ours; the cotton was dingy and coarsely woven. Then I turned it over and saw the eyeholes cut in the fabric, and bile rose in the back of my throat. I balled the hideous thing up quickly and stuffed it in the pocket of my robe. I would burn it in the stove later.

"What is it, Mama?"

"Just an old dirty pillowcase."

It was impossible not to picture the scene: the taunting men in their white hoods, the sweating and terrified brown face in their midst. I wondered how many others there had been, and where they'd done it; whether they'd hanged him or killed him some other way. Jamie must have found out about it—that was why he'd been so distraught last night. I wondered if he'd seen what happened. If he'd watched his father murder that poor boy.

"Is Pappy in heaven now?" asked Bella.

The old man's face was expressionless, and his untenanted eyes gave away nothing of what he'd felt in his last moments. I hoped he'd seen Florence coming for him and been afraid; that he'd begged and struggled and known the agony of help-lessness, as Ronsel must have. I hoped she'd taken pleasure in killing him, and that it would give her some kind of grim peace to know she'd avenged her son.

"He's in God's hands," I said.

"Should we say a prayer for him?" asked Amanda Leigh.

"Yes, I suppose we should. Come here, both of you. Don't be scared."

They came and knelt on either side of me. Mud from the

dirty floor oozed through the thin cotton of my nightgown. I felt a fat plop of water hit my head, then another; the roof was leaking. The girls waited for me to begin, their small, soft bodies pressing into mine from either side. I closed my eyes, but no words came. I would not pray for Pappy's soul; that would be the worst sort of hypocrisy. I could have prayed for Florence, that God would understand and forgive her a mother's vengeance, but not in front of the children. And so I was silent. I had no words to give them, or Him.

A shadow fell across us, and I turned and saw Jamie in the doorway. The light was behind him so I couldn't see his expression. Bella got up and ran to him, hugging him around the knees. "Pappy's dead, Uncle Jamie!" she cried.

"It's true," I said. "I'm sorry."

He picked Bella up and moved to stand at the foot of the bed. He was still in his dirty clothes from the night before, but he'd combed his hair and washed his battered face. There was bitterness in his eyes as he gazed down at his father's body, and sorrow. I'd expected the one but not the other. It tore at my heart.

"It looks like he went peacefully, in his sleep," I lied.

"That's how I'd like to go," Jamie said in a small voice. "In my sleep."

He looked down at me then, a look of such tender desolation that I could hardly bear to meet it. I saw a brother's guilt in that look, but none of the shame or contempt I'd feared to find. Just love and pain and something else I recognized finally as gratitude, for what I'd given him. Gone was the gallant and fearless aviator, the laughing cocksure hero of my imaginings. But even as I mourned his loss, I knew that that Jamie wouldn't have needed my comfort, or lain with me.

That Jamie had never really existed.

The realization stunned me, though it shouldn't have. He'd given me all the clues I needed to see the weakness at the core of him, and the darkness. I'd ignored them, preferring to believe the fiction. Jamie had created that fiction, acting the part almost to perfection, but I'd been the one who swallowed it whole. I was to blame, for having fallen in love with a figment.

I loved him still, but there was no longing to it, no heat. Already the memory of our lovemaking was beginning to seem distant, as though it had happened to someone else. I felt strangely empty, without all that carnal furor.

I think he saw it in my eyes. His own dropped to the floor. He set Bella down and knelt beside me, bending his head. Waiting for me to begin. For the second time, I was at a loss. What honest prayer could I, an adulteress kneeling with my lover beside the body of my hated, murdered father-in-law, possibly offer Him? And then I knew, and I clasped Jamie's hand in mine and started to sing:

> Praise God, from Whom all blessings flow;
> Praise Him, all creatures here below;
> Praise Him above, ye heavenly host:
> Praise Father, Son, and Holy Ghost. Amen.

My voice was strong and clear as I sang the familiar words of thanksgiving. The girls joined in at once—the Doxology was the first hymn I'd ever taught them—and then Jamie did as well. His voice was raw, and it splintered on the *amen*. I found myself thinking that Henry wouldn't have waited for me to begin. He would have led us in prayer unhesitatingly, and his voice wouldn't have cracked.

JAMIE

THE BIBLE IS FULL of thou-shalt-nots. Thou shalt not kill, that's one. Thou shalt not bear false witness against thy neighbor, that's two. Thou shalt not commit adultery, thou shalt not uncover the nakedness of thy brother's wife—three and four. Notice how none of them have any loopholes. There are no dependent clauses you can hang your sins on, like: Thou shalt not uncover the nakedness of thy brother's wife, *unless* thou art wandering in the blackest hell, lost to yourself and to every memory of light and goodness, and uncovering her nakedness is the only way back to yourself. No, the Bible's absolute when it comes to most things. It's why I don't believe in God.

Sometimes it's necessary to do wrong. Sometimes it's the only way to make things right. Any God who doesn't understand that can go fuck Himself.

Thou shalt not take the name of the Lord thy God in vain—that's five.

THE DAY AFTER the lynching passed with the slow heaviness of a dream. I hurt everywhere, and I had the mother of all hangovers. I couldn't stop thinking of Ronsel, of the knife flashing, the blood spurting, the clotted howling that went on and on.

I took refuge in work. There was plenty of it: the storm had wrecked the chicken coop, peeled half the roof off the cotton house and sent the pigs into a murderous frenzy. Henry hadn't returned from Greenville yet, but we expected him back any time. I'd gone earlier to check the bridge and found it just barely passable. From the ominous look of the clouds, it wouldn't stay that way for long. In weather like this Henry would know to hurry home.

I was in the barn milking when Laura came and found me. Venus hadn't been milked since the previous morning, and her udders were full to bursting. She'd already punished me for it twice by swatting me in the face with her cocklebur-infested tail. Still, it was good to sit with my cheek against her warm hide, listening to the snare-drum sound of milk hitting the pail, letting the rhythm empty my head.

"Jamie," Laura said. I looked up and saw her standing just outside the stall. "Henry will be back soon. We need to talk before he gets here."

With some reluctance I left the shelter of the stall and went to her. She had on lipstick, I noticed, but apart from that she was totally without artifice, probably the only woman I'd ever known who was. That would change now, because of me. I had turned her into a liar.

"How are the girls?" I asked her.

"Fine. They're both asleep. All this has worn them out."

"I expect it has. Death is unsettling. Especially the first time you see it."

"They wanted to know if you and Henry and I would die someday, and I said we would, a long time from now. Then they asked if they would die. I think it was the first time it ever occurred to them."

"What did you tell them?"

"The truth. I don't think Bella believed me, though."

"Good," I said. "Let her have her immortality while she can."

Laura hesitated, then said, "I need to ask you about something." She pulled a crumpled piece of white cloth from her pocket. Even before I saw the eyeholes I knew what it was. "I found this on the floor of the lean-to. I imagine it belonged to Pappy." When I didn't answer, she said, "You've seen it before, haven't you?"

I nodded, the memories exploding like grenades in my head.

"Tell me what happened, Jamie."

I told her. How I'd seen the light near the sawmill and gone over there. How I'd discovered Ronsel with a rope around his neck in a room full of hooded men, my father among them. How I'd broken in on them and tried to get Ronsel out of there. How I'd failed. "I didn't even fire my gun," I said.

"Listen to me," Laura said. "What happened to that boy isn't your fault. You tried to save him, which is more than most people would have done. I'm sure Ronsel knew that. I'm sure he appreciated it."

"Yeah, I bet he's just overflowing with gratitude towards me. He probably can't wait to thank me."

"He's alive?"

"Yes."

"Thank God," she said, her eyes closing in relief.

"At least, he was when I left," I said. And then I told her the first lie: how I'd come to with Sheriff Tacker bending over me, and the others gone, and learned they'd cut out Ronsel's tongue. Laura's hand flew to her own mouth. Mine, I remembered, had done the same.

"Tom Rossi drove him to the doctor," I said. "He'd lost a lot of blood." It had been everywhere: drenching his shirt, pooling on the floor, spattering Turpin's white robes.

"Why?" she asked. "Why did they do it?"

I reached in my pocket and pulled out the photo and handed it to her. She looked at it, then back at me. "Who are they?"

"That's Ronsel's German lover, and the child she had by him. There was a letter with it, I don't know what happened to it."

"How did they get hold of this?"

"I don't know," I said. Lie number two. "I guess Ronsel must have dropped it somewhere."

"And one of them found it."

"Yes."

"Who else was there, besides Pappy?"

"I didn't recognize any of the others," I said.

Lie number three, this one for her own safety. I'm sure she saw through it, but she didn't call me on it. She just gazed at me thoughtfully. I had the feeling I was being weighed, and found wanting. It gave me an unfamiliar pang. I'd cheerfully disappointed dozens of women. Why, with Laura, did it feel so bad?

"What will you tell Henry?" she asked.

"I don't know. He's going to be upset enough as it is, without having to know that our father was part of a lynch mob."

"Did Tom or Sheriff Tacker actually see Pappy at the sawmill?"

"I don't think so. But even if they did, this is the Delta. The last thing the sheriff wants to do is identify any of them."

"What about Ronsel?"

"He won't talk. They made sure of that."

"He could write it down."

I shook my head. "What do you suppose would happen to him if he did? What would happen to his family?"

Laura's eyes widened. "Are we in danger?"

"No," I said. "Not as long as I leave here."

She walked to the barn door and looked out at the brown fields and the bleak crouching sky, hugging herself with her arms. "How I hate this place," she said softly.

I remembered the strength of those arms around me, and the surprising sureness with which her hand had gripped me and guided me into her. I wondered if she was that fierce and sure with my brother. If she cried out his name like she'd cried out mine.

"I can't see any reason to tell Henry your father was involved," she said finally. "It would only hurt him needlessly, to know the truth."

"All right. If you think so."

She turned and looked at me, holding my gaze for long seconds. "We won't ever speak of it," she said.

WHEN HENRY GOT home he was already in a welter because of the storm. Laura and I met him at the car, but he barely gave us a glance as he brushed by us to kneel in the fields and examine one of the flattened rows of newly planted cotton. It had started to rain again, and we were all getting soaked.

"If this keeps up all the seed will be washed away, and we'll have to replant," he said. "The almanac predicted light rain in April, damnit. What time did it start here?"

"Around five o'clock yesterday," said Laura. "It poured all night long."

Her voice sounded strained. Henry looked from her to me and frowned. "What happened to your face?"

I'd forgotten all about my face. I tried to think up a story to explain it, but my mind was blank.

"Venus kicked him," Laura blurted out. "Last night, when he was milking. The storm agitated her. All the animals. One of the pigs is dead. The others trampled it."

Henry looked from her back to me. "What in the hell's the matter with the two of you?"

She waited for me to tell him, but I shook my head. I couldn't speak. "Honey," she said, "your father is gone. He died last night in his sleep."

She went and stood next to him but didn't touch him. He wasn't ready to be touched yet. *How well she knows him,* I thought. *How well they suit each other.* He bent his head and stared at his muddy boots. Eldest child, now the head of our family. I saw the weight of that settle on him.

"Is he . . . still in his bed?" Henry was asking me. I nodded. "I guess I'd better go and see him," he said.

Together the three of us walked to the lean-to. Henry went in first. Laura and I followed, coming to stand on either side of him. He pulled the sheet down. Pappy's eyes, vacant and bulging, stared up at us. Henry reached out to close them, but Laura took his hand and gently pulled it back.

"No, honey," she said. "We already tried. He's still too stiff."

Henry let out a long breath. I put an arm around him and so did Laura. When our hands accidentally touched behind his back, she shifted hers away.

I hadn't expected Henry to cry, and he didn't. His face was impassive as he looked down at our father's dead body. He turned to me. "Are you all right?" he asked.

I felt a flare of resentment. Did he never get tired of being the strong one, of being stoic and honorable and dependable? I saw in that moment that I'd always resented him, even as I'd looked up to him, and that I'd bedded his wife in part to punish him for being all the things I wasn't.

"I'm fine," I said.

Henry nodded and squeezed my shoulder, then looked back down at Pappy. "I wonder what he saw, at the end."

"It was a dark night," I told him. "No moon or stars. I doubt he saw much of anything."

Lie number four.

"NIGGER LOVER!" Turpin shouted. "Judas!"

Finally a boot connected with the back of my head, and that

was all—for five minutes or so. When I came to, somebody was none too gently slapping my cheek. I was lying on my side with the other cheek against the dirt. The room was a blur of legs and white robes.

"Wake up," said my father, giving me a hard shake. A half dozen overlapping hooded heads swam over me. I tried to push him away from me. That's when I realized my hands were tied behind my back. He pulled me to a sitting position and propped me against the wall. The sudden motion made the room spin, and I felt myself starting to topple over. Pappy yanked me back up again by my jacket collar. "Sit up and act like a man," he hissed in my ear. "You make one more wrong move, and these boys are liable to kill you."

When the room resettled itself I saw Ronsel, still alive, his head straining upward in an effort to keep the noose from choking him.

"What are we gonna do with him?" said Deweese, waving in my direction.

"No need to do anything," said Pappy. "He won't talk, he told you so already. Ain't that right, son?"

My father was scared, I realized. He was scared as hell, and he was trying to protect me. I think it was right then that I really began to feel afraid myself. My heart started to pound and I felt sweat breaking out all over me, but I made my voice stay calm and confident. For me and Ronsel to walk out of here alive, I would need to give the performance of my life.

"That's right," I said. "Just let him go, and as far as I'm concerned this never happened."

The hulking figure of Orris Stokes loomed over me.

"You ain't in a position to make demands, nigger lover. If I was you, I'd worry less about what happens to him and more about your own skin."

"Jamie won't go to the law," said Pappy. "Not when we tell him what the nigger did."

"What did he do?" I asked.

"He fucked a white woman and got a child on her," Pappy said.

"Bullshit. Ronsel wouldn't do any such thing."

"Is that a fact," said Turpin. "You think you know him, huh? Well, what do you say to this?"

He thrust a photo in front of my eyes, of a thin, pretty blonde holding a mulatto baby. It definitely hadn't been taken in Mississippi. The ground was covered with snow, and there was an alpine-style house in the background.

"Who is she?" I said.

"Some German gal," said Turpin.

"And what makes you think Ronsel's the father?"

He waved a piece of paper in the air. "Says so right here in this letter. She even named it after him."

My feelings must have shown in my face. "See?" Pappy said. "I told you boys he'd be with us on this."

I looked over at Ronsel. He blinked once, slowly, in affirmation. There was no shame in his eyes. If anything, they seemed to challenge me, to say, *What kind of man are you? Guess we're about to find out.* I looked at the photo again, remembering how shocked I'd been when I first saw Negro GIs with white girls in the pubs and dance halls of Europe. Eventually I'd gotten used to it. Soldiers will be soldiers, I'd told myself, and the girls were obviously willing. But I'd never been easy with it, and I still wasn't. And if *I* wasn't, I could only imagine what that photograph stirred up in these white-sheeted men. That, and Ronsel's quiet pride in himself, which must have infuriated them. I knew their kind: locked in the imagined glory of the past, scared of losing what they thought was theirs. They would make an answer. I understood that, and them, all too well. But I couldn't let them kill Ronsel. And if I didn't come up with something quick, they would.

"What do you fellows care about some Kraut whore?" I said.

That earned me a hard kick in the thigh from Orris's boot.

"Just tell em you won't talk," urged Pappy. I could hear the desperation in his voice, and if I could hear it, so could they. That was dangerous. Nothing goads a pack like the scent of fear.

"You're not taking my meaning," I said. "These fräuleins, they're not like our women. They're cold-hearted cunts who'll smile to your face then stab you in the back the first chance they get. They got an awful lot of our boys killed over there. So if Ronsel exacted a little vengeance on one of them and left her with a reminder of it, I call it justice."

There was silence. I began to have a little hope.

"You're good, boy," said Turpin. "Too bad you're full of shit."

"Listen, I'm not saying we should give him a medal for it. I'm just saying it doesn't seem right, killing a decorated soldier over an enemy whore."

Another silence.

"The nigger's still got to be punished," Pappy said.

"And kept from doing it again," said Stokes. "You know how these bucks are once they get a taste for white women. What's to stop him from going after one here?"

"*We're* gonna stop him," said Turpin. "Right here and right now."

He opened a leather case on the floor and pulled out a scalpel. Somebody whistled. Excitement crackled through the room. Ronsel and I started talking at the same time:

"Please, suh. I'm begging you, please don't—"

"You don't need that, he's learned his les—"

Doc Turpin's voice cut across ours like a whip. "If either of them says one more word, shoot the nigger."

I shut up, and so did Ronsel.

"This nigger profaned a white woman," Turpin said. "He fouled her body with his eyes and his hands and his tongue and his seed, and for that he's got to pay. What'll it be, boys?"

They all spoke at once: "Geld him." "Blind him." "Cut it all off!"

I caught a whiff of urine and saw a stain spreading across the front of Ronsel's pants. The smell of piss and sweat and musk was overwhelming. I swallowed hard to keep myself from throwing up.

Then my father said, "I say we let my son decide."

"Why should we do that?" Turpin demanded.

"Yeah," said Stokes, "why should he get to do it?"

"If he decides, he's part of it," said Pappy.

"No," I said. "I won't do it."

My father bent down to me, his eyes narrowed to slits. He put his mouth up to my ear. "You know where I found that letter?" he said. "In the cab of our truck, on the floor of the passenger seat. Only one way it could've got there, and that's if you let him ride with you again. This is *your* doing. You think about that."

I shook my head hard, not wanting to believe it, knowing it had to be true. Pappy pulled away and raised his voice so the others could hear. "You had to stick your nose in. Busting in here like Gary Cooper, waving that gun around and making threats. Threatening me, your own father, over a nigger! Well, you're in it now, son. You don't want him killed, fine. You decide his punishment."

"I said I won't do it."

"You will," said Turpin. "Or I will. And I don't think your boy here will like my choice." He made a crude stabbing gesture toward his crotch. There were hoots and chuckles from the others. Ronsel was shuddering, his muscles straining against the ropes that bound him. His eyes implored me.

"What's it gonna be?" said Turpin. "His eyes, his tongue, his hands or his balls? Choose, nigger lover."

When I didn't answer Deweese swung the shotgun around, pointing it at me. My father stepped away from me, leaving me alone in the shotgun's field. Deweese cocked it. "Choose," he said.

Here it was, the oblivion I'd been chasing for so long. All I had to do was stay silent, and I would have it—an end to pain and fear and emptiness. Here it was, if I just had the guts to reach out and grab hold of it.

"Choose, goddamnit," said my father.

I chose.

LAURA

I WENT TO SEE Florence the day after we found Pappy dead. I wanted to find out how Ronsel was. I also needed to have a private talk with her. I couldn't have her working for me anymore. I didn't think she'd want to in any case, but I had to be sure of it, and of her silence.

I told Jamie where I was going and asked him to watch the children for me. As I was about to walk out the door, he pulled something from his pocket and handed it to me: the photograph of Ronsel's German lover and their child. My arms broke out into gooseflesh; I didn't want to touch it. I tried to hand it back to him.

"No," he said. "You give that to Florence, for Ronsel. Ask her to tell him . . ." He shook his head, at a loss. His mouth was tight with self-loathing.

I gave his hand a gentle squeeze. "I'm sure he knows," I said.

I intended to drive, but both the car and the truck were mired too deeply in mud, so I took my umbrella and set out on foot. The rain had slackened a little since yesterday, but it was still coming down steadily. As I walked past the barn, Henry saw me and came to the open door. "Where are you going?" he asked.

"To Florence's. She didn't show up for work yesterday or today."

Henry still didn't know about what had happened to Ronsel. Hap hadn't come and told him, and we'd been cut off from town since last night. Jamie and I had said nothing, of course. We weren't supposed to know about it yet.

Henry frowned. "You shouldn't be out in this mess. I'll go over there later and see about it. You go on back to the house."

I thought quickly. "I need to ask her some questions. About how to prepare the body."

"All right. But take care you don't fall. The road's slippery."

His concern for me brought a lump to my throat. "I'll be careful," I said.

Lilly May answered my knock. Her eyes were red-rimmed and swollen. I asked to speak to her mother.

"I'll see," she said.

She closed the door in my face. I felt a clutch of fear. What if Ronsel hadn't survived his wounds? For his family's sake, and for Jamie's, I prayed that he had. I waited on the porch for perhaps five minutes, though it felt like much longer. Finally the door opened and Florence came out. Her face was drawn, her eyes sunken. I feared the worst, but then there came a long, guttural moan from inside the house. It was a horrible sound, but it meant he was alive. They must have brought him back home yesterday afternoon, I thought, before the river flooded the bridge.

"How is he?" I asked.

Florence didn't answer, just gave me a cold, knowing stare. I stared back at her, adulteress to murderess. Reminding her that I knew things too.

"We leaving here soon as the river goes down," she said curtly. "Hap'll be by later today to tell your husband."

Relief flooded me, overwhelming the small bit of shame that accompanied it. I would not have to see her, even from a distance; would not be reminded daily of how my family had destroyed hers. "Where will you go?" I asked.

She shrugged and looked out over the drowned fields. "Away from here."

There was only one thing I could offer her. "The old man is dead," I said. "He died night before last, in his sleep." I emphasized the last part, but if she was reassured her face didn't show it. If anything, she looked even more bitter. "God will know what to do with him," I said.

She shook her head. "God don't give a damn."

As if to prove her words, Ronsel moaned again. Florence closed her eyes. I don't know what was more terrible: listening to that sound, or watching Florence listen to it. It might as well have been her own tongue being torn from her body. I shuddered, imagining how I would feel if that sound were coming out of Amanda Leigh or Bella. I thought of Vera Atwood. Of my own mother, still grieving after all these years for Teddy's lost twin.

"I have something for him, from Jamie," I said. I took out the photograph and handed it to her. "It was taken in Germany. The child is—"

"I know who he is." She brushed her fingers lightly across the surface of the picture, touching the face of the grandson she would never see. Then she shoved it in her pocket and looked at me. "I need to get back to him," she said.

"I'm sorry," I said. Two words, pitifully inadequate to carry the weight of all that had happened, but I said them anyway.

Ain't your fault. Three words, a gift of absolution I didn't deserve. I would have given anything to hear Florence say them, but she didn't. All she said was goodbye.

JAMIE

THE FIVE OF US staggered through the mud to the grave. It was still raining lightly but the wind had picked up, coming in violent gusts that seemed to blow us in every direction but the one we needed to go. Henry and I carried the coffin and the ropes. Laura walked behind with the children, Bella in her arms and Amanda Leigh hanging onto her skirt.

When we got to the hole we set the coffin down and worked the ropes underneath it, one on each end. Henry moved to the other side of the hole and I threw him the two rope-ends. But when we tried to lift it, the ropes slipped to the center and the coffin teetered, then tumbled to the ground. The wood groaned, and there was a loud crack from inside the box—Pappy's skull, hitting the wood. One of the boards on the side had pried loose. I bent and pushed the nails back in with my thumb.

"This isn't gonna work," I said. "Not with just the two of us."

"It'll have to work," Henry said.

"Maybe if we stood at either end and ran the ropes lengthwise."

"No," he said. "The coffin's too narrow. If it falls again it could break open."

I shrugged—*so what?*

"No," he said again in a low voice, with a glance at the children.

Laura pointed at the road. "Look. Here come the Jacksons."

We watched their wagon approach. Hap and Florence sat up front, and the two younger boys walked behind. The wagon was piled high with furniture. As it got closer I saw they'd strung up a makeshift tarp in back. I knew Ronsel was under there, suffering.

When they came abreast of us Henry waved them down.

"Don't," Laura said. "Just let them go."

He shot her an indignant look. "It's not my fault, what happened to that boy. I warned him. I warned both of them. And now Hap's leaving me in the middle of planting season when he knows damn well it's too late for me to find another tenant. The least he can do is give us a quick hand here."

I opened my mouth to agree with Laura, but she gave a slight shake of her head and I swallowed the words.

"Hap!" Henry shouted over the wind. "Can you help us out here?"

Hap whoa'd the mule, and he, Florence and the two boys turned and looked at us. Even from thirty yards away, I could feel the force of their hate.

"We could use some extra hands!" Henry shouted.

I expected them to refuse—I sure as hell would have. But then Hap handed the reins to Florence and started to get down.

She grabbed hold of his arm and said something to him, and he shook his head and said something back.

"What are they dithering about?" Henry said impatiently.

Hap and Florence were really going at it now. Their voices weren't quite loud enough for me to make out what they were saying, but I could guess well enough.

"*No, Hap. Don't you do it.*"

"*It's the Lord's doing we passed by here just now, and I ain't gone argue with Him. Now come on and let's see it done.*"

"*I ain't helping that devil get nowhere.*"

"*You ain't helping him, he's already burning in hell. You helping God to do His work.*"

I saw Florence spit over the side of the wagon.

"*That's for your God. He ain't getting nothing more from me. He done taken enough already.*"

"*All right then. I won't be long.*"

Hap climbed down. He turned toward the two boys, and Florence spoke again. Her meaning was plain enough: "*And don't you ask the twins to do it neither.*"

Hap trudged to the grave alone, head bent, eyes on the ground. When he reached us, Henry said, "Thank you for stopping, Hap. We were hoping you and one of your boys could help us get the coffin in."

"I'll help you," Hap said, "but they ain't coming."

Henry frowned and his forehead knitted up.

"It's all right," Laura said quickly. "I can do it."

She set Bella down next to Amanda Leigh and took up one of the rope ends. Henry, Hap and I took the other three. Together we maneuvered the coffin over the hole and lowered it down. When it touched bottom we managed to wiggle one of the ropes out from under it, but the other one caught and wouldn't come loose. Henry cursed under his breath and let the ends fall down into the hole. He looked at Laura.

"Did you bring a Bible?" he asked.

"No," she said, "I didn't think of it."

I saw Hap look up at the sky, head cocked like he was listening to something. Then he bowed it and said, "I've got one right here, Mist McAllan." He pulled a small, tattered Bible from his shirt pocket. "I can send him on if you want. Reckon that's why I'm here." I searched his face for irony or spite, but I saw neither.

"No, Hap," Henry said. "Thank you, but no."

"Done this plenty of times for my own people," Hap said.

"He wouldn't want it," Henry said.

"I say we let him do it," I said.

"He wouldn't want it," Henry repeated.

"*I* want it," I said. We glared at each other.

Laura broke the stalemate. "Yes, Henry," she said, "if Hap is willing to do it I think we should let him. He is a man of God."

"All right, Hap," Henry said after a moment. "Go on then."

Hap leafed through the Bible. He opened his mouth to begin, then something flickered in his eyes, and he turned to an earlier page. I was expecting, "The Lord is my shepherd"; I think we all were. What we got was something else entirely.

"Call now, if there be any that will answer thee; and to

which of the saints wilt thou turn?" Hap's voice was strong and ringing. I saw Laura's head lift in surprise. She told me later the passage was from Job—hardly the thing to comfort the bereaved at a burial.

"Man that is born of a woman is of few days, and full of trouble," Hap went on. "He cometh forth like a flower, and is cut down: he fleeth also as a shadow, and continueth not. And dost thou open thine eyes upon such a one, and bringest me into judgment with thee? Who can bring a clean thing out of an unclean? Not one."

Henry was frowning. I think he would have put a stop to the reading if the clouds hadn't erupted just then, loosing their contents and drenching us all. While Hap shouted about death and iniquity, Henry and I grabbed the shovels and began filling the hole back up.

So it was that our father was laid to rest in a slave's grave, in a hurried, graceless ceremony presided over by an accusatory colored preacher, while the woman who meant to kill him looked on, stiff-backed and full of impotent rage that somebody else had beaten her to it.

If Pappy had woken up when I came in with the lantern, Florence might have gotten her chance. But he didn't. He slept on peacefully, his face relaxed, his breathing deep and steady, the way a man sleeps after a long and satisfying day's work. I stood there watching him for some time, dripping water and blood onto the floor, feeling the fury build inside me. I heard his voice saying, *You'd think I had three daughters and not two.* And, *My son don't have the balls to kill a man up close.*

And, *"The nigger's still got to be punished."* I don't remember picking up the pillow on my bed, just looking down and seeing it in my hands.

"Wake up," I said.

He jerked awake and squinted up at me. "What are you doing there?" he said.

"I wanted to look you in the eye," I said. "I wanted you to know it was by my hand."

His eyes widened and his mouth opened. "You—" he said.

"Shut up," I said, bringing the pillow down over his face and pressing hard. He thrashed and clawed at my hands, his long nails digging into the skin of my wrist. I cursed and let go for a second, long enough for him to turn his head and gasp in a last breathful of air. I pressed the pillow back down, smashing it against his face. His struggles grew weaker. His hands loosened and let go of mine. I waited another couple of minutes before I lifted the pillow off his face. Then I straightened the covers and closed his mouth. I left his eyes open.

I took the lantern and went to the barn. Laura found me there half an hour later, and Florence found us both not long after that. Laura thought I was asleep by then, but I wasn't. I saw Florence come in with the knife, saw her rage and knew what she meant to do. I wished there was some way to tell her it was already done, that he didn't die a peaceful death. I put my guilt in my eyes, hoping she would see it.

What we can't speak, we say in silence.

HENRY

THIS IS THE LOINS of the land. This lush expanse between two rivers, formed fifteen thousand years ago when the
glaciers melted, swelling the Mississippi and its tributaries
until they overflowed, drowning half the continent. When the
waters receded, settling back into their ancient channels, they
brought a rich gift of alluvium stolen from the lands they'd
covered. Brought it here, to the Delta, and cast it over the
river valleys, layer upon sweet black layer.

I buried my father in that soil, the soil he hated to touch.
Buried him apart from my mother, who'll lie by herself forever
in the Greenville cemetery. She might have forgiven me for that,
but I knew better than to think Pappy would. I didn't mourn his
death, not like I'd mourned hers. He wouldn't have wanted my
grief in any case, but he ought to have had somebody's. That
was the thought in my mind as I shoveled the earth on top of
his coffin: that not one of us was really grieving for him.

A few days later I lost Jamie too. He was hell-bent on going to
California, even though I'd made it plain I could use his help for
a few more weeks now that the Jacksons were gone. That was
a terrible business at the sawmill, but nobody could say I didn't

warn the boy. I wondered what he'd done, to make those men punish him like that. Had to been something pretty bad. I think Jamie knew, but when I asked him about it he just shrugged and said, "It's Mississippi. There doesn't have to be a reason."

In spite of everything that had happened, I would miss him, and I knew Laura would too. I figured she'd take his leaving hard, thought she'd probably end up mad at me over it. But when we finally talked about it—in bed, after the light was out—all she said was, "He needs to leave this place."

"And you?" The question just slipped out, but as soon as I said it I felt my mouth go dry. What if she said she wanted to leave too, to take the children and go back to her people in Memphis? I never thought I'd come to fear such a thing, not with Laura, but she'd changed since we moved to the farm, and not in the ways I'd expected she would.

"What I need," she began.

All of a sudden I didn't want to hear her answer. "We'll get a house in town after the harvest," I blurted out. "And if you can't wait that long I'll borrow the money from the bank. I know it's been hard for you here, and I'm sorry. It'll be better once we're living in town. You'll see."

"Oh, Henry," she said.

What the hell did that mean? It was pitch dark and I couldn't see her face. I reached for her, my heartbeat loud in my ears. If she turned me away—

But she didn't. She rolled toward me, settling her head in the hollow of my shoulder. "What I need, I have right here," she said.

I put my arms around her and held on tight.

LAURA

JAMIE LEFT US three days after the burial. He was
bound for Los Angeles, though he wasn't sure what he would
do when he got there. "Maybe I'll go to Hollywood and get a
screen test," he said with a laugh. "Give Errol Flynn a run for
his money. What do you think?"

The bruises on his face were starting to fade, but he still
looked haggard. I worried about him being all alone out there,
with no one to look after him. But then I thought, *He won't
be alone for long.* Jamie would find someone to love him, some
pretty girl to cook his favorite foods and iron his shirts and
wait for him to come home to her each day. He would pluck
her like a daisy from the side of the road.

"I think Mr. Flynn's in real trouble," I said.

The front door opened, and Henry joined us on the porch.
"We need to head out if you're going to make your train," he
said.

"I'm ready," said Jamie.

Henry gestured at the fields in front of us. "You wait and
see, brother. You're going to miss all this."

"All this" was a sea of churned earth stretching from the house to the river, bereft of crops and the furrows they'd been planted in. A newly hatched mosquito landed on Henry's outstretched arm, and he swatted at it irritably. I hid a smile, but Jamie's expression was serious as he answered. "I'm sure I will."

He bent and kissed the girls goodbye. Bella cried and clung to him. He gently pried her arms from around his neck and handed her to me. "I left you something," he said to me. "A present."

"What?"

"It's not here yet, but it will be soon. You'll know it when you see it."

"We'd better be off," said Henry.

Jamie gave me a swift, awkward hug. "Goodbye. Thank you for everything."

I nodded, not trusting myself to speak. Hoping he would comprehend all that was contained in that small movement of my head.

"I'll be back by suppertime," said Henry. He kissed me, and then Jamie was gone, down the road to Greenville, and to California.

In the days that followed, the girls and I looked everywhere for Jamie's present. Under the beds, in the cupboards, out in the barn. How could he have left me something if it hadn't yet arrived? And then, a few weeks after he'd gone, I found it. I was weeding the little vegetable patch Jamie had helped me put in when I spied a clump of small tender plants at the edge. There were several dozen of them, too evenly spaced to be weeds. I knew what they were even before I broke off a sprig and smelled it.

All summer long I slept with Henry on sheets scented with lavender.

AND NOW HERE we are at the ending of the story—my ending, anyway. It's early December, and I'm packing for an extended stay in Memphis. Henry and I agreed I should go home for the birth. The baby's due in six weeks, and at my age it's too risky to stay here in Tchula, two hours from the nearest hospital.

We moved here in October, just after the harvest. Our house isn't as nice as the one we lost to the Stokeses in Marietta, and there's no fig tree in the backyard, but we do have electricity, running water, and an indoor toilet, for which I'm profoundly grateful. Our days here have settled into a pleasant routine. We get up at dawn. I make breakfast for us all, and Henry's lunch to take with him to the farm. After he leaves I get the girls dressed and we walk Amanda Leigh the eight blocks to school. By the time Bella and I return home our colored maid Viola is here. She only comes half days; there's not enough work to warrant having her full-time. I spend the morning reading to Bella or running errands. At three we go and fetch Amanda Leigh, and then I cook our supper. We eat half an hour after sunset, when Henry gets home. Then I knit or sew while we listen to the radio.

Our life here is a world away from Mudbound, though it's only ten miles on the map. Sometimes it's hard for me to believe in that other life and that other self—the one capable of rage and lust, of recklessness and selfishness and betrayal. But then I'll feel the baby kicking, and I'll be forcibly reminded of that other Laura's existence. Jamie's baby, I have no doubt of it; I felt the tiny flare of its awakening that night, a few hours after we were together. I won't ever tell him the child's his, though he might wonder. It's a small bit of dignity I can give back to Henry, that he doesn't know I've taken from him. I give him whatever I can these days, and not just out of guilt or duty. That's what it is to love someone: to give whatever you can while taking what you must.

Jamie married in September. We weren't invited to the wedding; he let us know after the fact, in one of his breezy letters. And then, a week later, we got an almost identical letter telling us the news again, as if he hadn't remembered writing us the first time. Henry and I both knew what it had to mean, but we didn't say the words out loud. I pray his new wife will help him stop drinking, but I also know, as she doesn't, how much he has to forget.

I won't be allowed to forget. The baby will see to that. It will be a boy, who will grow into a man, whom I'll love as fiercely as Florence loves Ronsel. And while I'll always regret that I got my son at such terrible cost to hers, I won't regret that I got him. My love for him won't let me.

I'll end with that. With love.

RONSEL

IT'S DAYTIME, OR IT'S NIGHT. I'm in a tank wearing a helmet, in the backseat of a moving car with a burlap sack over my head, in the bed of a wagon with a wet rag on my forehead. I'm surrounded by enemies. The stench of their hate is choking me. I'm choking, I'm begging please sir please, I'm pissing myself, I'm drowning in my own blood. I'm hollering at Sam to fire goddamnit, can't you see they're all around us, but he doesn't hear me. I shove him aside and take his position behind the bow gun but when I press the trigger nothing happens, the gun won't fire. I have a terrible thirst. *Water,* I say, *please give me some water,* but Lilly May can't hear me either, my lips are moving but nothing is coming out, nothing.

Should my story end there, in the back of that mule-drawn wagon? Silenced, delirious with pain and laudanum, defeated? Nobody would like that ending, least of all me. But to make the story come out differently I'd have to overcome so much: birth and education and oppression, fear and deformity and shame, any one of which is enough to defeat a man.

It would take an extraordinary man to beat all that, with

an extraordinary family behind him. First he'd have to wean himself off laudanum and self-pity. His mama would help him with that, but then he'd have to make himself write his buddies and his former COs and tell them what had been done to him. He'd write it down and tear it up, write it down and tear it up until one day he got up enough courage to send it. And when the answers came back he'd have to read them and accept the help that was offered, the letters that would be written on his behalf to Fisk University and the Tuskegee Institute and Morehouse College. And when Morehouse offered him a full scholarship he'd have to swallow his pride and take it, not knowing whether they wanted him or just felt sorry for him. He'd have to leave his family behind in Greenwood and travel the four hundred miles to Atlanta alone, with a little card in his shirt pocket that said MUTE. He'd have to study hard to learn all the things he should have been taught but wasn't before he could even begin to learn the things he wanted to. He'd have to listen to his classmates talk about ideas and politics and women, things you can't fit on a little portable slate. Have to get used to being alone, because he made the others uncomfortable, because he reminded them of what could still happen to any one of them if they said the wrong thing to the wrong white man. After he graduated, he'd have to find a profession where his handicap didn't matter and an employer who would take a chance on him, at a black newspaper maybe, or a black labor organization. He'd have to prove himself and fight off despair, have to give up drinking three or four times before he finally kicked it.

Such a man, if he managed to accomplish all that, might one day find a strong and loving woman to marry him and give him children. Might help his sister and brothers make something of themselves. Might march behind Dr. King down the streets of Atlanta with his head held high. Might even find something like happiness.

That's the ending we want, you and me both. I'll grant you it's unlikely, but it is possible. If he worked and prayed hard enough. If he was stubborn as well as lucky. If he really had a shine.

ACKNOWLEDGMENTS

If James Cañón hadn't been in my very first workshop at Columbia. If we hadn't loved each other's writing, and each other. If he hadn't read and critiqued every draft of this book, plus countless early drafts of individual chapters, during the years it took me to write it. If he hadn't encouraged and goaded me, talked me off the ledge a dozen times, made me laugh at myself, inspired me by his example: *Mudbound* would have been a very different book, and I would be writing these acknowledgments from a nice, padded cell somewhere. Thank you, love, for all that you've given me. I could not have had a wiser counselor or a truer friend.

I am also grateful to the following people, organizations and sources:

Jenn Epstein, my dear friend and designated "bad cop," who was always willing to drop everything and read, and whose tough, incisive critiques were invaluable in shaping the narrative.

Binnie Kirshenbaum and Victoria Redel, whose guidance and enthusiasm got me rolling; Maureen Howard, friend and mentor, who told me I mustn't be afraid of my book; and the many other members of the Columbia Writing Division faculty who encouraged me.

Chris Parris-Lamb, my extraordinary agent and champion, for seeing what others didn't; Sarah Burnes and the whole Gernert Company team, for embracing *Mudbound* so enthusiastically; and Kathy Pories at Algonquin, for believing in the book and being such a thoughtful and sensitive shepherd of it.

Barbara Kingsolver, for her tremendous faith in me and in *Mudbound;* her help in turning the story into a coherent, compelling narrative; her passionate support of literature of social change; and the generous and much-needed award.

The Virginia Center for the Creative Arts, the La Napoule Foundation, Fundación Valparaiso and the Stanwood Foundation for Starving Artists, for the gifts of time to write and exquisitely beautiful settings in which to do so; and the Columbia University Writing Division and the American Association of University Women, for their financial assistance.

Julie Currie, for the price of mules in 1946 and other elusive facts; Petra Spielhagen and Dan Renehan, for their assistance with Resl's broken English; and Sam Hoskins, for lessons in orthopedics.

Theodore Rosengarten's *All God's Dangers: The Life of Nate Shaw;* Stephen Ambrose's *The Wild Blue;* Byron Lane's *Byron's War: I Never Will Be Young Again;* Lou Potter's *Liberators* (and the accompanying PBS series); and Joe Wilson's *The 761st "Black Panther" Tank Battalion in World War II,* for helping me put believable flesh on the bones of my sharecroppers, bomber pilot and tankers.

Denise Benou Stires, Michael Caporusso, Pam Cunningham, Gary di Mauro, Charlotte Dixon, Mark Erwin, Marie Fisher, Doug Irving, Robert Lewis, Leslie McCall, Elizabeth Molsen, Katy Rees and Rick Rudik, for their unwavering friendship and belief in me, which sustained me more than any of them will ever know; and Kathryn Windley, for all that and then some.

And finally, my family: Anita Jordan and Michael Fuller; Jan and Jaque Jordan; my brothers, Jared and Erik; and Gay and John Stanek. No author was ever better loved or supported.